The Last Samurai

Capt. Sakae Oba, twenty-nine-year-old veteran of Japanese victories in Manchuria and China, lay flat behind a pile of loose rocks and cursed his stupidity. He had led his entire force into a death trap. Behind them, a sheer wall of rock held them at the mercy of the enemy. Escape along the trail was impossible. He fired through an opening in the rocks at the muzzle blasts of enemy weapons until his pistol was empty, then tried to pull out his spare pistol without exposing himself to the bullets that chipped the rock in front of him.

To his left, Sano lay in a pool of blood. The top of his head had been blown away. His rifle lay on the trail in front of him. Oba could not see farther down the trail.

Am I alone? he wondered. He could see no others.

SAIPAN 1944–45

OBA
THE LAST SAMURAI
DON JONES

JOVE BOOKS, NEW YORK

This Jove book contains the complete
text of the original hardcover edition.
It has been completely reset in a typeface
designed for easy reading and was printed
from new film.

OBA, THE LAST SAMURAI

A Jove Book / published by arrangement with
Presidio Press

PRINTING HISTORY
Presidio Press edition published 1986
Jove edition / September 1988

ISBN: 0-515-09704-7

Jove Books are published by The Berkley Publishing Group,
200 Madison Avenue, New York, New York 10016.
The name ''JOVE'' and the ''J'' logo
are trademarks belonging to Jove Publications, Inc.

PRINTED IN THE UNITED STATES OF AMERICA

10 9 8 7 6 5 4 3 2 1

CONTENTS

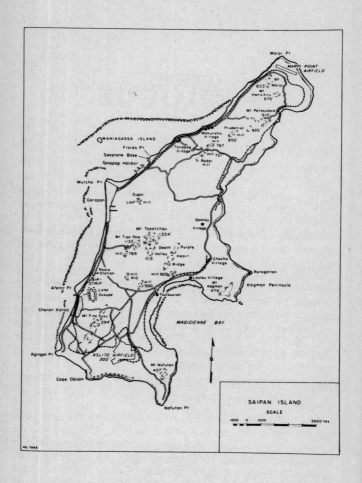

Morpi Pt

MARPI POINT
AIRFIELD

Mt
833' Marpi
Mt
Hanichiru 670'

Mt Petosukara
610'

Prudential
825' Hill
650'

MANIAGASSA ISLAND

Flores Pt

Seaplane Base

Tanapag Harbor

Mutcho Pt

Garapan

Sugar
Loaf Hill

Makunsha
Village

Tanapag
Village

Hill
767

Hill 721

Radar
Hill

Donnay
Village

Mt Tapotchau
554'

Mt Tipo Pale
1133'

Hill 789

Death
Valley

Purple
Heart
Ridge

Chacha
Village

Roragattan

Radio
Station

Hill
410

Hill 600

Loulou Village

Kagman Peninsula

Mt
Kagman
479'

AIR-
STRIP

Afetna Pt

Lake
Susupe

Tsutsuuran

Charan Kanoa

MAGICIENNE BAY

Mt Fina Susu
294'

Agingan Pt

ASLITO AIRFIELD
200'

N

Mt Nafutan
407'

Cape Obiam

Nafutan Pt

SAIPAN ISLAND

SCALE

1000 0 1000   5000 Yds

PD 7093

PROLOGUE

The unwashed, half-starved Japanese soldier cowered in front of a rifle held almost casually by a young Marine whose fair skin was nevertheless darker than that of his pasty-faced, emaciated prisoner. Months of hiding in caves and dense jungle had drained the man's face of its color, giving him an unnatural pallor.

He was lucky. We had surprised him a few minutes earlier as he was relieving himself in an opening of the jungle near the cave he had occupied. His disadvantageous position had left him no alternative but to raise his hands, saving his life.

I hunkered down to be at eye level with him and asked the same questions I had directed at other prisoners during the past year: "Where is Captain Oba? How many men does he have? When did you see him last?"

The answers were the same as the others I had received: "I don't know" to the first two, and "Several days ago" to the last.

Oba had become an acute embarrassment to the American military, who had proclaimed the capture of Saipan in July of 1944. Now, nearly a year later, his continued resistance in the hills surrounding Mount Tapotchau, the dominant peak of the island, was a threat to the lives of rear-echelon souvenir hunters who made unauthorized and sometimes fatal forays into the hills, and who had, more importantly, helped boost the U.S. military presence on the island to more than one hundred thousand.

With some 350 Japanese who had managed to avoid being killed or captured during the forty-five-day battle of June and July 1944, the wily army captain had continued to deprive the American military of absolute control of the island.

We had learned his name and rank from prisoners shortly after our first encounter, in September, when we began patrolling the hills for survivors of the fight. The discovery of his force was our first indication that the heavily jungled ravines and hills harbored more than the frightened and scattered civilians we had been finding.

Perhaps this book would never have been written had I not participated in that patrol or returned the following day to lead six other Marines into a Captain Oba ambush.

Fear leaves an indelible mark on the psyche. The mark left on me as I lay behind a rock with bullets from Oba and his men kicking up dirt and breaking branches around me will never be erased. We've had it, I remember thinking as I looked up the relatively open embankment we had descended, and up which we would have to climb in order to escape. Oba's force, meanwhile, was firing from a jungled height above us with some twenty rifles and at least two automatic weapons, pinning us behind whatever meager shelter we had found. (Our escape is detailed in Chapter 9.)

Later, when I had been assigned as an interpreter to a U.S. Navy hospital on Saipan for Japanese patients, the trauma of that event manifested itself in a growing interest in this man who continued to defy America's military might so successfully.

All prisoners captured in the hills by our patrols and ambushes, or during their attempts to raid American supply dumps, were brought first to the hospital for a physical. Civilians were then placed in an adjacent, sprawling compound of makeshift shacks that housed some fourteen thousand of the original sixteen thousand civilians who had lived on the island prior to our invasion. Military prisoners were transferred to a prison at the northern end of the island.

As interpreter at the hospital, I was able to interrogate all prisoners before they were questioned by military intelligence officers. And invariably, my first questions were of Oba. Many of those I spoke to had been members of his command. From them I learned of the strict control he maintained over those who shared his command post as well as those who lived in other camps.

Three months after the surrender ceremony on the deck of the U.S.S. *Missouri* in Tokyo Bay, on the day I was discharged in Chicago, a newspaper ran a front-page photograph over the caption "The War Is Finally Over." The picture was of Capt. Sakae Oba presenting his sword in surrender to Marine Col. Howard Kurgis. I knew Oba had survived. The accompanying story said he had come out of the hills with his remaining forty-six men, marking the end of organized resistance by Japan . . . and the end of the war.

Only later did I learn the extent to which my respect for Oba as a worthy opponent was shared by others. When he finally did come down—after setting his own conditions—he was feted at a Marine Corps officers' club as guest of honor.

In 1965, while working as a foreign service officer in Niigata, Japan, I told Oba's story to my staff. They suggested I write to a government army locater service. I forwarded all I knew of Oba and two weeks later received his last known address, in the town of Gamagōri, near Nagoya.

I checked with information, then dialed his number. A man answered, and I asked, "Is this Captain Oba?" During the long silence that followed, I realized that no one had called him "Captain" in twenty years. Finally, with an intoned question mark, he replied, "Yes?"

"You don't know me, Captain Oba, but I know a lot about you," I said, then proceeded to tell him of my long-standing interest in him and his eighteen-month battle with the U.S. military.

Two days later, he and his wife, Mineko, who had arranged for and attended his funeral service in 1945, when he was presumed dead, made a day-and-a-half train trip to Niigata to spend four days at my home. Far into each night Oba and I sat in the living room, sketching maps and reliving the battles we had fought.

My friendship with this man, who might have been awarded

the Medal of Honor had he been American, has endured to this day. Although I had toyed for many years with the idea of writing Oba's story, it wasn't until after I suggested it to him in 1980 that I learned of all he had experienced during those eighteen months. For nearly three weeks, I spent eight hours a day recording his recollections of that period. These events, combined with my knowledge of our efforts to kill or capture him, formed a saga I felt compelled to put on paper.

It's a privilege for me to tell you his story. Literary license has been kept to a minimum. The incidents are as they occurred, taken from Captain Oba's recollection, from my interviews with prisoners, and from my own memory of our efforts to capture the man who had earned the nickname ''the Fox.'' Some of the dialogue is as I imagined it must have been for the incidents to have occurred as they did. Some characters represent the melding of two or more persons, and some names have been changed to protect the feelings or reputations of those still living.

· 1 ·

SUBMARINE ATTACK

Running silently far below the surface of the Pacific Ocean, the S.S. *Bluefin* cruised southward one hundred miles east of Formosa. For twelve hours it had tracked three 10,000-ton transports and their three escorting destroyers by sonar. Auxiliary listening gear identified the destroyers' engines from those of the heavier and slower transports. Only once had the sub's captain ordered the boat to periscope depth, and then only for enough time to confirm the number of ships he trailed.

He waited now for the directional sonar to tell him when all three destroyers would be far enough away for him to safely fire his torpedoes.

Aboard the second of the three ships, a muscular twenty-nine-year-old Captain Sakae Oba watched as his company of 270 men clambered down a rope net from an upper deck, then climbed back to the top to repeat the exercise. Beside him, a younger and slightly rotund lieutenant also watched the drill.

"Let's hope there'll be no need for them to use this training," the chubby one said.

"Where they're going, they'll need every bit of training they can get," Oba replied. "We may be only a rear-echelon medical aid company, but we're going to make them combat-ready.''

''We'll never see combat on Saipan,'' Lt. Yoshihiro Banno protested. ''The whole island is rear-echelon.''

''Or maybe the staging area for another assault on the enemy,'' Oba speculated. ''In any case, we'll know in another week.''

The two officers had been ordered to form a medical aid unit shortly before they were ordered south from Manchuria three weeks earlier. Only half a dozen noncommissioned officers of the company had experienced any of the 18th Regiment's three years of combat in China. All others had been transferred to the regiment in the past six months.

''Whether it's on Saipan or somewhere else,'' Oba concluded, ''they will be ready.''

They had boarded the ship, the *Sakuhato-Maru,* at Pusan, Korea, on February 23, following a three-day train trip from Manchuria. They and two other regiments of the 29th Division had been detached from the Kwantung Army for what was said to be a special training exercise in Korea. Each regiment had boarded one of three ships for the voyage.

When they stopped briefly at a Japanese port to exchange their winter uniforms for tropical clothing, they all knew the next enemy they met would be the hated Americans.

The first morning out of Japan, Colonel Kakuma, the regimental commander, had called a meeting of all officers, at which he disclosed their destination: Saipan, second-largest island of the Marianas, and a key defense point in Japan's Pacific strongholds.

They were, the colonel explained, to bolster the island's defenses in the unlikely event the enemy assaulted the Marianas, and were to prepare themselves to further expand the Emperor's Co-Prosperity Sphere, which already included Formosa, the Philippines, Indonesia, and most of southern Asia.

That evening, in the dim light of the lower deck they shared with the men of their company, Oba and Banno sat on the hard planks of the deck with only crates of medical supplies separating them from the men. For six days they had been without a bath. The only water aboard was for drinking, and that was limited to a liter a day per man. The smell of unwashed bodies made the air in the unventilated compartment increasingly difficult to breathe.

The eight medical doctors assigned to Oba's unit and the enlisted medics had been busy treating the four thousand men of the regiment, first for seasickness, then for respiratory ailments and other complaints.

Because of limited space on the boat deck, only two companies were permitted on the open-air deck at a time, and then for only one hour. The other eight waited for four hours deep in the ship's hold for their next breath of fresh air. All officers, other than the colonel and his executive officer, shared the miserable conditions of the enlisted men.

The kitchen staff worked eighteen hours a day, serving their simple fare to each company as it returned below. The meals were eaten on the same cramped deck space in which the men lived and slept.

Banno had etched a calendar on the wooden deck of his sleeping area. Five squares, from February 24 to 28, were crossed by X's. Five more, to March 4, the date he estimated they would reach Saipan, were unmarked.

"We're halfway there," he said as he pocketed his knife. "In five days we'll be drinking coconut milk and sleeping under a tropical moon."

"Chances are," Oba replied, "we'll be busy for the first few days building shelters to protect us from tropical rains."

Banno spread his blanket, arranged his pack as a pillow, and stretched out. "I wish I could sleep for five days," he muttered.

Early the next morning, Oba reported to Colonel Kakuma on the status of the regiment's health, as reported to him by the chief physician, Captain Kodaka. He welcomed the excuse to obtain a few breaths of fresh air. The sky was clear, and long, gentle swells rolled under the ship perpendicular to its course.

He lingered on deck for a cigarette after making his report, then descended to his compartment. The brisk, cool breeze of the upper decks was snuffed out by the oppressive heat and stench of the living quarters. The yellowish pall from naked lightbulbs in the overhead revealed stacks of bedding, backpacks, rifles, and equipment piled haphazardly on the planked deck. Men sprawled everywhere. In the faint light, some saw the sword that marked Oba as an officer and moved to let him pass.

"Banno!" he said when he saw his subordinate propped up against his pack. "Get the men ready! We take over the security watch in one hour."

"Yessir," the second lieutenant replied, getting to his feet. "But what about the noon meal?"

"You don't need one," Oba smiled at the younger man's protruding stomach. "The men can pick it up at the galley now, but just be sure they're all on deck at noon. I'll be at the watch command post." Oba rummaged through his pack, pulled out a clean tunic, then picked his way toward the ladder.

The command post for the officer of the watch was just forward of a salon used by the crew during peacetime cruises, but now stacked with crates of materiel. An old easy chair was all that remained of the room's former furnishings, and it had been placed on the narrow passageway outside the salon. A captain from one of the battalions slouched in the chair with his feet on a lower railing and stared out at the sea.

Oba leaned against the railing next to the man and gazed at the swells. "It looks peaceful, doesn't it?" he observed.

"Yes, it does," replied the other. "But don't let it fool you. Do you have the next watch?"

"Right. The men are eating now and will report by noon."

The twelve-knot wind created by the ship's speed sent a chill through Oba's body, and he buttoned his tunic. "The air's still chilly, but nothing like it was five days ago."

"That's true. It's like spring now. In another five days we'll be in the tropics," the captain said. "And I, for one, won't miss those winters in Manchukuo." The captain looked at his watch, rose, and stretched. "There's the watch book," he said, indicating a ledger on the deck beside him. "I'll check my men, then be back to sign it over to you."

Oba settled into the chair, picked up the book, and turned to February 29. He was looking through the book when Banno appeared. The chubby lieutenant was one of the few who had not been affected by the rough seas during the first two days of the voyage and seemed to enjoy the rice, miso soup, and

occasional ration of canned vegetable that made up their mo-
notonous sequence of meals. Oba had fought a queasiness
until that morning and was hungry now for the first time since
their departure from Japan.

"We've finished lunch, and the men are on their way up,"
Banno reported.

"Good. We'll check them as soon as I sign in. When
they're in position, have one of them bring me lunch."

"Right, sir." Banno turned and went aft.

Oba settled back in the chair and put his feet on the railing.
His eyes scanned the calm sea. Overhead, a few fluffy clouds
cast shadows that darkened the blue water below them.

The clean air and warm sunlight gave Oba a sense of well-
being that he knew was deceptive. The almost unlimited visibility greatly increased the possibility of their detection by
enemy aircraft or submarines. Although he doubted that their
carriers would venture this far north, he knew their submarines could be anywhere.

For the next four hours, his company would be the eyes and
ears of the ship. The lives of all aboard could depend on their
vigilance. The thought brought him to his feet, and he walked
first to the port, then to the starboard side of the narrow passageway, searching sea and sky for signs of danger.

Ahead, the *Tozan-Maru* plowed through the wide swells,
its wake forming a frothy trail that was followed by their ship.
Far beyond the *Tozan* he could see one of the three destroyer
escorts, while another zigzagged ahead to his left. The third
transport, the *Aki-Maru,* was directly behind. Those two
transports, Oba knew, carried regiments destined to join Japan's defense forces on Guam.

Oba leaned over the starboard railing to watch a school of
porpoises frolic in the smooth water only a meter or two
ahead of the ship's bow. It seemed to him that they held a
military formation as they leaped, then paced the ship's speed
just below the water.

The sound of steps behind him broke his reverie.

"Captain," Banno was saying, "we've taken the watch.
Captain Yamana is here to sign over the duty." Captain Yamana was removing his life jacket for Oba.

Quickly the two men went through the ritual of changing

the guard. They signed the book and exchanged salutes, and the relieved officer repeated the orders of the day.

"All right, let's inspect the men," Oba said as he fastened the life jacket. He and Banno went aft to a ladder to the top deck.

His entire company was posted two meters apart on all sides of the upper deck. All wore life jackets, and every third or fourth man was equipped with binoculars, with which they slowly scanned the sea, horizon, and sky. As the two men slowly walked behind the sentries, they were joined by the regimental bugler, Corporal Oguro. Oba had heard that the thin musician had formerly played in a Tokyo dance hall. He didn't know if that was true, but the bugle calls were among the clearest he had ever heard.

Satisfied that all was in order, Oba turned to Banno. "Take over!" he ordered, then returned the lieutenant's salute.

During the next two hours, Oba forced himself to remain alert, sitting for only a few minutes at a time in the dilapidated but comfortable chair. Gradually hunger pangs made him aware that his order for lunch remained unfilled.

He returned to the upper deck, strode to where Banno was talking to the bugler, and growled, "Where's my lunch?" Without waiting for a reply, he returned to his command post.

It was shortly before 3:00 P.M. when a soldier appeared with a tray of the tin mess gear in which their food was served. Eagerly, he inspected the inevitable rice and soup and noted a serving of spinach greens and a half cup of diced sweet potato, presumably meant to be dessert.

Oba removed his tunic, sword, and pistol belt, made himself comfortable in the chair, and began his meal in reverse, starting with the diced sweet potato. He was reaching for a sip of the tepid water in his canteen when an explosion and a violent lurching threw him to the deck. He grabbed the railing, pulled himself to his feet, and looked quickly at the sea around him. The *Sakuhato-Maru* was swinging hard to starboard and vibrating wildly.

"What happened?" he shouted to a running sailor the next deck down.

"Submarine!" came the answer.

Grabbing his belt and buckling it as he ran, Oba hurried

to the ladder leading to the upper deck. Halfway up, a second explosion rocked the ship, and a cloud of steam blew an afterhatch high into the air.

"Banno," he shouted, "torpedo!"

"I know," the frightened lieutenant replied. "It came from the left. There were two, but one missed us."

Many of the sentries were already shrinking away from the towering cloud of steam and smoke.

"Back to your posts!" Oba shouted. He pulled his sword. "Find that submarine!"

A twin 20mm gun near the bow began firing to the left. Oba moved to the railing, snatched a pair of binoculars from a sentry, and focused on the area. Feathers of white water spurted about fifteen hundred meters distant, where the gun's shells were striking, but he saw no sign of a periscope.

Dead in the water, the *Sakuhato* had become a sitting target for another torpedo. Flames could be seen through the steam and smoke erupting from the afterhatch. Oba saw several bodies lying alongside it.

"Keep the men on watch!" he shouted at Banno, then ran to the ladder, motioning for Oguro the bugler to follow.

The main deck was chaotic. Men streamed from below until there was no room on the deck. A railing snapped and several men were crowded off the deck into the sea. A ship's officer shouted orders through a megaphone, but a wailing siren just above him drowned out his voice.

The regiment's commanding officer, Colonel Kakuma, descended a ladder from the bridge with the ship's captain. Oba ran up to him.

"We've taken a torpedo," the colonel said when he saw Oba. "Order the men to abandon ship!"

"Oguro," Oba called. He saw the little musician pushing his way through the throng. "Blow abandon ship!"

"But sir, I don't know the abandon ship call," the infantryman protested.

"Well, blow retreat, then. Get the men off the ship!"

Once again, Oba climbed to the upper deck. Banno and the men were still at their posts. The *Aki-Maru* was pulling past the paralyzed *Sakuhato* while the destroyers plowed at full speed in a tightened circle around the three ships.

"Get the men below! Prepare to abandon ship!" he yelled at Banno, then grabbed another pair of binoculars and slowly traversed the horizon in search of an enemy that had made the unthinkable a reality.

Oba waited until his men had descended, then returned to his command post and reached to retrieve the watch book. The futility of his action dawned on him, and he tossed it to the deck. He picked up the tunic he had discarded earlier. He realized he still had not eaten lunch.

Unable to find his *ohashi,* he scooped out a mouthful of rice with his fingers and attempted to eat it. But fear had drained his mouth of saliva, and the rice was like sand. He spat it to the deck, took a long drink from his canteen, and returned to the main deck.

Rope nets that had been dropped over the side were filled with men descending to the water. Some of the men were leaping directly into the sea. Bamboo rafts stowed along the deck to float machine guns ashore were being tossed over the side, some of them landing on the men floating below. In the true spirit of the Japanese code, all carried their weapons over the side with them.

A lifeboat had been lowered to the level of the main deck. Oba looked on in amazement as the regimental honor guard, in charge of guarding the unit's flag, boarded the boat and took seats. The half-empty boat was again lowered, and he watched the red sun of Japan, symbol of the Emperor's origin, slowly disappear from his sight.

Colonel Kakuma, who had declined an offer to board the lifeboat, stood beside one of the nets, urging his soldiers to be strong. The fifty-five-year-old man had commanded the 18th Regiment throughout its China campaign, and would not abandon his men now.

Oba looked for a familiar face among the soldiers on deck but saw none. He remembered his final order to Banno and hoped he and his men would not remain at their posts until it was too late to escape. He removed his sword from his belt and strapped it to his back under his life jacket, then climbed over the railing, lowered himself to the rope net, and began to descend. Below him, several bodies were already floating facedown, bobbing against the side of the ship.

He dropped the final meter, and his momentum carried him beneath the surface. He kicked frantically as bubbles from his uniform rose past his eyes. After what seemed an eternity, his head broke the surface. The icy water was coated with a thick layer of oil that he knew could erupt in a fiery hell at any moment. He began swimming at a ninety-degree angle from the ship but was pulled back with each stroke. A slow panic began to build within him. He changed from a breast-stroke to a crawl, but still with no result.

A sailor suddenly appeared in the water beside him. "How do I get away?" Oba called.

"Swim toward the bow," the man replied.

"Where is it?" Oba had become thoroughly disoriented.

"Follow me," the sailor said as he moved alongside the ship. Using his right hand and foot to push himself forward, Oba inched his way toward the bow. Once there, he kicked himself off and swam easily away to join a group of fifty or sixty others. He turned to look back. The ship's bow loomed frighteningly near. He watched with horror as a burning oil slick spread from the rear of the ship and smoke and flames engulfed the men still trapped alongside.

Hindered by the bulky life preserver, Oba struck out in the opposite direction, swimming hard until exhaustion forced him to rest.

During the next few hours, he attempted to conserve his strength by drifting on the wide swells that alternately raised him to where he could see the horizon and dropped him to a valley with walls of cold blue water. At each crest he scanned the horizon for help. The *Sakuhato,* with smoke and flames belching from her hindquarters, wallowed in the sea about five hundred meters distant.

Enemy submarines, he had heard, sometimes surfaced after a sinking to machine-gun survivors in the water. The appearance of neither friend nor foe was accepted with mixed emotions.

By the time darkness had replaced the short twilight, all feeling had left Oba's arms and legs. The numbness had come as a relief from the excruciating pain caused by the forty-degree water. The smooth swells had turned into choppy waves that frequently broke over his head.

Twice during the night he bumped into others. The first man muttered, "Be strong." The second said nothing, and when Oba reached out to rouse him, he felt the man's shoulder sink under his hand.

At one point he urinated and was encouraged that his body water momentarily warmed his groin and thighs. At least, he thought, he was still capable of some feeling. Earlier he had tried to open his gunbelt to discard his pistol and an extra clip of ammunition, but his numb fingers had been unable to manipulate the buckle.

At some point during the night the *Sakuhato* exploded with a roar and a shockwave he felt in the water. For several minutes it burned fiercely. Then, with bow raised, it slid slowly backward into the sea.

From a distance, he heard the strains of an army song. At first he feared he was hallucinating. As more voices joined in he felt pride in those who defied death with the stirring lyrics of an infantry march. Gradually, the sound of the voices diminished and was replaced by the sounds of rifle fire and a frantic slapping of water, then silence.

His awareness slowly returned to the fight to remain alive. The numbness of his body had invaded his mind. Only when his waterlogged life jacket allowed his face to slip beneath the surface did he order his limbs to respond, and even then he could not be sure they actually moved.

It wasn't until a solid object nudged the back of his head a second time that he had the presence of mind to notice it. Again, he directed his arms to move, but several agonizing moments passed before the object, a two-meter plank, was before him and he was able to get first one arm, then the second, over it. The buoyant board was a welcome replacement for his practically useless life jacket.

In the first gray light of dawn, he saw that the group that had surrounded him the previous evening had disappeared. A sense of despair flooded his being. With others around and fighting for life, there had seemed a chance of survival. Alone, there seemed to be none.

The choppy waves forced him to close his eyes against the stinging saltwater. His swollen tongue pressed against the roof of his mouth, making it difficult to breathe.

He awoke—or regained consciousness—with a start at the sound of voices. Twenty meters away, a soldier sat on a bamboo machine-gun raft, propelling it with a sheathed sword. Around him were bobbing heads and outstretched arms trying to reach the raft. Instead of assisting them, the man struck at the arms that threatened to grab his flimsy craft, then turned to paddle away from them.

Oba watched the drama of survival and gradually realized the raft was approaching him. His half-conscious mind recorded the scene but was incapable of emotion. Even when the soldier called to him, the words were barely comprehensible: "Captain, come aboard!"

He simply stared at the stranger aboard the raft.

"Come here!" the voice shouted again. The raft, if it wasn't a hallucination, came nearer. He felt the man pull at the collar of his life jacket and was aware of bamboo scraping his cheek. He tried to move higher on the light craft, but his muscles would not respond. He was rolled roughly onto his back, and he looked into the face of the man who had beat off others, yet had selected him to be saved. He dimly wondered why as he slipped once more into unconsciousness.

A sharp pain in his back brought him to. He had no idea how long he had been there, but he was still aboard the raft. Feeling had returned to his hands and feet. The soldier was beating his back with the sheathed sword, and shouting, "A ship! A ship!"

Oba rolled onto his side and saw the slim outline of a destroyer moving toward them. He tried to smile, but his cracked and swollen lips resisted movement. From his slightly elevated position, he could see a dozen heads bobbing in the water, all moving toward the now still ship, less than fifty meters away. Lines were being lowered from the deck. He could hear the grunting breath of the soldier behind him as he paddled furiously with the sword. Twenty meters from the ship, the man said, "Come on," and dove into the water. Slowly Oba pushed himself off the raft and began to swim.

A rope dangled before him, and the fingers of his left hand closed around it. A wave jerked it from his grasp and threw him against the steel hull of the ship. As the wave rebounded,

Oba was pulled away and felt himself slip into a trough before a wall of water closed over his head.

Panic took over for the first time since the explosion eighteen hours earlier. Again his body banged against the steel of the ship, and he had only a fleeting glimpse of the sky before he was once more submerged. With the next wave, a rope brushed his face, and he grabbed blindly. Quickly he twisted it once around his wrist and felt a jerk as another wave attempted to pull him away. With two hands now he clung to the lifeline, then felt it slip as it was pulled from above.

He looked up the smooth, curved wall of steel at the faces that peered over it and shook his head. "I can't!" was all he could say or think. He wondered if the ship would leave him because he was unable to pull himself aboard.

Then he saw another line being lowered toward him. At its end, a loop dangled, and he was able to grasp it with one hand, then maneuver it under both arms. He relaxed as the weight of his body tightened the loop around his chest. His sword, still strapped to his back, grated against his spine as he was pulled to the destroyer's deck. Around him lay the exhausted bodies of other survivors. Oba took one step. His knees buckled, and he slipped into oblivion.

Oba tried to ignore the voice that called to him, "Captain, wake up!"

He closed his eyes more tightly. The voice persisted, and he heard himself say, "Shut up!"

"He's awake," another voice said, and Oba opened his eyes. The cherubic face of Lieutenant Banno smiled down at him. For a moment, he wondered why. Then the whole nightmare flooded into his memory. He looked around him. There was a canvas bunk above him. Banno and another man stood alongside him.

"Easy, Captain, you must rest," the other man said. Banno continued to grin.

Oba closed his eyes and allowed the details of his rescue to fall into place. He was alive. So was Banno. He savored the thought for several seconds, then opened his eyes and said, "Thank you."

"Your heart has had a severe strain, Captain," the other man was saying, "and we're going to keep you here in the

hospital ward for a few days.'' Then Oba saw the bottle of
colorless liquid hanging from the bunk above, with a tube
attached to a needle in his arm. "All right," he mumbled,
and fell asleep.

The passage of time during the next five days was marked
only by periods of wakefulness and sleep, with occasional
visits by Banno. They had been rescued, the lieutenant said,
by one of their three escort destroyers. It had returned before
dawn but, unable to use its lights, had failed to discover them.
Only after circling the area for several hours the next morning
did it spot the oil slick and floating wreckage of the *Sakuhato*
with its survivors. Of the 4,000 men of the regiment, plus
the ship's crew, 1,720 had been rescued. More than 500 of
them, like Oba, were crammed into the hospital ward and
other quarters with injuries.

Oba told Banno of the soldier who had saved his life and
asked him to locate the man among the survivors. His friend,
however, was unsuccessful, and Oba was not permitted to
leave the hospital ward to conduct his own search. Only when
the destroyer dropped anchor in Saipan's harbor was Oba allowed to dress and go on deck.

In the distance, a city was nestled at the foot of a green
mass that rose irregularly to an evenly sloped peak that dominated the island. Lesser hills tapered toward each end of the
island, giving way in the south to a flat expanse of land.
There the smokestacks and square framework of a factory
rose above the shoreline.

A lighter was brought alongside, and the survivors descended a gangway to board it. Although hatless, Oba wore
the pistol belt and sidearm he had been unable to discard in
the water, as well as his sword. Banno had cleaned and oiled
both weapons the day after their rescue, returning them to
serviceable condition. Most others were without weapons,
and many without shoes.

They were landed at a pier near a seaplane base where
several amphibious four-engined planes floated offshore. The
soldiers formed groups representing their original companies
and were marched away. The seriously injured were transported to a hospital. Oba and others wearing walking casualty
tags were loaded onto trucks and driven through a city that

more closely resembled a Japanese seacoast village than a south sea island community.

The neat concrete and stucco homes, surrounded by green lawns and flower gardens on tree-lined streets, were a far cry from the grass huts and half-naked natives he had expected. Japanese civilians turned to watch them pass, and children waved.

The truck stopped before one of the several two-story buildings in the city, and Oba saw a group of kimono-clad women bowing low from its entrance. As he and the others disembarked, one of the women stepped forward, dropped to her knees, and with her head bowed almost to the ground, thanked them for the hardships they had endured to protect the island from the enemy.

Inside, while they were served coffee, ice water, and tapioca cakes, Oba learned that nearly ten thousand Japanese inhabited the capital city of Garapan, and that most were engaged in sugarcane production at one of the two sugar mills to the south, or in fruit and vegetable production. Except for the large number of soldiers on the island, the women told him, they had been unaffected by the war.

The survivors were still wearing their oil-soaked clothing. Oba and the other lesser-wounded men were taken to the Garapan middle school, where sleeping quarters were arranged in hastily vacated classrooms. There, they washed for the first time in a week and were issued marine uniforms. After several futile attempts to wash out the oil, their original clothing was burned.

Oba returned to the pier the following morning. Banno was there with the 100 remaining men of the medical aid company, and some 125 other soldiers.

"They're what's left of the engineering and tank companies," the lieutenant explained. "They're to be under your command."

"Medics, engineers, and tankmen. All without equipment, many without shoes, and some only half-dressed," snorted Oba. "What am I supposed to do with them?" He walked through the squatting soldiers, still wearing their oil-soaked uniforms, and greeted several from his company. He refrained from asking about those he did not see, not wanting to hear the answer.

During the next two days he arranged for quarters and uniforms for his 225-man, poly-talented command. He and Banno remained billeted at the middle school, where he became friends with the headmaster, a scholarly man named Baba who had come to Saipan four years earlier to teach at the school he now headed. During the two-week recuperative rest he and his men had been granted, Oba took long walks with the headmaster, learning of the island's history and observing the defenses under construction. Frequently they were accompanied by Baba's two small children, Emiko, age nine, and her brother, Akira, seven.

Following the two-week rest, they were ordered to join a defense construction battalion of the 31st Army to work on half-completed gun emplacements in the hills above Garapan.

The contrast of conditions there to the equipment available to them in China and Manchuria was frightening. Heavy tractors, explosives, cement, and steel were nonexistent. "We can dig holes by hand," he complained a week later to the battalion commander, "but there's no material to fortify them with."

The commander, already well aware of the problem, drafted a message that was dispatched a few days later to the chief of staff, Central Pacific Fleet, complaining, "We cannot strengthen the fortifications appreciably now unless we get materials suitable for permanent construction. Specifically, cement, barbed wire, lumber, etc., which cannot be obtained in these islands. No matter how many soldiers there are, they can do nothing. . . . I would like this matter of supply dealt with immediately."

The sense of impending danger among the command at Saipan came as a surprise to Oba. From their victorious and isolated position in Manchuria, they had known nothing of Japan's reverses in the Pacific. Many of the officers on Saipan were certain the invasion would take place soon, possibly before the defenses were scheduled for completion in November.

With the remainder of his regiment attached to various units already on the island, Oba sought permission to reestablish his medical aid group in order to utilize the talents of his one remaining physician and enlisted medics. Eventually he was given a fraction of the medical supplies they had lost and told to establish a base with his 225 men one kilometer east of the village of Matansha on the west coast, halfway between Garapan and the northern tip of the island, Marpi Point.

In a narrow valley, they erected a thatched-roof treatment room capable of protecting twenty-four stretchers from the weather and enlarged two natural caves in the valley wall for supplies. Several smaller caves were used as living quarters by the men. By mid-May, their aid station was as complete as it ever would be.

While the Japanese high command grew increasingly concerned with its inability to complete its defenses of Saipan, Adm. Chester A. Nimitz, commander-in-chief of U.S. naval and Marine forces in the Central Pacific, was revising his plan of attack. On March 13, he sent a secret dispatch to major subordinate units, directing that highest priority be assigned to the preparation for the assault on Saipan, Tinian, and Guam.

From that point on, the staggering logistics of the operation began to fall into place. The 5th Fleet, the largest ever assembled in the Pacific, would contain more than eight hundred ships to transport, protect, and land the ground forces of the task force. Vice Adm. Richard K. Turner was placed in overall command of all units to be employed in the amphibious assault.

By mid-May, the 2d and 4th Marine divisions had boarded troop transports in Hawaii to prepare for their critical role. On May 17, some forty thousand Marines from the two divisions assaulted a beach of Maalaea Bay at Maui in the Hawaiian Islands. Although their weapons were not loaded, because of the civilian populace, the two divisions landed abreast in a tactical maneuver that simulated the planned invasion of Saipan, scheduled for a little less than one month from then. Two days later, on May 19, the same troops again climbed down rope nets from transport ships to board amtracks and move in waves against the Hawaiian island of Kahoolawe under actual naval gunfire and aerial support. The amphibious vehicles approached to within three hundred yards of the shore before returning to their transports.

Maj. Herman H. Lewis clung to the side of the bucking amtrack he rode and grimaced against the salt spray from the choppy Hawaiian waters. The thirty men in the tractor with him watched Grumman Wildcats streak from the sky in dummy runs on imagined targets. Despite the planes and naval gunfire, Lewis was unable to simulate the fear he expected to have on a real landing. Later, when he reboarded the Coast Guard ship with the designation PA-3, known to her crew as the *Zieland*, his first thought was of a shower.

Most of the 6th Regiment of the 2d Division was jammed into racks of six-level bunks in the lower decks of the ship, but Lewis and three other officers shared a stateroom that at least allowed some light to enter through a small porthole.

Lewis had joined the division shortly after it had arrived to lick its wounds in Hawaii six months earlier, following a bloody victory at Tarawa in the Gilbert Islands. Two of his cabinmates were strangers to him, officers from one of the battalions. The third, Capt. Merle Acton, with whom Lewis had trained on Hawaii, was from Regimental Plans and Operations, better known as R-3. It was with Acton that he usually stood in the long line leading to the officers' mess and discussed women, politics, the war, and their probable destination.

Acton, who had been privy to some top-level meetings at division headquarters, was convinced they would be sent to Guam. "Where else could it be?" he asked, leaning against a steel bulkhead with his hands palms-up to accentuate his opinion. "We've taken all the atolls we need for forward air bases, and we don't dare go for Iwo Jima until the Marianas are neutralized."

"We'll know in a few days," Lewis replied, "but it wouldn't surprise me if we hit Truk or even the Philippines."

"No way, buddyboy." Acton gestured with his broad hands and stubby fingers as he spoke. "The objective of the game now is to get closer to Japan." He glanced around to determine no one could overhear, then leaned closer to Lewis and spoke in a low voice. "There's a new bomber coming off the lines in Seattle and Los Angeles right now that has a range of nearly three thousand miles. Sure as hell, we're going to take some place that puts them in range of Tokyo."

Three days out of Pearl Harbor, maps were distributed to all intelligence officers. Within the hour, everyone aboard the *Zieland* knew its destination was Saipan. Everything known—and in many cases it was very little—was passed to all hands through briefings by intelligence officers. Enemy strength consisted mostly of the 43rd Division and the 47th Mixed Brigade. Another regiment, the 18th, was reported to have arrived either at Saipan or Guam three months earlier from China.

"At least," Acton observed when they had begun to digest the information, "they're not Jap marines. Those bastards at Tarawa just wouldn't stop."

Lewis did not reply immediately. He hadn't been at Tarawa, but he had acquired some knowledge of the Japanese language and culture at a Boulder, Colorado, language school during a two-month intensive course there. His impression was that all Japanese military—army and marines—were certain Japan could not lose and were more than willing—even happy—to give their lives for that victory. "They've got a psychological advantage, Merle, that I think will make all of them tough as hell."

"What's that?"

"They're not afraid to die. They think it's an honor. After all, to them, the Emperor is a descendant of God. And how can God be a loser?"

Lewis was one of the first to brief other officers of the regiment on what little was known of Saipan. Lewis had been named regimental intelligence officer while the 6th Regiment was in Hawaii. At twenty-eight, he was young for the job, but capable. He had been among the top 10 percent of every Marine Corps school he had attended, from OCS to the Japanese-language school at Boulder. Standing on the cover of an afterhold, he used maps that showed the location of Saipan in relation to Guam, 90 miles to the south, and to Tokyo, 1,250 miles to the northwest.

On a larger scale map, he pointed out the known physical features of the island. Sweat stained the shirt he had donned for the occasion as he pointed to the color-coded landing beaches on the southwest side of the island.

"We'll be going ashore on red beaches one, two, and three, together with the Eighth Regiment," he said as his pointer came to rest on a portion of the shoreline midway between the town of Garapan and another to the south called Charan-Kanoa. "The Fourth Division will land at the blue and yellow beaches down here, south of Charan-Kanoa."

The forty or so young men who clustered around Lewis followed his every word and motion. The maps he displayed were of an island where many would face the enemy for the first time. Some, they knew, would die there. But none among them would allow himself seriously to consider the prospect of being one of those who would lose their lives.

"The army's Twenty-seventh Division will be in reserve, eventually landing on the southern beaches. As the Fourth crosses to the east coast and swings north, the Twenty-seventh will secure the airfield and the south end of the island."

"What about defenses?" asked one of the men.

"We estimate the enemy force at somewhere between twenty-five and thirty thousand," Lewis replied, and waited for the impact of this figure to register on his audience. "We know the Forty-third Division is the principal defense force, and that it's supported by a mixed brigade and possibly by another regiment recently arrived from China.

"The most recent aerial reconnaissance photographs were taken in April," Lewis continued, "and the identified defensive positions are marked here near the beaches, and here." He moved his pointer to the western slopes of Mount Tapotchau, the fifteen-hundred-foot peak that dominated the spiny ridge of the central northern half of the island, where red circles and markings indicated suspected gun emplacements.

"Air strikes from carriers are scheduled to begin June twelfth," he went on, "three days before the landing, and to continue right up to D-day, when they will be joined by naval gunfire. I'm sure we will get additional and up-to-date information on defenses and troop placement from camera planes that will accompany the air strikes," he said in an effort to brighten the dismal prospects he had presented.

Lewis was shirtless an hour later as he sat on an ammunition box and leaned against a davit on an upper deck, letting the sun darken his already tanned skin, and discussed the invasion with Acton.

"We got 'em by the short hair," Acton was saying. "Once we take the Marianas, we'll have broken their inner defense line. Those new bombers will be able to hit Tokyo and everything in between." Acton sat on the deck, cushioned by a life preserver. The twelve-knot speed of the twenty-one-thousand ton transport created a breeze that dulled the tropical heat. "Hell, this may be the last amphibious operation of the war."

"Well," Lewis replied without taking his eyes from the water and the distant ships, "from what I've read, there are worse places to sit out the war. Still, there are a helluva lot of Japanese soldiers spread around the Pacific. And if they're dug in like they were at Tarawa, bombs aren't going to eliminate them."

"Neither will a bunch of Marines, except at a hell of a high price." Acton stubbed out his cigarette. "And I'm not anxious to be part of that price."

"That's where the Japs have a jump on us. They're happy to pay the price." Lewis turned to look at the younger captain.

"If that makes 'em happy," Acton's face broke into a grin, "I hope we spread one helluva lot of joy when we get to Saipan!"

The monotony of long days in the cramped quarters of the transport was broken by unending poker games, reading, writing letters home, and long conversations about women, hometown anecdotes, and the war. Lewis read and reread a classified intelligence book translated from the original German that was written in 1913, just before Japan seized the Marianas, except for Guam, from German control. The seizure, later recognized by the League of Nations, terminated some thirteen years of control by Germany, which had purchased the islands from Spain at the conclusion of the Spanish-American War.

The author had gone into great detail describing the history, inhabitants, and physical features of the Marianas, not-

ing that they had been named after Queen Maria Anna of
Spain, who sent missionaries and soldiers there in 1668.

A prologue to the original text pointed out that little was
known of the islands after 1935, when Japan withdrew from
the League of Nations and discontinued the annual reports
she had made since 1920 to Geneva. From that point on,
Japan had jealously guarded the islands against visits by for-
eigners. But by 1938, it was known that Japanese immigrants
outnumbered the Chamorro natives, and that Japan was planning powerful naval and air bases throughout the archipelago.

Japan's complete sovereignty over the islands was frustrated by the American presence on Guam. One of her first
moves at the outbreak of World War II was to remove that
frustration with the occupation of that island.

It was that portion of the book that dealt with Saipan on
which Lewis focused most intently. The seventy-two-square-
mile island was a narrow north-south strip, roughly fourteen
miles long and six miles wide. Together with its sister island
of Tinian, three miles to the south, Saipan had become the
key point of the Marianas defense, and an important supply
base and communications center for Japan's operations in the
Central Pacific. Two airfields and a seaplane base on Saipan
and two airfields on Tinian served as stopovers and refueling
points for Japan's aircraft ferry route to the south.

Steep cliffs dropped to the ocean on the island's east coast,
while the coastal plain on the west side was fringed by reefs
that extended from one to two miles from the shoreline. It
was over these reefs that the initial assault waves would travel
in the lumbering tracked landing vehicles that rode low in
the deep water but were able to grind their way over the coral
reefs to deposit their passengers ashore. Support troops and
the much needed materiel for continuing the assault would
follow in shallow-draft landing craft that could maneuver to
within a few feet of the shoreline.

More recent estimates of the Japanese civilian population
on the island placed it at considerably more than ten thousand, and that of the Chamorros at about four thousand. The
capital city, Garapan, housed most of the Japanese community on the west coast flatland, while the town of Charan-
Kanoa was occupied by some three thousand Chamorros.

The most outstanding feature of the island was its fifteen-hundred-foot Mount Tapotchau, surrounded by a maze of jungle-covered hills and depressions and dominating the hilly backbone that ran from the south to Marpi Point at the north, a sheer cliff to the sea.

Lewis studied the topographical maps that he would carry ashore and realized that their landing would be made under the eyes and guns of any artillery forces stationed on the rocky slopes of Tapotchau or the surrounding hills.

On the southern flatlands, about a mile from the south coast, the Japanese had built a 3,600-foot airfield which would accommodate medium bombers as well as fighter aircraft. Aerial reconnaissance photographs disclosed that fighter strips also were under construction just north of Charan-Kanoa and near Marpi Point.

The 6th Regiment, according to the battle plan, would land between Garapan and Charan-Kanoa with the 8th and fight inland to a low ridge line about one mile from the shore, designated 0-1, before swinging north.

There was no identification of beach defenses among the intelligence documents. Although the most recent aerial photographs, dated April 18, 1944, gave no hint of emplacements along the beach, Lewis knew that sand-covered and well-hidden pill boxes there would be the first sources of fire to strike the invading Marines.

The armada of which the *Zieland* was a part sailed steadily westward during the early days of June. Increased attention was given to the cleaning and checking of weapons as the fifteenth grew near. Lewis attended a series of meetings with other regimental officers at which contingency plans were methodically organized.

The attack on Saipan was to be only half of the American campaign in the Marianas. While the three divisions would land at Saipan, the largest island of the chain, Guam, would be hit and captured by the 3d Amphibious Corps, consisting of the 1st Marine Provisional Brigade and the 3d Marine Division.

The gigantic task force headed toward the horizon from all directions. Troop transports, cargo ships, and destroyers were identifiable from the *Zieland*'s decks. Beyond the horizon, sixteen carriers, seven battleships, thirteen cruisers, and most of the fifty-eight destroyers assigned to the Marianas operation steamed under battle colors.

On the night of the fourteenth, Lewis spent six hours in restless sleep, fighting the growing tension that had been gnawing at him, and finally arose at 2:00 A.M. Thirty minutes later, in full battle gear except for his carbine and helmet, Lewis stood at the chest-high table of the officers' mess and nervously devoured the traditional D-day breakfast, a steak topped by two fried eggs. Beside him was Captain Acton, but neither spoke. Only as they turned to leave did they shake hands. "Keep your ass down," Lewis said.

"Yeah, see ya ashore," Acton replied.

Thirty minutes later, together with riflemen and others from regimental headquarters, Lewis clambered down a rope net in total darkness, dropped into a bobbing amtrack, and quickly moved to make room for those still climbing down. He found himself pushed into the rear port side of the vehicle. He crouched there, slightly benumbed by the realization that he was about to fight for his life.

With a roar of its engine, the amtrack moved away from the ship to join the eight hundred similar craft and more than nine hundred landing craft that would spend the next two hours making large circles as they completed formation for the assault. Salvos of naval gunfire roared over their heads and erupted in flashes of light in the distant blackness. Fires at several points on the island gave a pinkish glow to the columns of smoke above them. Lewis leaned against the corner of the rocking vehicle. He could see the spurting fire from the big guns of the battleships before he heard their heavy missiles pass overhead. Around him, men crouched in silence and clutched their weapons. The amtrack rocked gently in the churned-up waves as its noisy treads propelled it at a little more than one mile an hour.

With the first light of dawn, the naval support ships increased the enfilading fire they threw at the island. Below the hazy silhouette of Mount Tapotchau the island was cloaked in a pall of dust and smoke. At shortly after 8:00 A.M., the signal was given and the long lines of amphibious tractors began to move toward the shoreline, four thousand yards distant. Minutes later, Lewis's tractor climbed onto the shelf of an outer reef, then bounced and lurched over the coral formations and shallow pools that ringed the beach.

Naval gunfire had ceased, Lewis noted, and had been replaced by carrier-based SBD-3 dive bombers and Grumman Wildcat fighters that streaked low over the beach, hitting Japanese defenses with machine-gun bullets and bombs. Simultaneously, enemy artillery and mortar shells began exploding among the vehicles. The slow-moving craft were sitting ducks for the Japanese gunners. Twice, screaming shrapnel flew overhead as near misses rocked Lewis's amtrack to the point of capsizing.

From his crouched position, Lewis saw treetops in the distance, then directly overhead. The tractor stopped, and someone yelled, ''Let's go!'' He threw himself on the ledge of the vehicle, swung his legs, and landed on sand. He lunged for a fallen tree trunk a few feet away. Momentarily secure behind the coconut log, he looked about him. Tractors on both sides of him were depositing running men on the beach as their .50-caliber machine guns sent steady streams of fire into the island ahead of them. Shell and mortar fire exploded in both directions along the water's edge. Bodies of Marines floated in the shallow water or lay sprawled on the sand. A momentary awareness of each spectacle seared itself in Lewis's memory, then was replaced by another. His only continuing thought was that he was alive, and would have to fight to remain so.

A machine-gun squad slid to the ground beside him and set up its weapon to fire over his protecting log. Through occasional holes in the smoke and dust he could see uprooted trees and patches of shrubbery, but nothing of the enemy.

Calls for corpsmen were passed up and down the crowded thirty-foot strip of beach into which Japanese gunners were directing their fire.

Marines to his right heaved hand grenades into the greenery ahead, then rushed forward immediately after the explosions, firing at a still-invisible enemy. To his left, Lewis saw the antenna of a field radio and began inching his way toward it.

Sgt. Oswaldo Parades, a soft-spoken draftsman from Los

Angeles, was lying next to the radioman, studying a map on which he would be responsible for noting all changing troop positions. The sight of Parades already at work suddenly made Lewis aware of his own role in the battle.

"Where do you figure we are, Parades?"

"The best I can tell, we're smack-dab on Red-Two, sir."

"Have you seen Colonel Risley?"

"Yessir, he just moved down to the left. The Third Bat just took some mortar fire."

Lewis had just begun worming his way in the direction taken by the regimental CO when a barrage of rifle fire to his front froze him with fear. Beyond the Marines prone on the sand, he saw about twenty Japanese running toward them from the north. Peering over the sights of his carbine, he watched the Japanese approach, firing as they ran. Then a barrage of rifle fire from Marines on the beach stopped them in mid-step. The group crumpled almost en masse as they neared the rallying Marines. The last three collapsed only a few steps beyond their comrades.

Again, the cry for corpsmen, and this time Lewis could see that Colonel Risley was one of the objects of concern. Someone was tying a tourniquet around the upper part of the colonel's left arm, just above a blood-gushing bullet hole. As Lewis crawled toward him, he could see the colonel trying to write on a message pad with his good hand.

"Lewis," he said when he saw the major. "Take this! Get back to the radio and pass the word to operations to bring the First Battalion in behind the Third. They took mortar hits on their CP!"

On the island for the first time, Lewis rose to his feet and ran in a low crouch toward the radioman. The situation was already changing for the better. Forward elements of the attack had penetrated the green beyond the beach, and others were moving up to take advantage of the additional cover. Slowly the regiment advanced up the gently rising ground toward 0-1.

· 2 ·

SAIPAN

Sgt. Yuki Nakano's face tilted upward as he studied the vine-covered protrusions of coral and black rock that formed the fifty-meter-high cliff to his right. He then returned his gaze to his front and continued to peer through the dense foliage that limited his view of the valley before him. He had been lying in the same prone position for nearly two hours as the sounds of battle on top of the cliff had grown nearer. Now they were almost overhead. Captain Yamashita and the rest of the company had fallen back. He knew his turn to stand or fall was approaching.

He once again checked the curved clip of ammunition that held forty-five polished bullets in readiness above his machine gun, then turned to see that the two remaining men of his squad were prepared to replace it with fresh ones. His mission was to hold this ravine while the rest of the company blocked the enemy advance on the cliff above. He had chosen this position because the ravine narrowed to thirty meters here, and he had a good field of fire from the cliff to the jungle-covered hill on his left.

Here, he thought with confidence, the tanks, naval bombardment, and aircraft the Americans had used to crush Japanese defenses in their advance from the beach to the hills, would be useless. Here they would have to fight like soldiers. And here they would be defeated.

His body stiffened and he lowered his head as a camouflaged helmet moved into an open area one hundred meters down the ravine.

"They're coming," he whispered to the men on each side of him. His finger rested lightly on the trigger of the machine gun. His heartbeat grew more rapid as he saw other figures move in and out of the concealing jungle. He had already selected a clearing fifty meters distant as his target area. It was only a matter of waiting until they reached it.

Second Lt. William Stephens, of the 3d Platoon, G Company, 2d Marine Regiment, listened to the exchange of fire atop the cliff above him and controlled his advance to stay abreast of it. He knew that F Company was encountering a well-entrenched enemy on the high ground which, as it slowly withdrew northward, was inflicting heavy casualties on the Marines.

Stephens's platoon, ordered to clear the narrow valley at the foot of the cliff, had as yet met no resistance but had slowed to maintain a line with the embattled F Company. He halted his force at the edge of a natural clearing, then motioned for the squads on his left and right flanks to continue their advance.

Suddenly, to the sounds of the battle above him, were added the sharp staccato cracks of a Nambu light machine gun. Stephens and his entire platoon hit the ground before a second burst split the air above their heads. Rolling on his side to check the men around him, Stephens saw one writhing in agony.

"Corpsman! Where in the hell is the corpsman?" The call was echoed back by others until a voice in the distance called that he was moving up.

The young lieutenant shouted to a squad leader, "Dombrovski, take a couple of men and move around to the right! Get that sonofabitch!"

The corporal signaled to two of his squad and began making his way in the direction indicated by Stephens. A sharp burst of bullets ripped into the trees above them as the trio sought to become invisible behind any bush, rock, or rise of earth that offered cover or concealment. Working with their elbows and a twisting motion of their bodies, they moved slowly toward a position they hoped would give them a shot at the machine gun that pinned them.

Sergeant Nakano had seen four men drop as bullets from his weapon struck their bodies. The rest had disappeared behind rocks hidden by heavy undergrowth. He fired two more bursts at the sound of shouting, then waited for the enemy to react.

He had hoped they would charge. But now, as moments became minutes, he knew they would attempt a flanking movement. He bellied his way backward and motioned to one of the squad to bring the machine gun. Retrieving his rifle, he led the other two toward the cliff where he had selected his secondary defensive position, a well-concealed indentation in the cliff about ten meters above the valley floor.

Still hidden by jungle foliage, the three men flattened their bodies against the cliff as they searched for footholds. When they were within a few meters of the ledge, Nakano could see that instead of stopping under an overhanging projection of coral, the indentation swung to the left, forming a narrow cave.

It was the cave's natural concealment that had led Yoshi Aono to select it as a hiding place for his family. For five days he had struggled to keep them alive, first from the artillery shells and strafing planes that attacked the hills above the city of Garapan where they had taken refuge before the invasion, then from the advancing Americans.

The frail man had brought his small family to Saipan fifteen years earlier, when he went to work as a chemical engineer at the island's large sugar processing plant. They had been without food for two days. Mitsuko, their younger daughter, was feverish, and could go no farther. His wife and Chieko, the elder daughter, who had been a nurse at Garapan's hospital, also were reaching the point of exhaustion.

Aono's thin fingers played nervously at the rocks that lay around him on the floor of the cave. His eyes remained on the entrance and the mass of greenery that formed a wall of foliage over the valley floor.

He, his wife, and their daughters had fled their comfortable home in Garapan on June 13, when enemy planes rained bombs on the city in a preinvasion assault while warships hurled shells at more selective targets. The army had been misinformed. They had boasted, almost until the attack began, that the Americans were being defeated throughout the Pacific. Aono and his family had run from their home with only the clothing they wore, spending the next two days with sugar farmers in a secluded valley above the city.

The increased bombardment that accompanied the enemy's landing on June 15 had forced them to flee farther into the hills. Others who had shared their terror at the knowledge that the enemy had broken through the beach defenses had fled farther north to the caves of Mount Tapotchau or beyond that toward Marpi Point at the northernmost tip of the island.

But now he knew they would die. The Americans, he had been told, preferred not to take prisoners. And if they did, it was for the amusement to be had in raping the women and torturing the men. He was without a weapon and wondered how he and the women could take their own lives to avoid capture. He had heard the firing directly below his hiding place and knew the moment was near. Hurriedly, he began to gather fist-sized rocks he could use to throw at the Americans or, if necessary, to destroy the family.

He heard the scrape of boots moving up the cliff toward the cave. The first rocks—the largest—would be used to kill the first American whose head appeared at the cave entrance.

As he waited, he heard a whisper in Japanese. It was from a soldier urging his men to move quickly but quietly. A momentary sense of relief was replaced a second later by the realization that their hiding place would not only be discovered, but would soon be the focal point of a fight to the death by the soldiers who were beginning to set up their machine gun at the cave's entrance.

"What are you doing?" Aono whispered from the recess of the cave.

Startled, the first soldier to enter swung and pointed a rifle at the frightened man. "Who are you?" he asked. Then, seeing they were civilians, he whispered, "Stay quiet!" and turned to peer over the edge of the cave's entrance.

Chieko Aono cradled her teenage sister, who occasionally moaned in a near-delirium. Her mother knelt in prayer, silently voicing the words that she hoped might save them from the death that seemed inevitable.

Despite her fear, the girl felt anger and frustration at having no control over what was to happen to them. As she looked about for some positive action she could take, the interior of the cave exploded in sound. It was the opening burst of the Nambu. One of the soldiers was firing into the jungle below.

Corporal Dombrovski, who had called a moment before that the machine gun was no longer there, had stood to make his voice heard by his lieutenant. Five bullets from the first burst of machine-gun fire had ripped through his body.

Shouts were followed by a volley of fire that poured into the cave. Like a hundred angry hornets, ricocheting bullets whizzed from wall to wall. Several of them found their mark in Aono's thin body.

Chieko Aono felt the impact of the bullet that killed her sister. She watched in horror as the girl coughed and blood streamed from her mouth. She heard her mother scream. Two of the soldiers lay beside their machine gun. A third rose, shouted an obscenity, and began firing his rifle at the enemy. She neither heard nor felt the exploding grenade that blew the standing soldier to the rear of the cave, where he landed on top of the sisters—one dead and the other still alive.

The American who inspected the cave a few minutes later cautiously examined the bodies of Nakano and the two soldiers, then looked briefly at the battered bodies of what had been the Aono family. Only the eldest daughter, covered by the bodies of Mitsuko and the soldier, continued to breathe. But the American did not notice.

It was nearly an hour later when Aono—Chieko had refused to allow any but her immediate family to call her by her first name since she had turned eighteen—looked up and recoiled in horror. Her sister's sightless eyes stared at her only inches away. Struggling to escape the weight of the soldier whose body pinned her to the floor, she stifled another scream. Sobbing, she pushed the body from her, then stumbled blindly toward the cave's mouth.

There she stopped, ducked back inside, and dropped to the

ground. Barely one hundred meters away, Americans were setting up camp. Some unloaded supplies from a jeep and trailer, several were cooking over an open fire, and others slept.

Gradually, as she recalled the events up to the moment of the explosion, her fear turned to anger, then to hatred for those who had killed her parents and sister.

Three feet away, the machine gun sat, poised. She pushed aside the body that lay with one arm draped over the firing mechanism and aimed the weapon at the unsuspecting Americans. Carefully she pulled the trigger. Nothing. She pulled again, then collapsed beside it, her body wracked by silent sobs.

Slowly and inexorably, the combined might of one army and two Marine divisions rolled northward over the frequently fanatic, but underpowered, defenders. Several kilometers to the north, Japanese who had yet to feel the might of the attacking infantrymen died under the relentless barrages of naval gunfire directed by circling observer planes. By D plus 3, eight-inch guns were in place on the southern end of the island, throwing their huge projectiles at targets ahead of the American advance. Strafing planes from carriers further impeded efforts by the Japanese high command to move its forces to strategically defensive positions.

Two weeks after the landing, the narrow valley in which Capt. Sakae Oba had established his aid station was still six kilometers ahead of the American advance. The thatched-roof treatment room had long since been destroyed, and casualties were being tended in caves lining the south bank of the canyon.

The moans of a delirious dying man, whose head was covered in bandages that hid a gaping hole where part of his left jaw and ear had been torn away, were the only sounds in the cave. Captain Oba turned his head toward the dim interior where more than a dozen other wounded lay on makeshift stretchers or on the bare ground. Most were conscious, but uttered no sound.

Four medics and one army physician divided their time

between this and a larger cave ten meters away that held even more wounded, many of whom would not survive the day.

Some of the forty men Oba still commanded were boiling the foul-smelling water they drew from a cistern near the ruins of a house that once stood in a small clearing at the base of the cliff in which they hid. Others guarded the position's perimeter while still others slept before taking over the guard duty at sunset.

Faintly, Oba heard the explosions of shells falling to the south. He hunkered close to the cave's entrance and tried to judge the distance. Although the entrance faced in that direction, the cliff that formed the south side of the ravine blocked his view of everything except the cloud of smoke that floated over the island.

His headquarters building and the ten-bed medical ward he had supervised at the mouth of the ravine had been destroyed eighteen days earlier, when the enemy's planes and warships began blasting the island in preparation for the troop assault two days later.

He heard his name and turned back to the gloomy interior of the cave. Dr. Kenji Ishikawa motioned to a still figure and said simply, "Here's another." The gaunt physician, whose high cheekbones accentuated his thinness, had once been on the staff of a hospital in Tokyo. Now his expertise was being used to try to keep life in bodies that had been slashed, broken, and mangled by instruments of war.

Oba signaled to two of his men who had been assisting the medics, and they half carried, half dragged the body to the cave entrance. Stepping outside to check the sky for aircraft, he grunted a command and the two soldiers moved with their burden toward the ditch fifty meters distant that had become a mass grave for fatalities. Occasional shifts in the wind brought the nauseous stench of death to his nostrils. Oba knew that already more than thirteen bodies lay in the depression, thinly covered by layers of dirt. He wondered for a moment if it would become his final resting place, too.

He turned back to Ishikawa, who sat on a wooden box, smoking a cigarette and staring at his patients. "You should take some rest," he told the doctor. "We can't afford to lose you through exhaustion."

"It's not the fatigue, it's the frustration," Ishikawa replied without turning his eyes from the wounded soldiers. "We're supposed to be a field hospital, but now we don't even have enough supplies to keep our own wounded alive. None of us has even seen an American, yet we're destroyed as a unit. What kind of a war is this?"

Oba studied the demoralized physician. The two of them—the only two captains of the 18th Regiment to survive the sinking of their ship off Taiwan in March—had been drawn together by that force that links those who have endured and survived an ordeal. Of the twelve medical officers of the company, Ishikawa alone had survived the sinking, and now had only the assistance of an enlisted medic, Corporal Hayashi.

He grunted a sympathetic reply to the doctor, who was in the process of snubbing his cigarette out and placing the butt in a silver case. Oba was about to say something encouraging when he heard someone scrambling up the rocky slope leading to the cave.

Pulling his pistol, he walked quickly to the entrance. A soldier, more properly dressed and equipped than his own men, appeared at the opening.

The soldier's eyes took in Oba's captain's insignia, and he snapped to attention and bent from the waist in a formal, stiff-armed bow. "Orders from regimental headquarters for Captain Oba," he said before returning to an erect position.

"Give it to me," Oba gruffed in a military tone.

The soldier saluted, produced a message blank from a dispatch case and handed it to Oba, saluted again, and took one pace backward. Quickly, Oba scanned its contents. His unit was to join that of a Major Hanai, then move south to the town of Donnin near the east coast of the island. As he read, his mind's eye saw the map of Saipan he had memorized. Although he had never been on the eastern side of the island, he knew immediately the route they would follow. The orders were to move out that night. Major Hanai and his force were to join them later in the day.

From his dispatch case, Oba removed a message blank and wrote an acknowledgment of the order, returning the soldier's salute as he handed it to him.

The message had been initialed by Colonel Suzuki, commanding officer of the 135th Regiment. Although it was only one kilometer to the west, Oba had had no contact with the island headquarters for three days and had begun to fear that the shells he had heard bursting in that direction had destroyed the command post.

"Soldier," he snapped to one of his men who stood waiting expectantly, "tell Lieutenant Banno to report here immediately." Then he showed the message to Ishikawa.

The chubby Lieutenant Banno, whose sense of humor had buoyed Oba's spirits during the first days of Saipan, arrived quickly. He saluted militarily, but with the usual twinkle in his eyes.

"We have orders to move against the enemy," Oba said. "We're going to Donnin tonight."

"At last," Banno smiled. "They realize they need us to win. Are we going as infantry or as a hospital unit?"

"A little of both. We'll carry what medical supplies we can, but once there, we're to attack as infantry."

"Good. Once they see how well we can fight, maybe they'll put us back in the infantry and give this aid station to people who don't have our combat experience."

Oba showed his friend the orders, and together they studied their maps, planning the six-kilometer trip.

By the time Major Hanai, an officious little man with a sharp nose and a long face, arrived late in the afternoon, Oba and those who were leaving with him were ready to move. Corporal Hayashi and four soldiers were to remain with the wounded. Dr. Ishikawa and the remaining men would advance with Oba to the south.

Earlier in the afternoon, Oba and two soldiers had climbed to the top of the far side of the ravine, and then to a hill two hundred meters beyond it. From there they could see the smoke and occasionally a shell-burst on the slopes of Mount Tapotchau. Most of the action was on the southern slopes. He knew, even without looking at his map, that Donnin lay directly east of the area he watched. The enemy would be approaching Donnin.

A sense of satisfaction at being able, at last, to meet the enemy brought a smile to his lips. The long, frustrating days of simply hearing the sounds of others inflicting their toll on the enemy were over. Tonight or tomorrow morning, he thought, I will strike my first blow against the American enemy. And if I should die, it will be with a bloodied sword in my hands.

At sunset, Oba assembled his small force with the soldiers who had accompanied Major Hanai for a briefing of their mission. The men squatted outside the larger of the two hospital caves while the major, in polished boots and a sword that barely cleared the ground, paced back and forth in front of the entrance, pausing to turn and speak, then continuing to pace as he formed his next point.

"The ungodly enemy has succeeded in getting ashore," he said, "but his back is to the sea. His weaponry, which has won him a foothold, is no match for Japanese courage. Even now, our forces, inspired by their dedication to our Emperor, are regrouping to drive the foreign devils into the sea. Tonight, we will take part in that honorable battle. We will halt this barbarous attack that is an insult to our Imperial forces.

"Our role will be in coordination with other units of the Imperial Army. We will establish our headquarters just north of Donnin, then prepare to join our comrades in dealing a death blow to the American devils."

He finished his address with his voice rising to a climax that brought the entire group to its feet shouting, *"Dai Nippon, banzai!"*

The 240 men were divided into three groups, which departed at fifteen-minute intervals starting at 11:00 P.M. Oba, with Doctor Ishikawa and about 100 men, formed the first group. Lieutenant Banno and a young tank company lieutenant named Morita, who had joined them after the rescue at sea, took the second. Hanai and his headquarters staff of some 40 men were to follow.

A high layer of clouds blocked the dim light of a half moon, but flares over Tapotchau four kilometers to the south gave them faint but almost constant illumination. Two kilometers from their base, they crossed a road that bisected the island. They then located a dirt road that skirted the spiny ridges rising toward Mount Tapotchau. The road was clogged with the human debris of battle, mostly moving in the opposite direction, away from the horror of combat. Women, many of

them with infants on their backs and two or three crying
children in tow, moved doggedly northward. At one point a
young woman, seemingly oblivious to the fact that she was
naked to the waist, sat at the side of the road and dazedly
watched the parade of humanity. Unarmed soldiers, many
wounded, wandered aimlessly along the narrow road. The
flashes of distant flares flickered across their expressionless
faces.

Huge shells fired from the southern end of the island
crashed at random in the hills and jungle around them. Blindly
fired to harass the Japanese forces, they were ignored by Oba
and his men. Twice, explosions were close enough for them
to feel the concussion, and screaming hunks of hot metal
crashed into the valley below them.

At 2:00 A.M., they crossed the east-west road across the
island, and Oba halted the procession to check his map with
a penlight. Then he angled the unit left down a gently sloping
jungle-covered flat that would bring them to the rendezvous
area just north of Donnin. An hour later he halted and deployed his force, sending two scouts ahead to establish contact with the other groups.

The sounds of battle had become distinct. Rifle and automatic weapon fire came in sporadic bursts from the south at
what seemed to be about five hundred meters. Flares from
enemy ships popped almost directly overhead, turning night
into day and throwing stark, slowly moving shadows as they
drifted eastward.

"Attention," Oba rasped. He discerned three figures moving up the slope toward him. He suddenly realized he had
not arranged a coded password for the night and wondered
for a moment how to challenge the approaching trio. When
they were within twenty meters, he pointed his pistol and
growled in a low voice, "Who are you?"

He recognized the voice that replied as one of his scouts.
The three stopped as they reached his position, and one tried
to salute as they took cover in the darkness of the jungle.

"Lieutenant Banno and his men are in a canyon about two
hundred meters in that direction," the scout reported. "We
have not located Major Hanai."

Oba ordered his force to join Banno's, then supervised them

as they unloaded and set up their meager medical supplies in various caves in the face of the canyon. A dry creek bed formed the center of the ravine, and most vegetation had been swept away by the rain-fed torrents that frequently tumbled down the canyon.

By 4:00 A.M. he was as organized as possible. After posting guards and ordering scouts to check to the east, west, and north for Major Hanai's group, he told the others to get some rest. He fell asleep to the sharp, high-pitched cracks of a Japanese light machine gun and the lower-throated bark of an American .30-caliber air-cooled machine gun.

At dawn a lull settled over the front as soldiers of both sides concentrated on relieving themselves over hastily dug slit trenches and finding some sort of food to ease their hunger pangs.

Oba arose at the first light of dawn. The ominous silence belied the fact that within a half kilometer lay a wave of violence which, even at that moment, was advancing steadily toward them. Should they attack? Should they build defensive positions? How close was the enemy? Where were the other units they were supposed to join? All these questions needed immediate answers if Oba was to carry out his mission.

A narrow dirt road divided a sugarcane field from the jungled hills that formed the ravine in which they slept and meandered south toward where Oba knew the enemy either lay in wait or was silently moving toward them.

"Sergeant Bito, get your rifle and come with me. Let's find out what's happening. We'll move parallel to the road until we locate the enemy, then decide what to do."

The dense jungle slowed their progress as they pushed their way through the undergrowth a few meters from the road. Both men moved as silently as possible, stopping every few meters to listen for enemy activity.

A sound of movement to their right front sent both men flat on their stomachs. The sound grew rapidly to become the unmistakable noise of a large group of men forcing their way through the resisting jungle.

Oba looked at the sergeant beside him who lay with his rifle pointed in the direction of the growing sound. Bito's face gave no indication of the emotional storm that Oba knew must be raging within him. Oba crept forward to a jagged rock and waited, pistol in hand.

He almost fired as the first of the men entered a clearing only twenty-five meters away, then released the pressure on the trigger when he saw they were Japanese. A full platoon of soldiers, crashing their way through the undergrowth, heedless of the noise they made, crossed the road and disappeared into the cane field to the east.

Moments later, the heavy sound of American machine guns shattered the silence. They were close, probably no more than two hundred meters. Rifle fire and the whomp of exploding mortars to his left front told him the enemy had advanced to a point almost due east of where he lay. The fleeing platoon had probably walked into their line.

The chattering of enemy machine guns was suddenly interspersed with the crack of rifles directly ahead. Twice he saw oily black smoke rise above the greenery where flame-throwers hurled their fiery death at his countrymen.

Satisfied that his men were not in immediate danger of attack, Oba motioned to Bito to withdraw, and the two men returned to their would-be aid station in the ravine. They reached the station in half the time it had taken on the way out. Lieutenant Banno had most of his men and equipment set up in a large, shallow cave a hundred meters up the canyon, but he and a few of his noncoms were in a deeper cave near the one in which Oba had spent the night.

The high whine of a single-engine aircraft suddenly made itself heard over the other noises of war, and Oba looked up as a pontooned biplane passed overhead, then banked and dove to within two hundred meters of their aid station before turning on a wing and circling southward.

"Inside the caves!" he shouted at the men, who stood motionless, shocked by the audacity of the American pilot. A few had recovered sufficiently to fire their rifles at the plane as it flew to the south.

But Oba knew the damage had been done. A few minutes later the plane returned at a much higher altitude and circled for several minutes. The craft's pontoons made it obvious that it was a navy spotter plane, and it was safe to assume it had already reported their position to the battleships and cruisers that threw their huge missiles at the island with impunity.

The first shell shattered the air with no warning. It turned the upper end of the canyon into deadly chaos, uprooting trees and shattering coral rock into jagged, deadly slivers, and unleashing shards of hot steel that slashed through anything that lay in their unpredictable trajectory. For sixty seconds the canyon was silent. In the distance, the tiny biplane circled to observe and correct the fire of the navy ships. The second, third, and fourth explosions followed within seconds of each other, splitting eight-inch tree trunks and gouging huge holes in the canyon floor and sides.

Oba and a half dozen others hugged the rocky floor of the first cave, Banno and about twenty men were in the next, and the rest cringed in the uppermost of the three caves. All clasped their hands over their ears to prevent the concussion from shattering their eardrums. Occasionally the razor-sharp pieces of steel would slice into one of the caves, ricocheting until it found the unprotected flesh of an occupant.

The ground heaved and sank with the impact of each bursting shell. Oba felt his anger and frustration overcoming the numbing fear he had sensed with the opening salvo.

This is no way to fight a war, he told himself. How can we be expected to fight when we can't move a hand or a foot outside the caves? There is no honor in hiding like frightened children, but it's equally useless to step outside and die by the hands of an enemy you can't even see, let alone fight. War has always been an honorable pursuit, he reasoned, where a man could prove himself against an enemy. If he were victorious, he reaped the glory of victory. If he died, it was an honorable death, which came only after he had inflicted his share of casualties on the enemy. But this, this was not war. This was a one-sided slaughter. Somehow, he had to get the men to a position from which they could fight like soldiers.

A thundering roar and a brilliant flash of light were accompanied by the angry buzz of red-hot metal as shrapnel flew into the cave. He was barely aware of a nearby scream as he fought to regain control of his senses. A wave of panic overtook him as he realized he could no longer see. A reptile of fear coiled about his innards, immobilizing him. The scream had turned into a gurgling whimper, but he couldn't even be sure of the direction from which it came. Gradually he controlled his trembling and then, as the air cleared, realized he wasn't blind. The smoke from the last shell had obscured the cave's interior. Explosions continued to rock the narrow ravine as he crawled toward the source of the scream. In the dim light he made out the form of the man and reached out to him. His groping hand encountered a still-hot piece of metal, the size of a shoe, protruding from the man's intestines. He wondered what he should do, but a moment later the man's whimpering ceased. Slowly Oba crawled back to the defile in which he had been lying and cursed the cowardly enemy who killed only from a distance, who was afraid to fight as a soldier should.

It was mid-afternoon before the bombardment was lifted. By then, nearly half of the force he had brought to the ravine were dead or were so badly wounded they would never again fight. The upper cave had taken a direct hit, killing many of the men in it. Lieutenant Banno and those with him had escaped without injury, but most of their equipment was useless. Doctor Ishikawa's mangled body lay next to that of a man he had been trying to drag to safety.

Shortly after dusk, a force of about twenty soldiers approached their base from the upper end of the ravine. Led by a sergeant, the group seemed stunned by the intensity of the American onslaught. Many wore makeshift bandages over wounds they would have been hospitalized for under other conditions. The sergeant, with a bloodstained cloth wrapped around his left hand, was brought to Oba. He saluted and said his name was Iijima.

"Why are you retreating?" Oba asked angrily. "Why don't you stand and fight?"

"We're under orders to move north to Matansha," the exhausted sergeant replied. "The One Thirty-fifth is planning a counterassault from there, and we are to join it."

Oba had just come from less than two kilometers away from the small village north of Tanapag Harbor, and he had not been told of a counterattack. Instead, he had been ordered to where the Americans were attacking. "How near is the enemy?" he asked.

"Five hundred meters to the south," Iijima answered, "but they have already taken the lower land east of here, and by tomorrow we'll be encircled."

Oba directed his men to share their remaining rations with the ravenous soldiers who, Oba learned from the sergeant, had been without food for thirty-six hours. While they ate, Oba was told that the attack, to be launched in two or three days, was to sweep the enemy from the western coast and to cut their supply lines from the sea.

Flares from the same warships that had turned the morning into a massacre were bursting overhead, casting an eerie light over the ravine.

Oba ordered those who could walk to prepare to return to their aid station near Matansha. Some of the injured were carried in improvised litters, and others, who were more critically wounded, were left in protected firing positions from which they could kill as many of the enemy as possible before they, too, gave their lives for their country.

The injustice of this war sickened Oba. Sixty percent of his regiment had been lost at sea before they had even reached Saipan. This afternoon, half his remaining unit had been destroyed. Only a few of his unit still functioned, yet neither he nor his men had seen even one of the enemy. And now, regardless of what the sergeant said about regrouping, he was ordering his men to retreat without having fired a round at the enemy.

The sergeant and his platoon collapsed from exhaustion after eating and slept in hollows of tangled underbrush while Oba and what remained of his force repacked for a return trek to the site of their aid station. At 10:00 P.M. Oba roused Iijima, and the group started northward, avoiding open areas and exposure by the ever-present flares.

Firing to their right front told them that the Americans had, indeed, advanced along the coastal areas far ahead of them. Oba ordered three of the sergeant's soldiers to form a point a hundred meters ahead of the main body, to purposely draw the fire of any enemy they should discover. Random artillery from the eight-inch guns on the south end of the island continued to explode around them throughout the night, but no enemy was encountered.

The blackness of the sky was giving way to the gray of dawn when they half walked, half slid down the bank of the ravine where they had been hiding since the invasion. Even from the ridge, Oba could see the station was much more crowded than it had been two days earlier. Stretchers and bandaged men filled both caves, overflowing out into crude shelters camouflaged by greenery.

He found Corporal Hayashi, whom he had left in charge, working in one of the overcrowded caves. Hayashi said an artillery barrage the day before had almost wiped out a company of soldiers moving toward the front. They had been assigned to defend Marpi Point, the high cliff overlooking the northern tip of the island, but had been ordered to move south against the enemy. Most were killed, and the survivors had been brought to the aid station.

Oba studied the corporal. He knew that the young man had just begun to study medicine in Sendai when the war broke out. Exhaustion prevented his eyes from focusing, and his speech was slurred. The last of his supplies had been used on yesterday's casualties. Hopelessness and frustration were reflected in his every sentence. Oba ordered him to leave the wounded and get some sleep, then visited the other two caves. Each presented the same picture of torn bodies, many bandaged with ripped-up portions of uniforms.

He directed Banno to detail men to bury the growing number of dead, whose putrefaction was already saturating the camp, but to first remove those portions of their uniforms that could be used as bandages.

The normally jovial Banno had changed since the shelling at Donnin. The horror of this kind of warfare had taken the twinkle from his eyes and had given a cast of seriousness to his round face. Oba felt the man who accepted his order was almost a stranger, rather than one he had come to consider a close friend.

Late that afternoon, Oba received orders to abandon the aid station and move all personnel to Matansha, by now a much battered community about two kilometers west. From there, it was confirmed, a counterattack was to be launched that would sweep the enemy from the entire western shoreline, cutting them off from their supply ships and isolating them inland.

Oba learned from the runner who brought the order that the Americans had swept northward to Tanapag Harbor, about three kilometers south of Matansha, and were moving down the ridge of hills from Mount Tapotchau. He knew firsthand of their advance on the eastern side of the island.

"The choice for counterattack is a good one," he told Banno. "In less than three weeks the enemy has broken all our defenses and has taken most of the island. Our only chance is to cut their supply line. Get the men ready to move!"

Oba knew that less than half the station patients, even with the aid of improvised crutches, would be able to travel the two kilometers to Matansha. He was forced to make one of the most difficult decisions of his life.

Lieutenant Banno and Iijima, who had joined them in the previous night's march, were preparing to move to Matansha when Oba approached them. He called the lieutenant aside.

"Issue orders that all patients who can walk are to join the march to Matansha," he told his subordinate. "No man is to be carried." Banno's eyes reflected the obvious question. "The remainder"—Oba lowered his voice—"will be assisted in taking their own lives in the manner of their choice." The lieutenant gave a stiff bow and walked briskly toward the caves.

Slowly, and with an oppressive weight in his chest, Oba followed a meandering trail leading up the valley. When he was well out of sight of his men, he slumped to the ground. Tears of frustration filled his eyes. What kind of hell had fate forced him into? he asked himself. He was a good soldier. He had proved that during his years in Manchuria and China. Yet on this godforsaken island he had done nothing but run and hide. He had not yet seen the enemy, let alone drawn its blood. The first lives he was responsible for ending were those of his own people. Without meaning to, he had betrayed his Emperor and the families of his men. His mind flashed back to his wife, who had smiled so proudly that last day in Nagoya. He closed his eyes and recalled how he had returned home for a hurried goodbye before boarding a train for the port where ships were waiting to transport his regiment to their unknown destination somewhere in North China.

Mineko-san had presented him with a small box of almost impossible-to-find *osembe* crackers. Her beautiful and intelligent eyes, when not downcast in respect, had shown no tears, but did not reflect the brave and artificial smile on her lips. Nervously, she had twice removed bits of lint from his uniform in an attempt to touch him without appearing forward to neighbors who stood nearby.

Oba could think of little to say, and the words he had uttered sounded stilted and foolish to him. Finally, he had exchanged bows with Mineko-san and had strode quickly toward the depot. He had not looked back. He would not know for years that Mineko's father, who had been cited for bravery in the Russo-Japan War, had earlier cautioned his daughter not to cry when her husband left for war. "It's a bad omen," he had told her. "It will affect his morale as long as he's away."

Oba sat against a tree trunk with his head in his hands. A muffled pistol report reverberated across the small valley. Oba raised his head and opened his eyes. A moment later, the sound of a second shot echoed off the cliff opposite him. The wounded for whom he was responsible were dying. Dying on his orders.

He walked back to where Banno was directing preparations for the move and motioned for the lieutenant to follow him. Together, they moved to the upper end of the ravine. Oba turned to the younger man.

"I've failed the Emperor," he said flatly. "Now I'm going to give him my life. I want you to be my second."

The two exchanged a solemn look for several seconds before Banno lowered his eyes and said, "Yes, sir."

Carefully, Oba removed the cloth emblems of his rank from his collar and slipped them into his pocket. "Take them when I'm dead. If you survive, give them to my wife." He sat down. His hand slowly unlocked the holster that held his army-issue automatic. He removed it, checked to see that a round rested within the chamber, and clicked off the safety. He looked again at Banno.

"I'm sorry, my friend. May your death be more honorable than mine."

"Yours is the more honorable," Banno replied. "What greater tribute can one pay the Emperor? Perhaps I, too, will follow your example . . . for the good of our country and the Imperial Army."

A frown creased Oba's forehead. He looked sharply at Banno. "What did you say?"

"I said I may follow your . . ."

"No, about helping our country and the army. You said it would help by sacrificing our lives . . ."

"Yes . . ."

"But don't you see? That's wrong. What if every soldier in the army were to kill himself?" Realization of the obvious contradiction brought Oba to his feet. "We will die," he said with renewed vigor in his voice, "but in battle, and after our swords have tasted enemy blood." A smile broke over his face. "In two days, Banno, in the charge! We will prove our worth as soldiers, then die in a manner that will give pride to our families."

Suddenly a weakness overcame him, and Oba sank on watery knees to the ground. It was only for a moment, and then his mind was cleared and his thinking keener than it had been in weeks, but he found his knees would not support his weight when he attempted to rise. The calmness and resolution of purpose that had so suddenly replaced the earlier anguish was limited to his mind. His body had not yet recovered from the shock of impending death. He looked at the pistol he still held, then smiled and replaced it in its holster. Still smiling, he reached for a cigarette and lighted it, exhaling with a strong breath that sounded like a sigh of relief. Analyzing his emotions, he decided he was happier at this moment than he had been since entering the army. At last, he knew how and where he would die. The shock just suffered by his body, he realized, was not from a fear of death, but from a subconscious knowledge that it was not an honorable one. He welcomed the death he would meet in two days' time, because it would be honorable. It would be his ultimate sacrifice for the Emperor.

He ground out his cigarette and got to his feet more resolute than he had been since arriving on Saipan. "Come on," he said to the stunned Banno. "Let's get ready to move."

They strode briskly to the aid station and began issuing orders in preparation for the walk to Matansha. Oba tried to ignore the occasional rifle report from the two caves.

The flares that burst almost continuously over the forward American position four kilometers to the south cast a pale light over the dirt road they followed to Matansha. Fragments of units from the front, reserve companies and small groups of soldiers who had been separated from their companies, materialized from the jungle to join the march. Oba sensed a new confidence among them; they shared a destiny, and together, perhaps they would have the strength to succeed.

· 3 ·

"TENNOHEIKA, BANZAI!"

On July 6, twenty-two days after the invasion, an American intelligence report stated that the Japanese had two courses of action remaining: "To fight a withdrawing action ending in complete annihilation on the northern tip of the island, or to attempt to muster their disorganized and crumbling forces into one all-out countercharge."

The American high command was convinced that if an all-out "banzai" attack were to be launched, it would take place on the coastal plain that stretched from Tanapag Harbor north to the upward slope of Marpi Point, the northernmost point of the island. It was here that remnants of the Japanese forces dislodged from the heights of Tapotchau had fled.

It was here, too, that Lt. Gen. Yoshitsugo Saito, commander of the Northern Marianas Army Group and 43d Division Headquarters (combined), had moved his headquarters.

Lieutenant General Saito was nominally commander of the 43d Division. But now, in the absence of Lt. Gen. Hidoyoshi Obata, the island commander who had flown to Palau a few days before the invasion, he had been elevated to commander of all army forces on the island. He would personally lead the charge, and every available man was to take part.

During the predawn hours of July 6, Genenal Saito and the greatest concentration of Japanese troops left on the island

51

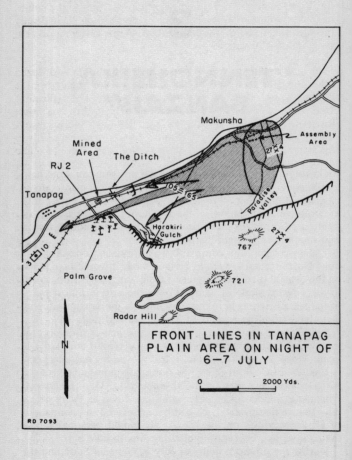

FRONT LINES IN TANAPAG
PLAIN AREA ON NIGHT OF
6—7 JULY

0   2000 Yds.

RD 7093

were crowded in the caves of an area known as "the Valley of Hell," one kilometer south of Oba's aid station, and were under one of the heaviest artillery bombardments of the battle. Eight-inch guns mounted twenty kilometers to the south, near the village of Charan-Kanoa, were hurling their deadly missiles under the direction of a U.S. Army observation post overlooking the valley.

As he crouched in one of the caves with some two dozen other men, Master Sgt. Toshio Kitani's eyes burned from the cordite smoke that grew more dense with every explosion. Under attack by enemy forces along the eastern sea coast three days earlier, he and others from the 135th Infantry Regiment had followed General Saito's orders to move north to the narrowest portion of the island where they were to make a final united stand. They had arrived under the cover of darkness only hours before, just in time to be submitted to a bombardment that now threatened to destroy them all. Gigantic explosions created a constant, bone jarring roar.

Hissing shrapnel from a nearby explosion knifed into the cave, embedding itself in the soft dirt walls of the man-made cavern in which Kitani had taken refuge. He rolled to his side to check on the others and looked into the fear-filled eyes of a private still in his teens. "Hang on," he whispered. The boy nodded and replied in a voice surprisingly low-pitched for his small, thin frame. The stocky master sergeant turned again to look at the boy in the dim light of the cave, and forced a smile that he hoped was encouraging. The boy, Chiba, had somehow attached himself to Kitani during the hectic withdrawal from Tapotchau, and had not been more than five meters away since. Part of Kitani's responsibility, he knew, was to inspire young soldiers like the one behind him. But it wasn't easy when you were cringing in fear from indiscriminate shrapnel that could slice clear through a body before its ugly sigh of death was heard.

Kitani had heard the whisper of exploding shrapnel in both Manchuria and China. But never, in the four years of combat there, had he been subjected to a barrage of this intensity. Only after two hours of steady shelling did the devastating attack cease. Suddenly and ominously, a silence cloaked the narrow valley. For almost a minute, not a man moved. Then, cautiously, Kitani rose to a sitting position and looked at the dozen or so soldiers around him.

"Don't move, any of you," he said in a low voice. On his hands and knees, he moved to the entrance, from where he could see the devastation around them. Several mangled bodies lay among the shattered tree trunks that had provided concealment a few hours earlier. As he retrieved his rifle and stepped into the sunlight, he saw others emerging from caves on both sides of the valley.

A hundred meters up the ravine, near where General Saito had established his command post, Kitani could see a crowd gathering. In his characteristic rolling gait, Kitani walked toward the scene of activity.

"What happened?" he asked the first soldier he approached.

"The general has been wounded," the man replied, then hurried on toward the lower end of the valley.

Normally Kitani would not dare to enter the command post unless ordered to do so, but anxious to see what had happened, he took advantage of the confusion to step inside the two-meter-high entrance. It was the first time he had seen General Saito, and he was shocked by his appearance. Frail and gaunt, the commander of all army forces on Saipan was obviously near the point of exhaustion. The sleeve of his shirt was blood-soaked and torn where a bandage had been applied to a shrapnel wound. But he was on his feet and, in a weak but authoritative voice, was ordering his staff to assemble all unit commanders for a conference. Kitani, feeling it important that he, too, know what was to happen, took a place with officers who, in the gloom of the cavern, failed to see the stars of his rank. Gradually the large cave became filled with men, many of whom wore fresh bandages.

A hush fell over the cave as Saito stepped onto a small platform. In a voice that occasionally trembled with emotion, the aged warrior began to deliver the most difficult speech of his life. Two candles, mounted on the wall of the cave behind him, cast a flickering light upon the paper from which he read and silhouetted the defeated general, catching highlights in his graying hair. His hands were steady, and his eyes burned with the determination for which he was famous.

"I am addressing the officers and men of the Imperial Army on Saipan. For more than twenty days since the American devils attacked, the officers, men, and civilian employees of the Imperial Army and Navy on this island have fought well and bravely. Everywhere they have demonstrated the honor and glory of the Imperial forces. I expected that every man would do his duty.

"Heaven has not given us an opportunity. We have not been able to utilize fully the terrain. We have fought in unison up to the present time but now we have no materials with which to fight, and our artillery for attack has been completely destroyed. Our comrades have fallen one after another. In spite of the bitterness of defeat, we pledge our lives to repay our country.

"The barbarous attack of the enemy is being continued. Even though the enemy has occupied only a corner of Saipan, we are dying without avail under the violent shelling and bombing. Whether we attack or whether we stay where we are, there is only death. However, in death there is life. We must utilize this opportunity to exalt true Japanese manhood. I will advance with those who remain to deliver still another blow to the American devils, and leave my bones on Saipan if that is how it must be.

"As it says in the *Senjinkun,* I will never suffer the disgrace of being taken alive, and I will offer up the courage of my soul and calmly rejoice in living by the eternal principle.

"Here I pray with you for the eternal life of the Emperor and the welfare of the country, and I advance to seek out the enemy. Follow me!"

The statement had been written the night before during a joint conference of army and naval leaders. Saito and other army representatives had favored a suicide attack. The navy, headed by admiral Chuichi Nagumo, had opposed the idea, arguing that a prolonged and strong defensive action might win them time for help from navy forces. The bitter controversy had continued most of the night, but the navy had failed to convince the headstrong Saito and his officers.

Kitani thought he detected a sense of relief in Saito's features as he concluded the statement and looked at the sixty-odd men sitting cross-legged before him. An aide stepped to the general's side and whispered. Saito nodded, then took a seat in the same manner as those around him. The aide, a colonel, told the assembled group that the suicide attack would take place before dawn on July 7, the following day.

Confusion greeted Oba at Matansha. Hundreds of leaderless men milled about the clearing, seeking someone from their home units. Oba turned over the command of his approximately one hundred soldiers, including those of Sergeant Iijima, to Lieutenant Banno, and set off to find the headquarters of General Saito. Finally he located the command post of the deputy regimental commander, Major Matsushita of the 18th Regiment, who was seated at a table in a small cave with several subordinates, studying a map by the light of a kerosene lamp. The colonel hardly glanced up as Oba stood at attention and reported the arrival of his force. Fortunately, he had inventoried the weapons of his men so that he could reply promptly when Major Matsushita barked the question. Noting the figures on a pad beside the map, the colonel ordered Oba to bivouac his men in a draw about two hundred meters inland and to prepare to join in the counterattack at midnight on the following day. A young lieutenant pointed to the draw on the map, and Oba noticed that it was within three hundred meters of the island's navy headquarters at Matoisu. He stepped back one pace and saluted with a military bow, then returned to where Banno was waiting.

From the lieutenant he learned that General Saito had moved his headquarters to the Valley of Hell and would lead the attack from there. Sergeant Iijima reported he had located his company commander and had been ordered to return to that unit.

Oba regretted the loss of Iijima's men, but he regretted even more the loss of twenty rifles. But even so, the eighty-odd men of his command were better armed than most of those he could see at Matansha.

Arriving at the draw where he was to bivouac his men, Oba discovered it had been the campsite of a much larger force and that living areas had been carved out of the jungle for concealment from aerial observation. Cooking utensils had been abandoned beside charred holes over which food had been prepared, but the previous occupants had not left a scrap of food. He knew his exhausted troops would need nourishment for the coming battle.

When the camp was quiet and most of his men asleep, Oba called Kato, a sergeant he had inherited from the survivors of an engineering company, and pointed out the location of the navy headquarters he had seen on Major Matsushita's map. He instructed him to take two men and bring back any food the navy could spare. "Try to get enough for at least one good meal," he said. Then he rested.

He was awakened by a voice shouting in the stilted military manner used in issuing orders to a large body of men. For a moment, he couldn't relate the voice to the vine-covered hole he had chosen for a bed. He raised himself on his elbow and looked at his watch. It was a little after 6:00 A.M. His back was stiff from the hard ground. He listened to the voice.

". . . to act otherwise is not only cowardly, but evidence of a lack of faith in the ultimate and unquestioned victory of Japan over the barbarous enemy. . . ."

Oba jumped to his feet and rushed out of the thicket. He could not see the speaker because of the crowd around him. But he could hear him as he walked toward them, and he recognized the voice of the sergeant he had sent to navy headquarters for food.

". . . all Imperial forces, whether navy or army, are therefore ordered, by the authority of Vice Admiral Chuichi Nagumo's headquarters, to continue fighting and to avoid participation in an obvious suicide attack. Only by continued resistance can we provide assistance to our naval forces that are even now en route to this area to drive out the invading American devils and to retake the island."

Kato! That officious fool! What the hell did he think he was doing? "Clear the way!" Oba shouted as he pushed through the men to where the sergeant was reading from a paper he held at almost full-arm's length.

"Shut up, fool," he snarled as he snatched the paper from the cowering noncom. "You men," he shouted at the assembled group, "return to where you were and stay under cover! Kato! Come with me!"

He did not bother to examine the paper in his hand until he reached a point well out of hearing of his men. He turned to Kato. "You stand at attention and don't say a word until I order you to speak!"

The paper in his hand was from naval headquarters and was signed by a Commander Onodera for Admiral Nagumo. In effect, it countermanded the order of General Saito to launch what it termed a suicide attack that would result only in complete victory for the enemy.

"Where did you get this?" he snapped at the sergeant without turning.

"A commander at navy headquarters personally ordered me to read it to everyone I met," he stuttered. "I was only following orders, sir."

"Go!" Oba ordered as he sat to reread the document.

Was it possible? Were the Imperial Landing Forces really returning to recapture the island? Even so, what could the disorganized, demoralized, and poorly armed fragments of the army do from their toehold on one-tenth of the island? And to whom did he owe allegiance? To the Imperial Army of which he was an officer or to a naval commander who knew nothing of ground combat?

The clearness of purpose that had accompanied his decision to die in the coming night's attack began to fade. His studies of military tactics had taught him the advantage of prolonging a battle, especially when reinforcements were expected. But the honor of dying in battle, wasn't that even more important? Important, yes. But not compared with possible victory. There was no doubt of their ultimate victory. This was simply a battle, not the whole war. And as long as the rest of the Imperial forces were continuing the attack elsewhere, what right did he have to purposely end his life and deprive the Emperor of one more soldier?

Only half-convinced and feeling a need to discuss it with someone, Oba returned to where his men were gathered in small groups under the protective jungle canopy. He could hear the heated discussions as he approached. Each man was apparently interpreting the message Kato had carried according to his own feelings. Oba saw the young tank commander, Morita, speaking with some noncommissioned officers. "Lieutenant Morita," he called. "Come here, please."

"I was just coming to see you, sir. Have you heard . . ."

"Yes, I've not only heard, but I've read the navy orders."

"No, sir. I mean about General Saito?"

"What about General Saito?"

"He gave a beautiful speech, urging us all to a suicide attack against the enemy tonight. He will then commit hara-kiri. He showed us the way, sir. Now we can all die with honor as we attack."

Morita was a good soldier. Oba suspected he came from a samurai family. His military bearing and the natural authority of his voice seemed to be inbred rather than acquired. He could see the dedication of the young man shining in his eyes. He hesitated to dampen Morita's enthusiasm but finally shook his head slightly and said, "It will be useless death."

Morita recoiled as if he had been struck. Oba was sure that if his rank had been lower than the lieutenant's, the man's sword would be arcing toward his neck at that moment.

"What the hell do you mean?" asked Morita, his face a mixture of incredulity and anger. "That is . . . ah, did you say our death will be useless, sir?"

"Sit down, Lieutenant," Oba said as he lowered himself to a log and removed one of his few remaining cigarettes. The young officer hesitated, then, declining the offer, sat on a rock facing the captain.

"We are in a war." Oba began slowly because he was not sure what he was about to say. He only knew that he wanted to convince this headstrong young man that he was wrong. "To win this war, we must be stronger than the enemy. If not at one place, like Saipan, then overall, in the entire area of combat. It is the duty of all of us to take as many enemy lives as possible before laying down our own for the Emperor. By committing hara-kiri or by taking part in a suicide attack, we fail the Emperor, because we lessen Japan's strength by our death. If every soldier in the army were to follow Saito's order, where would we be? The war would be over immediately, and we would have betrayed our Emperor, our country, and our families."

"You are wrong!" Morita blurted, forgetting the rank that separated them. "There is no greater honor than to give your life for your country. We will not kill ourselves tonight. We will die fighting the enemy."

"But even now"—Oba kept his voice low—"the Imperial Navy is on its way to recapture Saipan and to sink the enemy warships that have been shelling us. What if you die fighting tonight, and our fleet should arrive tomorrow? What help will you be to them? They will need us alive, not dead. I believe every man on this island should fight to remain alive until they arrive."

"Tonight's attack will help," the lieutenant countered. "We will cut them from the beaches, then wipe them from the hills."

Oba's eyes locked on those of the young man. "How many rifles do we have? About half of the men at Matansha have none, and even those who do are low on ammunition. We're short of machine guns and mortars, and our artillery is limited to a few field guns. You've seen the strength of the enemy." He slowly shook his head again. "Tonight's attack is nothing more than suicide. To hit the enemy in a frontal assault is only to ensure their victory."

"But General Saito said, 'Whether we attack or whether we stay where we are, there is only death. But in death there is life. We must utilize this opportunity to exalt true Japanese manhood.' "

"Saito is an old man. He has ordered a charge he is too frail to lead. He is doing the only honorable thing. Listen to me, Morita, we can win this war, and we will. I've been a soldier eight years. I've known what it is to fight against unbeatable odds. I've done it. The men around me did it. And we won. We can do it here, too. But not if we're dead!"

Morita's lips drew back from his teeth, and his face was a mask of hatred as he jumped to his feet. "Captain Oba, you're a coward." His right hand flashed to his sword and began to withdraw it as Oba sprang to his feet in a turning motion that brought the heel of his right hand to the lieutenant's neck, knocking him to the ground. Oba placed his hand on his own sword, but made no movement to draw it.

"You, Morita, are the coward. You're afraid to fight. You

would rather take the easy way out and think of yourself as
an honorable soldier. But you won't be. You'll have weakened
our ability to fight just as surely as if you were to kill one of
your own men. Don't worry, we will attack, and we will
attack tonight. But we will not expose our weakness to the
enemy. We will hit him silently, and we will move to his rear
from where we can strike again and again until he is unable
to oppose our returning navy landing forces. The jungles and
hills of Tapotchau will become our stronghold. We will know
every ravine and hill. We have caches of food and ammunition hidden throughout the area. Regrouped, the forces in
Matansha could hold Tapotchau forever."

The hostility in Morita's eyes remained as he rose to his
feet. But his training as a soldier forced him to stand at attention. "Yes, sir," he grunted.

Again Oba was in command of his thoughts. "You will
order the men to rest after cleaning their weapons for tonight's attack. No one is to leave the area except on my orders. I will brief all of you on our mission at sundown. Send
young Iwata and one other to me immediately. Dismissed!"

Morita saluted again, turned smartly, and walked toward
the men.

Oba was pleased Iwata was still among the survivors. The
boy was barely eighteen, but as eager a soldier as any in the
unit. His father, Oba had heard, was a wealthy landowner in
Niigata. He set the youth and another soldier to clearing an
area he had seen in the upper end of the ravine, and to fashioning a shattered door into a table for his command post.
When they were finished, he directed them to take a post
some ten meters distant and to stand by for orders. After
several minutes, he called to Bito. "Bring Lieutenant Morita
here!"

"Morita," he said when the young officer had arrived and
saluted, "here is a message I want you to take to Colonel
Matsushita at headquarters in Matansha. It tells him that I
have decided to attack the enemy tonight from this position,
rather than with the *gyokusai*. Tell him we will rejoin the
main unit in the hills north of Garapan."

Oba knew the suicide charge would never make it that far,
and that there was only a slim chance that he and his men

would. He knew also that there was little likelihood that Morita would return after delivering his message.

Kitani's regiment, the 135th, had arrived on Saipan only three weeks before the invasion. After four years of fighting in the barren terrain of Manchuria and China with the 6th Regiment, he had been transferred shortly before the 135th left Japan. He was unaccustomed to the damp, tangled jungle in which he had been fighting for the past month. The oppressive heat, the constant withdrawal, the superior power of the enemy, all were handicaps under which he had never fought. But now, for the first time, he had been told, they were going on the offensive. They would hit the unsuspecting flank of the enemy along the beach over which they received their supplies. If they managed to cut off the flow of weapons and ammunition, the enemy would be trapped in the hills they now occupied.

Kitani walked slowly through the mob of disorganized soldiers to the cave where he and the others had waited out the barrage. "Gather up your gear and follow me!" he called inside from the cave's entrance. He stepped aside as the men filed out. Chiba flashed a smile of gratitude as he walked past Kitani.

Kitani formed the dozen men into two ranks and led them through the mass of confused and leaderless troops that had arrived in the valley from their earlier hiding places. He stopped each time he saw armed soldiers.

"What's your unit?" he asked repeatedly. "Where is it?"

If the reply indicated the man was separated from his unit, Kitani ordered him to fall in line. By the time he had reached the mouth of the valley and had found an area in which he could bivouac his force, he had collected thirty-two men, including two corporals and a sergeant. All were armed, although several were without ammunition.

"You men," the burly master sergeant said, stepping to a rock that enabled him to get the men's attention, "are now members of the 1st Platoon, Saipan Infantry." He was pleased with the name he had invented and hoped it would help to restore a sense of belonging to the leaderless soldiers. "From now on, I, Sergeant Kitani, am your commander. I want you all to clean and check your weapons, because we will soon take part in an offensive against the enemy that will turn the tide of this battle. General Saito is finalizing plans for an attack that will cut the enemy's supply line from the sea and deprive him of the superiority of firepower that has given a temporary advantage.''

The soldiers, whose confidence had been restored by a leader who had made them part of a unit instead of frightened stragglers, reacted positively to Kitani's remarks. Satisfied that they would follow his orders, he turned the platoon over to the sergeant and returned to Saito's headquarters to learn what more he could do to prepare for the impending attack.

There, instead of last-minute preparations for a battle, a feast was in progress. Candles illuminated several low tables at which field- and staff-grade officers sat cross-legged while enlisted men served a meal of canned crab meat, squid, rice, and sake.

General Saito, bathed and attired in a dress uniform, sat at the head table, flanked by Vice Adm. Chuichi Nagumo, head of the combined navy in the Mariana, Marshall, and Caroline islands; Brig. Gen. Keichi Igeta, Saipan chief of staff; and Rear Adm. Hideo Yano.

Kitani did not recognize the naval officers, but he knew the white bands all four wore around their heads signified they were about to die. The men were exchanging toasts and final words with officers of their command who stood in line to offer their farewells. Most of the exchanges were solemn, but there was an occasional chuckle as friends recalled an incident they had shared.

Among all present there was an air of calm resignation. They knew when and how they would die. The four senior officers would end their lives in the traditional and honorable style of hara-kiri, and the others would lay down their lives the following morning on the field of battle.

How could this be? Kitani wondered. He was shocked that the four ranking military officers on the island would choose to die in this manner rather than in battle with the enemy.

''Why are they doing this?'' he asked softly of the man standing next to him. In the gloom, he was unable to see the man's rank and hoped his was equally invisible.

"General Saito is too old and weak to lead the *gyokusai*," the man replied without looking at Kitani. "He has turned his command over to Colonel Suzuki. Our navy forces on the island have been destroyed, so Admirals Nagumo, Yano and General Igeta are sacrificing their lives because of their failure."

It was the first time Kitani had heard *gyokusai,* the word for "suicide charge," used so directly to describe the planned attack. With a sinking feeling in his stomach, he realized that the battle was lost. Rather than attacking with a hope of victory, they were to charge into certain death.

Still not satisfied, Kitani sought out a naval uniform in the semidarkness. "Why are Admirals Nagumo and Yano joining General Saito?" he asked a man with navy commander insignia.

"Nagumo wanted to continue fighting," the man replied with only a cursory glance at Kitani. "He even issued orders that he received yesterday from Tokyo that we were not to launch a *gyokusai*. But he was overruled last night during a meeting of the high command."

And rightly so, Kitani thought to himself. The battle was lost. The only alternative to dishonorable surrender is death, either in the manner of these brave leaders or by an enemy bullet.

The line of waiting officers dwindled as the last of the men paid their respects. Saito nodded to a major, who in turn motioned to two enlisted men standing in the background. Solemnly they spread four white sheets on the ground near where the officers now chatted among themselves. On each sheet was placed a pillow covered with white cloth, and in front of the pillows were placed short swords, also wrapped in white.

Kitani did not see the signal that prompted all four men to rise from their tables and walk to the sheets, but he watched as each kneeled on a pillow. All kneeled, with heads high and eyes closed. Kitani could see the general's lips move as he silently mouthed his last prayer. There was no sound in the cave for a full minute. Even the enemy's distant exploding shells seemed to cease while the officers prayed.

Then Saito rose and bowed slowly and reverently toward

the northeast, where fifteen hundred miles distant the Imperial Palace housed the man for whom all Japanese were willing to give their lives. The other three officers followed his example, then resumed their kneeling posture, this time with their eyes closed.

Two majors and two naval officers stepped up behind the kneeling officers, and each withdrew a pistol and held it pointed at the ground.

Slowly General Saito, followed by the others, picked up the wrapped sword before him. Carefully all four pulled back the white cloths until they had exposed above five inches of gleaming blade. As Saito placed the point of his sword against his stomach, his fragile but piercing voice filled the cave.

"Tennoheika, banzai!"

Three times the salute to the Emperor rang out, then, in swift, simultaneous motions, the four swords plunged through stomach walls, and the cave rang with explosions as pistols fired bullets into the heads of the men who paid a grisly final tribute to their country.

The bodies of General Saito and the two admirals rolled to their sides as death spasms jerked their legs. Igeta's body remained motionless, with his forehead resting on his knees.

· 4 ·

VALIANT DEFENDERS

Two thousand yards to the south, at a point inland from Tanapag Harbor, a jeep ground to a stop at the base of a hillock where Marines of the 7th Artillery Regiment were digging emplacements for their 37mm field guns. The driver was older than the young Marines around him, but he wore no insignia of rank.

"Where's Colonel Donovan?"

One of the Marines pointed toward the top of the hillock. "The CP's behind those rocks, sir." The driver got out and strode toward the command post.

A reddish-faced man in his forties was puffing on a pipe as he studied a map spread on the hood of a jeep.

"Colonel Donovan?"

The man looked up. "Yeah."

"Major Herman Lewis, sir, division intelligence. We've been trying to raise you on the radio but couldn't get through."

"Yeah, I know. The damn thing's been out all afternoon." He nodded toward two Marines working on metal radio boxes attached to either side of the jeep's rear seat. "But they're workin' on it."

Lewis moved closer to the colonel and lowered his voice.

"Colonel, we're concerned about the possibility of a major attack in this sector in the next twenty-four hours."

The colonel smiled at the younger officer. "Are you kiddin', Major? Hell, we got 'em on the run. We'll be all the way up to Marpi Point in twenty-four hours."

"That's my point, sir. They've been pulling back for three days. We've got them bottled up. Now they either allow us to wipe them out, or they attack. We suspect the latter."

Colonel Donovan pulled on his pipe, then tapped out the ashes on the jeep. "Well, let 'em come. We got the infantry dug in to our front, and we got plenty of guns on high ground to give 'em support. Don't you worry none, Major, we'll take care of those little bastards if they come this way."

"But Colonel . . ."

Donovan straightened to his full height, still an inch below that of Lewis. "I said, don't you worry none. We're in good shape. You go on back to division and tell 'em that."

Lewis started to say something more, then turned and walked back to his jeep.

The quadruple suicide, while honorable, seemed to Kitani to be an admission of defeat for all of them. With mixed emotions, he returned to where he had left his small force. He ordered them to rest, sleep, if possible; they would need their energy that night.

He explained to the men what had happened in the headquarters cave, but omitted the word *gyokusai*. He told them the attack would be launched sometime after midnight and ordered all of them to be ready. Then he returned to the headquarters area to find Col. Takuji Suzuki, named chief of staff after Saito's death.

Kitani was pleased that Suzuki, with whom he had fought in Manchuria, would be leading the charge. He would be content to die fighting beside him.

The colonel greeted him as an old friend, obviously happy that Kitani was still alive. When the sergeant explained that he had organized a platoon of unattached men, the colonel motioned for him to sit at the table he used as a desk, and produced a map of northern Saipan.

"I have an assignment for you," Suzuki said, "that could

make the difference between success or failure of our attack.'' He pointed to the reported positions of the forwardmost American forces that roughly bordered a narrow road extending from the mountains westward to the coastal road between Matansha and Tanapag Harbor. ''I want you and your platoon to probe the enemy's line from here''—he indicated the high ground one thousand meters from the sea—''to here.'' He pointed to the juncture of the coast road. ''Find their weak points, then report back by midnight so we can pick the most favorable points of attack.''

The sergeant made a rough copy of the map, then asked for and was authorized ammunition for those of his men who needed it.

Alone in the jungle-covered streambed, Oba studied his map for several minutes, then directed an orderly to fetch Sergeant Bito, one of the few men of his original unit still with him. He told the sergeant to select one other man, then report back in fifteen minutes to accompany him on a reconnaissance patrol. As Bito left, a soldier carrying heated navy rations entered the clearing and placed them on his improvised table. He forced himself to wait until the soldier departed before wolfing the food. He had forgotten how hungry he was until the sight and smell of it had assailed his senses.

Trusting that Morita had delivered his message to the colonel, though not expecting Morita to return from Matansha, Oba prepared for his attack. He opted not to proceed directly south, choosing instead to lead his reconnaissance patrol up the ravine from where they could establish an observation post in the hills to the east. They followed a dried creek bed, bearing to the south each time they encountered a branch. Eventually they left the winding ravine to move directly up a steep hill until they reached a rocky cliff. Oba and the sergeant climbed the jagged face of the cliff and reached a natural ledge upon which they dragged themselves, panting from the effort.

From their elevated position, the sounds of battle were surprisingly near. Earlier, in a gully where the sounds were muffled by jungle, they had seemed distant. But from here, he knew they came from within a kilometer. There was little smoke, but the crash of mortars and the sharp reports of rifle and automatic weapons fire told him the Americans were continuing their advance. With his binoculars, he studied the terrain. From this hill, the jungle seemed to stretch directly up to Tapotchau, about five kilometers distant. He knew, however, that deep ravines and impassable cliffs lay in the path, making a successful night attack close to impossible.

He could see the Valley of Hell to his right, where preparations were being made to lead the late general's suicide attack. He could see shells bursting in and around the valley and wondered how many men would be left to take part in the charge.

As he scanned the terrain, his glasses suddenly caught a movement. Slowly and ponderously, the domes and long barrels of two huge tanks appeared over a grassy rise four hundred meters from his position. They were coming directly at them. Immediately behind the tanks appeared the tops of helmets; then the men wearing them appeared. Flattening his body on the rocky shelf, Oba waited until around a hundred American infantrymen had appeared, then, ordering Sergeant Bito ahead of him, began to scramble and slide down the cliff.

The three men trotted down the dry streambed, stumbling now and then in their haste to reach the camp. When they reached the clearing in which Oba had established his command post, the captain ordered Banno to assemble the men immediately and have them ready to move out in five minutes. He checked his watch. It was almost five o'clock.

He stuffed his jacket pockets with extra ammunition for his pistol and attached as many grenades as he could to his belt. He studied his map briefly, looking for the best way to escape the approaching tanks, then walked to where his soldiers were forming into a double line and climbed atop a rock to address them.

''A large enemy force is within four hundred meters and heading in this direction. We will move immediately up this ravine and remain hidden until nightfall. Then we will launch an attack through their lines, continuing until we are in their rear areas.''

He moved to the head of the column and followed the same route he had taken an hour earlier. This time, however, he passed the hill with the rock cliff face and continued until they had gone some five hundred meters. There he ordered a halt and sent two men up a hill to check on enemy activity. When they returned a short time later to report no sign of the advancing Americans, Oba posted sentries and ordered the men to rest until nightfall.

At 10:00 P.M., when the American shells falling on the Valley of Hell had been reduced to sporadic harassment, Kitani checked once more with Colonel Suzuki. He had spent nearly an hour briefing his men.

"The X's mark the positions from which we will attempt to draw enemy fire," he had told them. "Every man will find cover before opening fire, and none of you are to return the enemy's fire. We will wait until they become quiet before moving to the next position."

"What if they attack us?" a corporal had asked.

"Our mission is to report back with information on enemy defenses. You will withdraw if attacked. Your chance to meet the enemy will come later tonight."

Kitani worried about the flares that burned occasionally in the sky between them and the American positions. After their first burst of fire, he knew, additional flares, both from local mortars and from ships offshore, would turn the area into a false but possibly fatal daylight.

Colonel Suzuki approved his plan and told him, "We will depend on you to find the path that will lead us to the unprotected heart of the enemy. Your success will mean our success."

Kitani returned to the edge of the encampment, then began leading his men toward the enemy lines, a thousand meters to the south. They went directly to the point where the hills gave way to the coastal plain, about a thousand meters from the beach, took cover, and sent a volley of fire toward what they hoped were American positions.

Immediately, bursts of machine-gun fire from their immediate front forced them to flatten themselves in the dirt. Flares began bursting in the sky above them, and mortar shells exploded among them. Kitani twisted on his side to be sure that none of his men returned the fire and that they made no move to further excite the enemy. After the mortars had ceased falling and the flares popped less frequently, Kitani and his platoon began crawling toward the next X he had marked on his map.

Twice more they moved two hundred meters toward the coast road with machine guns and rifles answering their attempts to draw enemy fire. On the third try they were fired upon from their left and right fronts, but not from a two-hundred-meter gap between two small hills on which the Americans were concentrated. A few minutes later they discovered that the area between the second hillock and the beach, only a hundred meters away, also was unprotected.

Again Kitani waited for the flares to subside before he and his men began making their way northward. Halfway back to the Valley of Hell he stopped to check on his platoon and discovered that three had been wounded by mortar shrapnel and two had been killed in the enemy's first response to their provocative assault.

He found Colonel Suzuki near headquarters in a cave with several staff officers. The colonel interrupted the meeting to hear Kitani's report.

"We've found a gap," he told the colonel. "The Americans have gun positions here and here"—he indicated the two hillocks—"but we received no fire from the area between them, nor from between the second one and the shoreline."

"Good work," Suzuki patted the sergeant's muscular shoulder, then added, "stay nearby. I want you to spearhead the assault." The colonel turned back to the officers around him and, using the map Kitani had marked, began explaining the new strategy of their attack.

"Our main thrust will be between these two hills," he told his subordinates, "with enveloping movements to overrun both of them. The main force will continue south to Tanapag Harbor, where we will consolidate our position, then resume the attack to Garapan. If we are strong, we will vindicate the honorable death of our leaders and comrades. We will launch the assault"—he looked at his watch—"in two and a half hours, at oh two hundred."

He waited until the officers had started back to brief their respective units before turning again to Kitani. "Many of us will die tonight, but thanks to you, enough of us may survive to accomplish the task that an hour ago even I thought impossible.''

Kitani, who had snapped to attention when the colonel addressed him, relaxed slightly when he realized Suzuki was talking to him man to man, rather than as colonel to sergeant. ''What do you want me to do, sir?'' he asked.

''We will attack on a narrow front that will give us strength in depth as well as enable us to follow your platoon through the gap you have discovered. You will continue attacking southward. If you reach Tanapag, hold up and wait until we arrive. Do you understand?''

''Yes, sir. I understand.''

''Good luck to you, Master Sergeant Kitani. Your country is indebted to you.''

Kitani saluted sharply, turned, and walked to where his platoon waited. As he pushed his way through the crowd of soldiers, Kitani wondered about their prospects for success. This was not the first time he had been prepared to give his life for his Emperor and his homeland. But it would be the first time he had entered into a battle with little expectation of emerging victorious. Although he would die gloriously, he knew the disorganized and poorly armed force that readied itself behind him was no match for the seemingly invincible enemy that had crowded them into this small portion of the island. He knew that many of those who would join in the charge were without weapons of any kind. Others had only bayonets they had fastened to poles. He was grateful that he and his platoon were well armed. It would be an honor to lead the attack and, probably, to be among the first to die. He was determined, however, to carry out the orders of General Saito.

Hidden with his small force just north of where he was sure the Americans had dug in for the night, Oba tried to sleep. But the weight of responsibility for what he was about to do and his doubts about the correctness of his actions pounded at his brain.

Explosions echoed through the hills, and Oba heard the distant rattle of machine-gun and rifle fire, interspersed with cracks of cannons. The sounds came from the direction of the shore, and he wondered if the tanks had found the force at Matansha. He regretted that he had been unable to convince Morita to join him.

The sky was still light in the west when the first flares popped above them. Oba waited, however, until 10:00 P.M. before rousing his men. He knew the main attack along the beach was scheduled for 2:00 A.M. and wanted to launch his before the enemy in his sector had been alerted. "Stay close to me," he whispered to Banno, hoping they would either succeed or die together.

He divided his men into two platoons, each under a noncom, and stressed the necessity of remaining together. Separated, he knew, they would be powerless against the enemy's guns, but as a solid force, their firepower would give them temporary safety and mobility. He ordered the noncoms to be certain that each of the men knew the password, *yama*, and the counterpassword, *kawa*.

With a four-man point a hundred meters to its front, the small force began to move slowly and quietly up a lightly jungled grade from where Oba hoped to travel on the eastern slopes of the island's backbone. The Americans, he thought, were more likely to be atop the ridges or on the valley floors. They used the light of the flares to pick their way over rocks and between trees through the jungle.

They had only traveled two hundred meters when red tracers stitched the air above them and the sound of bullets from at least two machine guns cracked just over their heads. The nearly one hundred men dropped as one, squirming to find something solid to deflect the bullets cracking around them. After a few more tentative bursts, the machine gun ceased firing. Two of the four men on point returned, reporting that the others had been killed by the first burst of bullets. Oba whispered to those behind him that they would move to the right in an effort to flank the guns. Then he began to crawl toward a slope that would place them below the gunners' line of vision. He had no way of knowing, however, if he was leading his men directly into a stronger enemy position.

Ten minutes later, rifle fire opened up in front of them from their right, followed by a machine gun. The red tracers fell short of their position, but ricocheting bullets whined over their heads.

A flare burst directly overhead, and Oba could see at least twenty American soldiers lying in shallow foxholes not more than ten meters away. Half of his men were standing when the flare turned the area into day, and he had been in the process of getting to his feet.

"Charge!" he shouted, pulling his sword and rushing toward the Americans, who had been as startled as he at seeing the enemy so close. Rifles began firing in front and behind. He heard shouting and some screams but couldn't tell whether they were in Japanese or English. He swung his sword at the first American he came to, but the man, still in his hole, deflected the blade with his rifle. Cursing, Oba lashed a backhand blow that sent the blade under the man's upraised arms and into his rib cage.

Ahead, two men grappled furiously in another hole. Oba hesitated; for a moment he could not distinguish Japanese from American. Switching his sword to his left hand, he pulled his pistol and fired at the flash of a rifle that had burned his cheek with the heat of a bullet. As the American rose to his knees and prepared to fire again, Oba covered the three meters in as many steps and kicked the rifle from his hands, simultaneously firing two rounds at the figure.

Suddenly remembering the grenades attached to his belt, Oba dropped to the ground and began lobbing them to his front. With each explosion he would jump to his feet and dash forward ten meters, then repeat the process. Eventually he saw no more foxholes and was no longer being shot at. Falling into a shell hole, he turned with his sword as a figure loomed from his rear. The blade had started its sweep when the man cried, *"Yama!"* Unable to stop the sword's momentum, Oba turned the blade so that it struck the man broadside, knocking him to the ground. *"Kawa,"* he said, relieved that he had turned the blade. By the light of another flare, he saw other members of his company running crouched toward him. He smiled when he recognized the short, sturdy figure of Lieutenant Banno.

Behind them, sounds of machine-gun and rifle fire were

punctuated by hand grenade explosions. Smoke and dust hovered over the area, reflecting the nearly continuous light of the flares. He watched for several minutes for additional members of his unit, then made his decision. "This way," he whispered hoarsely and began crawling toward a wall of jungle.

For the next two hours, Oba and the men who had survived the breach of the American front line skirted back and forth through jungle, ravines, and enemy positions. Machine guns and rifles fired from the hillocks on either side of them. Each time, they changed their direction to avoid direct confrontation. Their progress was slowed by the frequent halts they had to make when flares floated overhead.

Shortly after 2:00 A.M., the flares from warships were shifted to the west, where they burst almost continuously. Oba could hear the sounds of small arms and artillery from the beach area and knew the main attack was in progress. He cursed General Saito, Colonel Suzuki, and Morita for not wanting to continue the fight and for not choosing to attack in the hills, where the defense was so light.

They were, Oba knew, well behind the enemy lines, and the battle to the west made it easier for them to move undetected. His force had been reduced to twelve men, but he was determined to keep them alive and fighting as long as possible.

Shortly before 2:00 A.M. a runner had arrived from Colonel Suzuki's headquarters, ordering Kitani and his men to begin the advance. Silence was to be maintained as they walked to within one hundred meters of the enemy positions. At that point, Suzuki would give the signal to charge.

They had only walked a short distance when Colonel Suzuki and two officers overtook them. "Slow your pace," he ordered. "The others are still getting organized."

Kitani halted while the colonel ordered a subordinate to check on the formation behind them and report back.

"Let us hope that gap you discovered is still clear," he muttered to Kitani. "It's our last chance."

Kitani looked at the face of the man who now held responsibility for Japan's defense of Saipan. It was barely discernible in the white light cast by the flares bursting in the distance off to their front. He was impressed by the man's stoic calmness and recognized it as a willingness to accept death, mixed with a determination to inflict maximum damage on the enemy and, perhaps, emerge victorious.

Moments later, the major he had sent to the rear returned. "All is ready, sir," the man said.

"Good. Resume the advance!"

More slowly now, Kitani led his platoon through the scrub growth and sugarcane fields that separated them from the enemy line. Although flares continued to burst sporadically in front of them, the Americans gave no indication they were aware of the impending attack. When the two hillocks could be seen by the light of the flares, Colonel Suzuki ordered Kitani to wait for his signal, then walked back toward the main body.

Kitani crawled under a bush that hid him from the brilliant white light of enemy flares that illuminated an area of several hundred meters around them. He had instructed his men to remain still while the flares floated to earth under their small white parachutes. As he looked around him, he noticed that young Chiba was bareheaded. "Where's your helmet?" he asked.

"I lost it," the youth replied, more frightened of the sergeant's wrath than of the enemy.

"Fool!" Kitani growled. Then, in the moments between flares, he removed his own and threw it at the young soldier. "Wear this. And don't lose it!"

Finally, from somewhere behind him, a pistol shot signaled the charge. Amid shouts for the Emperor, Kitani jumped to his feet and sprinted into the darkness. Behind him, fifteen hundred shouting soldiers charged against the enemy in a valiant but futile effort to hold the island of Saipan for Japan.

Rifle and machine-gun fire cracked from the two hillocks to his left and right. Almost subconsciously, Kitani noted from tracer bullets that it was directed at those behind him.

"Keep moving!" he shouted at those around him. He glanced over his shoulder and saw only a few figures running close behind him. He could hear the shouts of the main body not far to his rear. Running in a crouched position, with his bayonetted rifle at the ready, he saw spurts of fire to his left as enemy field guns opened fire at point-blank range.

"Over there!" he shouted, and veered to the left toward the weapons that were spewing death into the main body. Peripherally, he saw young Chiba on his left. They were close to the rapidly firing field guns, but had not yet seen a single American.

He almost lost his balance as his right foot landed on something soft, and a hand grabbed at his leg. Turning on the captured foot, he jabbed his bayonet into the area next to it, then withdrew his leg as the grip relaxed.

Unable to see the enemy that he now knew were in their foxholes around him, Kitani moved cautiously forward. A bullet, fired from so near that the muzzle flash temporarily blinded him, passed under his left arm. Hardly pausing, he lowered his rifle, fired at the point of the flash, and continued his forward movement until his bayonet point glanced off something metallic and sank into flesh.

Breathing heavily, he moved forward at a half-trot, swinging his head back and forth and scanning the ground ahead of him. The darkness was suddenly replaced by stark black and white outlines as a flare burst almost directly overhead. Kitani molded his body to a tree trunk as more flares threw unnatural light and moving shadows over the area around him. He could see others of his platoon using the sudden visibility to speed their charge. He watched as most were cut down by fire from the entrenched positions.

Chiba suddenly appeared in the opening beside him. Again his helmet was gone, and the right side of his face was darkened from blood that flowed from somewhere above his hairline. The youth was firing his rifle from the hip, working the bolt to insert a new round as he ran. As Kitani watched, a bullet spun the boy completely around, but his momentum carried him forward for two steps before he crashed to the ground. Kitani shifted his attention to the enemy.

Several hundred yards to the south, Maj. Herman Lewis dozed on a poncho spread on the ground beside a communications jeep, surrounded by the various units that comprised Headquarters Company, 2d Marine Division. They were located on a forward slope of a hill that during the day gave a commanding view of the northern half of the island. But now, only an occasional flare dotted the blackness of the night.

In the rear seat of the jeep, a radioman sat with headphones clamped to his ears. He watched the distant flares and was kept half-awake by the crackling of static in his earphones. Suddenly he was wide awake.

"Sir, it's Parrot. They're under attack."

Lewis was on his feet in an instant, grabbing the microphone from the operator. "Turn on the speaker," he ordered. "Hello, Parrot, this is Eagle, over."

The crackling over the radio increased as the speaker carried the voice of Colonel Donovan. "Give us some damn flares. They're comin' in by the hundreds."

Lewis aimed a penlight at a map on the front seat. "Tell the Navy to saturate Sectors P and M with flares. Now!" He turned to a signalman with a field telephone. "Get me the old man!" Then back to the mike: "Roger, Parrot. Illumination on the way. Are you holding? Do you want artillery? Over."

"Negative, negative. They're comin' through the infantry positions. We're already firing the shortest fuses we've got!"

Crackling took over the transmission, then died down as Donovan's voice continued. ". . . We need infantry, fast! Send us some . . ." Again interference drowned out the metallic voice of the colonel.

"Hello, Parrot. Hello, Parrot. This is Eagle. Do you read us? Hello, Parrot. Hello, Parrot . . ." Lewis's knuckles were white as he gripped on the radio's microphone. He looked at the radioman.

"Looks like their radio's gone out again, sir."

"Yeah. I hope to God that's all it is."

· 5 ·

AFTERMATH OF BATTLE

Kitani instinctively knew that his time was limited.. He was still fighting only because he had survived earlier battles, and believed a soldier ended his effectiveness with death. He would die eventually, he knew, but not before inflicting many more casualties among the enemy.

The battle still raged around him. An American 37mm field gun ten meters away was firing with rapid regularity explosions that sent shrapnel into the bodies of men behind him. He heard shouting. Among the voices he could not understand was one that said, "Hello, Eagle. Hello, Eagle. Damn it, Eagle, come in!"

Kitani tapped the primer of one of his grenades on a tree and lobbed it toward the shadowy figures. The voice was cut off with "Oh, mother of God" as the grenade exploded.

Ignoring the shrapnel that shrieked over his head from the explosion, he sprinted toward a jeep and trailer, lifted the trailer canvas and dropped in a grenade.

He had run only another twenty meters when a shock wave lifted him from his feet and threw him into a hole. A blast of heat seared his skin as two tons of 37mm ammunition exploded in a fireball that rose into the sky, overpowering the light from the flares that still swung gently overhead. Dazed, but protected by the hole, Kitani lay where he had fallen.

American voices shouting unintelligible words brought his senses back into focus. He pulled himself painfully to a crouched position to look around him. Flames from the demolished jeep and trailer lighted the immediate vicinity. Screams mingled with shouted orders behind him where other 37mm shells, with timed fuses, exploded with devastating effect among the charging Japanese.

After reloading his rifle, Kitani marshaled his thoughts and strength and bounded from the hole. Four steps later, he swerved to dive behind a tree. Nearly a dozen of the enemy were running toward him. Frantically he pulled the pin of a remaining grenade and banged it against the tree trunk until the pop of the fuse told him the primer was burning, then lobbed it toward the still-advancing Americans. The explosion rang in his ears as he resumed his charge. He raced through the dead and wounded, firing from the hip.

He ran on almost blindly, gasping for breath and waiting for the bullet that would end his life. A black shadow suddenly loomed in front of him. Instinctively, he lunged with his bayonet, the weight of his body driving the blade toward the enemy. His momentum carried him crashing into metal. The impact jarred his teeth as the bayonet snapped with a crack. Stunned, he slumped to the ground, then turned to face the foe who had finally blunted his attack.

But there were only the flares and the noise of battle. He realized he had run headlong into a truck. The ''enemy'' at which he had thrust his bayonet had been the truck he had not seen. He listened groggily to the war that raged behind him. Behind him? That meant he had pierced the enemy lines and was at their rear.

He noticed the flares were beginning to pale. Dawn was breaking. To return to join his pinned-down and trapped comrades would be to throw away his life. If fate had meant him to survive, why should he deny it?

In the gray light of the eastern sky he could see the dark outline of the hills surrounding Mount Tapotchau. Hardly caring whether he met the enemy, the chunky sergeant got to his feet, slung his rifle, and walked calmly to the jungle that extended upward toward the mountain.

At dawn, Lewis and others from Headquarters Company roared north along the dusty coastal road toward Tanapag. They turned inland through the troops who still fired sporadically as they mopped up remnants of the attack. Several Americans who had fled the Japanese assault by swimming to a small offshore island could be seen making their way to shore.

An officer in command of the mopping-up operation approached the jeeps.

"What were our casualties?" someone asked him.

"I don't know for sure, sir, but we counted over seventy bodies. Some of them are buried under Jap bodies."

"My God, look at that!" They had just topped a small crest that overlooked the positions of the American infantry from the previous night. Bodies of Japanese soldiers sprawled in grotesque positions for more than a hundred yards, some piled three or four deep.

"What happened to Colonel Donovan of the field gun outfit?" Lewis asked the officer.

"They overran the positions, sir. He's dead."

Too far away to hear them or to be seen by them, a young Japanese soldier lay bleeding in a clump of thick undergrowth. His eyes opened occasionally, then closed in semiconsciousness.

Oba kept his small force moving southward. Enemy defensive positions became less frequent as they followed various trails that traversed the relatively open areas and led them to the more heavily jungled foothills of Mount Tapotchau. The more distance he could put between them and the front line, he knew, the less chance there would be of encountering battle-ready American troops. In the foothills, they stood a chance of surviving. The Americans who had captured the hills a week earlier had been replaced by rear-echelon support troops who were relaxed and confident in the victory that was supposed to have cleared the area of Japanese.

Twice they skirted large enemy encampments with several supply vehicles without being seen. By the dim light of flares that still illuminated the northern end of the island, they spotted the Americans by their trucks and tarpaulin lean-tos and were able to avoid any sentries that may have been posted.

They almost blundered into the second encampment without realizing it. Emerging from a jungle hillside, Oba dropped to one knee and studied what appeared to be a cliff a few feet away. With a shock, he realized it was a large canvas-covered truck. As silently as possible, he and the others turned on the narrow trail and made their way back up the hill.

The next hour was spent trying to avoid the Americans, who seemed to be everywhere. Oba tried to stay close to the top of the ridges, as most of the enemy seemed to be in valleys. With only an hour left before dawn, they were skirting a clearing in which the ruins of a small farmhouse was bathed in the bleakly reflected light of distant flares.

"Captain," Sergeant Bito whispered, "it looks deserted. There might be food inside." It had been eighteen hours since they had eaten the navy rations, but it seemed like days. Oba could not predict what the coming day held for them, but he knew they would be unable to search for food.

"Tell the others to cover us. Let's go!"

The two men crept toward the half-demolished structure until they could see it was deserted. In a crouch, with his pistol extended, Oba entered, then whispered to Bito to get the others. Quietly the men searched the two rooms of the house that remained standing. They discovered a jug of water and a half jar of miso, but nothing to ease the hunger pangs that had grown more severe with the prospect of food. Even the stench of rotting bodies brought by an occasional shift in the breeze could not take their minds from their hunger.

As he sifted through the debris of the ruined portion of the house, a slight movement overhead caught Oba's eye. A chicken roosting on a remaining rafter turned to cock one eye at him. Taking care not to frighten the bird, Oba stepped over a collapsed wall. He was directly below the now suspicious chicken. He grabbed its legs with his left hand and snapped its neck with his right before it could utter more than a surprised squawk.

With the chicken, miso, and a full canteen of water for each man, the group was preparing to leave, when Banno noticed what sounded like the mewing of a cat.

"Maybe it's trapped in that rubble," Banno said as he pulled back some boards leaning against a partially toppled wall. He stooped to look inside a wooden box, then turned to call Captain Oba.

"They're alive," he said in an astonished voice.

"What are?" Oba replied, annoyed that a lieutenant should be so concerned over a litter of kittens.

"Babies," Banno said in the same unbelieving voice.

"What the hell are you talking about? Let me see!" He watched as Banno carefully picked up the box and carried it to where the others stood. Cupping his left hand to conceal the flare, Oba struck a match above the box.

Two infants, both less than six months old, stared up at him.

One made a faint whimpering sound. Both were too weak to cry.

"What should we do?" Banno asked. "We can't take them with us, and if we leave them they'll die of starvation. They're already half-dead."

Tenderly, Oba picked up one of the infants. Its body sagged, and its arms hung limply as he carried it to the pale light near the door. The sky was already growing light in the east, and he knew he would have to make a decision quickly.

One of the men brought the second infant. "Bring the box," Oba ordered as he removed his canteen, wet a finger, and allowed one of the babies to suck the moisture. Banno followed suit. The infants sucked greedily at their fingers.

"We'd better kill them and put them out of their misery," someone said. There was a rumble of dissent from the soldiers who crowded around the two tiny beings.

"Quiet!" Oba whispered. Killing them was out of the question. How to keep them alive was the problem. But he had to smile at what was happening: surrounded by the enemy, and with daylight only minutes away, he and his lieutenant were playing wet nurse to two starving infants.

"Collect every bit of clothing in the house," Oba said to the men standing around him, "and put it in the box." As they did, he selected two pieces that were cleaner than the rest. After the babies were as comfortable as they could make them, he moistened the cloths and gave each a corner on which to suck. Then he placed the box under a tree that would shade them from the sun, and where they could be seen by passing American soldiers. As an afterthought, he tied a bright red piece of cloth to a pole and stuck it in the ground beside the box.

"We've done all we can do," he said to no one in particular. Then, to Banno, "Let's go!" He glanced at the lightening sky, then at the silhouetted Mount Tapotchau, and began walking south toward it.

A sugarcane field bordered the farm, and they entered the six-foot-high wall of green, moving single file through the stalks that hid them from hostile eyes. A gentle slope was taking them into a valley that Oba was certain would be alive with enemy activity. The sound of heavy trucks ahead soon confirmed his fears.

Cautiously, with pistol in hand and prepared to make the final stand if that was to be his fate, Oba led his men forward until the sound of passing vehicles was only meters away. He signaled to halt. As they crouched where they had stood, he crawled forward to the edge of the cane field.

A ten-meter-wide road of crushed coral reflected the light of the rising sun. This is impossible, he thought. I crossed here just a week ago on the way back from Donnin. This was a narrow dirt road. The Japanese army would take weeks or months to build a road like this. A heavy truck rolled by, engulfing him in a billowing cloud of dust. As the sound of another truck grew louder, he turned and crawled back to the cane field where Bito and the others waited.

Fate had protected them once more. Secure in their conquest, the enemy was no longer looking for Japanese. For the moment, at least, Oba and his men were safe. Oba reached in his gas mask bag and brought forth the chicken they had gutted three hours earlier. One of the men produced the half jar of miso and a can. Then, in a move that brought smiles to all of them, Private Naito pulled two candles from his pocket. Bito used his bayonet to skin the bird after a futile try at plucking it clean of feathers. Others, meanwhile, fashioned a stove from green cane that held the can just above the candle flame.

Later, after a small, but welcome lunch of miso chicken,

the group spent the rest of the day sleeping—within several meters of the hundreds of Americans traveling the new highway they had bulldozed across the island.

Shortly after nightfall, Oba crawled back to the road. Jeeps and trucks still passed occasionally, but they were usually several minutes apart. He signaled to Banno and waited until his band of twelve soldiers had joined him at the road's edge before leading them across. Heading once more for high ground, Oba avoided the larger trails that might bring them into a surprise meeting with the enemy, and stuck to less-traveled paths along ridge lines leading to what he hoped would be the safety of Tapotchau.

At daybreak they were well within the jungled slopes of the mountain. Exhausted and with nothing to sustain them for thirty-six hours since their meager meal, they stopped to rest in a clearing on the western side of the mountain.

At mid-morning, Oba was awakened by Lieutenant Banno. "Captain," he said in a whisper, "there are voices below us. Many voices!"

Oba snapped awake. With drawn pistol, he accompanied Banno down the side of the ridge to where the voices could be heard. "Send someone down to see how many there are and in which direction they're moving," he ordered. He searched the terrain for a defensive position, in case they were discovered.

At Banno's order, Private Iwata slipped into the jungle and headed toward the valley floor. Ten minutes later he returned smiling. "They're Japanese soldiers," he said. "There must be a hundred of them."

Oba suspected a trap. Why were a hundred unmolested Japanese soldiers in a valley only two kilometers from Garapan? How could they have been missed by the enemy advance? He and his men had not seen a single Japanese since breaking through the enemy line. He had almost convinced himself they were all that was left of the nearly thirty-thousand-strong army and navy forces that had been on the island.

He led his small band to a vantage point a hundred meters from the soldiers who were milling about as if they were unaware that the Americans had captured the island. Oba studied them through his binoculars. Yes, they were Japanese, not Americans in Japanese army uniforms as he had thought possible.

Relieved, but curious, he led his men into the midst of the group, stopping when he met a slightly built major with a bandaged head. He identified himself with a formal bow which was only partially returned. The men, he learned, were survivors of a mountain artillery regiment who had somehow been by-passed by the Americans as they swept northward three weeks earlier. Since then, they had been living undiscovered, awaiting orders. The major did not seem particularly interested in what had happened at the Valley of Hell and only motioned with his chin toward a nearby hill when Oba said he and his men would like to join his force.

"Go see Colonel Nakajima," he said. "He and a major are up there in a cave." Then, ignoring the officer's sword and pistol that Oba carried, he stepped closer and stared at Oba's collar. "If you're a captain," he said, "where are your stars?" Oba remembered that he had removed them when he had considered shooting himself. Embarrassed, he searched his pockets.

"It looks like I may have to borrow a set," he smiled. "Mine seem to have disappeared."

The little major looked as if he wanted to challenge Oba's offhanded reply, but changed his mind. Oba's unwavering look convinced him that the man before him was an officer.

Oba, who had already noticed the large stockpile of food at one end of the encampment, said he would see the colonel after he and his men had been fed. He was abrupt with the man partly because he disliked his attitude, but mostly because he was too hungry to be polite.

A little later, after enjoying the first hot rice he had had since the invasion, Oba watched a warrant officer enter the encampment from the head of the ravine and ask Banno for food. The man sat apart from the others as he ate with unusual formality, kneeling erectly as if at a formal dinner. Eventually he arose, walked a few meters to the jungle's edge, and disappeared into it. Banno and the others were already sleeping in the shade of a low tree. Oba was looking for a spot where he, too, could take a much needed rest when the sound of a nearby shot startled him into full wakefulness. He dropped behind a rock with his pistol drawn as the entire camp reacted to the report. Seconds passed without another sound. Some of the men moved into the jungle to investigate. Moments later they returned. The warrant officer, they said, has placed the barrel of his pistol in his mouth and pulled the trigger.

That's an honorable way to die, Oba told himself. The man's final meal was a ceremony in which only he had participated. And his death, although unseen by others, was probably equally formal. He looked about him at the soldiers who had returned to inactivity. Some were lying in the shade, others wandered aimlessly around the camp. These men, too, are waiting to die, he told himself. They're no longer interested in the war, only in making their final days as comfortable as possible. Unlike the warrant officer, they lack the courage to end their lives honorably.

Once again, Oba considered taking his life. Perhaps this is to be my fate, too, he thought. Perhaps I should conduct my own private ceremony preparatory to ending my life. The island is lost. The will to fight has left these men, and even my own determination seems to be weakening. But should it be my fate to die as the warrant officer did, what will happen to Banno and the others? What were the colonel and major, somewhere up on that hill, planning? Why hadn't they tried to turn these demoralized soldiers into a spirited fighting group? Are they really waiting for orders? Orders from whom? To do what? No, now is not the time to end my life. Perhaps later, but not yet.

Physically tired, but too disturbed by the warrant officer's death to sleep, Oba rose and walked to where Lieutenant Banno sat talking with an officer of the artillery regiment.

"Let's find a place to set up camp," he said to his once-again jovial friend. "I'd feel safer up near the ridge line than down here in the valley." As they walked up a trail that led through the bush-covered north wall of the valley, Oba offered a cigarette to Banno, who declined, then lighted one for himself.

"What do we do now?" the younger man asked. "The Americans are bound to discover us sooner or later."

"Without their artillery pieces, these men can no longer fight," Oba replied. "Let's spend another day or so with them, then find a place where we can establish a base."

They were passing small groups of men clustered on the hillside. They climbed in silence until a private who had been talking to another soldier arose as they passed and called, "Hey!"

Oba turned, saw the man was addressing him, and began to bristle. He had seen how lax military discipline had grown here, and understood that men who were waiting to die, and whose officers showed no inclination to lead them, could lose their inspiration. But for a private to shout "hey" to a captain could not be accepted. He turned to the man who was walking toward him. He was short, heavy to the point of being fat, and wore a thick black beard below unusually round eyes. He came directly to Oba, showing no inclination to either bow or salute.

"Give me a cigarette," he said in a surly tone. The man's eyes met Oba's in a steady gaze that did not reflect the hostility in his voice. He's not being insolent, he is shell-shocked, Oba thought, and reached into his pocket for his nearly empty pack of cigarettes. The man extended his right hand, and Oba saw the purple and red band of tattoo around his wrist. No, he's not crazy, he told himself, but he's no ordinary soldier, either. Even though I'm not wearing my stars, he could tell by my sword and pistol that I am an officer. But to a *yakuza* it would make little difference. Still studying the man, Oba withdrew one cigarette from the pack and handed it to the tattooed stranger who muttered his thanks and walked back to his waiting friend. Oba watched him and was aware of a sense of uneasiness.

"Why did you give him a cigarette?" Banno asked indignantly. "Why didn't you punish him for insolence? He could see we were officers. I think I'll . . ." Banno turned to go back where the private had rejoined his friend.

"Just a moment." Oba grabbed Banno's arm. "Didn't you see his tattoos?"

"No, but what does it matter? He was insolent."

"True, but he's also a *yakuza*. If he ever was a disciplined soldier, he certainly isn't now. A man trained in crime, as he has been, could be a valuable friend or a dangerous enemy. And for a cigarette, I'm not going to eliminate either one of those possibilities at this point.''

They continued to the top of the ridge and found a spot several meters removed from the other soldiers, which Oba selected as a site for himself and his men.

During the next three days Oba and his small group lived among, but separate from, those of the artillery regiment. He learned that the valley above which they camped was known as Chikko no Sawa. He watched his men surrender to the lassitude of the others. He made no effort to stop them, because food was plentiful and their bodies needed rest.

On the third day, Oba lay down under a low-hanging bush after lunch to rest. He had just fallen asleep when he was shocked awake by the angry crack of automatic weapons fire that ripped leaves from a bush inches from his head. Instinctively, he rolled to the right down an incline, then rose to a crouching run. Automatic fire exploded with the reports of rifles behind him. He saw no one. A compelling fear gripped his mind as his pumping legs carried him toward a small ravine bordered on one side by a sheer rocky cliff. He was not running to anything, but simply away.

Then, to his right, he heard shouting. His heart pounding, he saw about thirty Americans moving down the draw toward him. To his left was an open area which he could not hope to cross before enemy bullets cut him down. Blindly, hopelessly, he ran on. From the brush at the base of the cliff two figures emerged and began to climb its rocky face.

''Get down!'' Oba tried to yell, but his vocal cords were constricted by fear. ''They'll see you,'' he tried again, but still with no sound. The two figures continued slowly to climb the wall.

Then, he too was at the base. The bodies of two Japanese soldiers lay in the dry wash. The enemy was only fifty meters away, and although he was momentarily hidden by bush, he had no place to hide or run.

Quickly he removed his sword, pistol, and gas mask bag, threw them into some bushes, then crawled between the bodies of the two soldiers and feigned death. He could hear the Americans approach.

"There go two of them up the cliff!" He heard the shout, then a volley of fire. As he listened to the voices without understanding the words, he came to a conclusion: he would be dead soon. Very soon. But it was not the way he wanted to die. To die while pretending to be dead is to die without honor. But to act otherwise is to give up all hope of living. He was waiting for the impact of the bullet that would end his life.

Suddenly something struck him with a force that pushed his face into the sand. He did not know where the projectile had entered his body because it shook his frame from head to foot. He waited for unconsciousness, hoping it would close his mind before a searing pain replaced the initial shock of a mortal wound. But neither came, only the suffocating feeling of a weight pushing him into the sand.

The voices around him spoke in unintelligible sounds. Am I already dead? he wondered. He held his breath, conscious that he still had sufficient life to direct his actions.

"Well, at least we got five of 'em," one of the voices said.

"Sounded like the Second Platoon had a field day up on the ridge," another voice replied.

Oba felt another weight, this one on his left leg, and realized one of the enemy soldiers was resting the butt of his rifle there. He tried to identify the weight on the rest of his body and gradually realized it was the corpse of one of the people he had seen trying to scale the cliff.

I'm alive, he thought, and slowly allowed the breath trapped in his lungs to escape. Equally slowly, he replaced it with another. I'm not cowering. I'm fighting them with my wits. The thought made him feel better. The panic that had gripped him earlier subsided. Even if I die now, I will have been fighting until the end. He was tempted to smile but remained motionless in case his face was visible to the enemy.

Eventually the weight on his leg was removed, and the enemy voices receded. Still, he continued to lie unmoving among the dead. After what he estimated to be a quarter of an hour, he opened his eyes, then very slowly turned his head until he could see down the draw. They were gone.

This is like rising from the dead, he thought, as he rolled on his side to dislodge the body on his back. He remained on his hands and knees to crawl to the bushes where he had thrown his weapons. Armed once again, he looked up the hill toward where he had been sleeping thirty minutes earlier. At least two dozen bodies were visible from where he stood. He looked at each as he walked up the hill, hoping that some of them, too, were only pretending to be dead. But he knew from their unnatural positions that none was acting.

Near the crest, Banno's body lay where it had been thrown by a burst of automatic fire. The glaze of death gave a pale cast to one eye. Where the other should have been, a gaping hole, already lined with blackened blood, marked the exit point of a bullet that had torn its way through his head. Oba closed the remaining eye. Reverently, he placed the dead man's hands on his chest even though the fingers of one had been partially sheared by another bullet.

Desperate for some way of demonstrating his sorrow, Oba impulsively pulled a bayonet from a body nearby and sawed through the sinew of Banno's nearly severed left thumb. He wrapped the dismembered digit in his handkerchief and placed it in a pocket of his tunic. If he could, he would return at least a portion of his friend to the man's family.

As he topped the crest, it became apparent that most, if not all, of what had been left of the mountain artillery regiment had been caught unaware and killed before they had fled more than a few meters. He looked for his original force of twelve but could not find them amid the carnage. The arrogant major who had challenged his rank was sprawled between two rocks. Oba noticed that both his pistol and sword were missing, but the bandage on his head was still in place.

Suddenly he became aware that the casual way in which he was walking among the bodies made him an excellent candidate to join them. He returned to the ridge, from where he could see or hear the enemy should they return, and selected a rocky formation that would give him an opportunity to make a stand before he was overwhelmed. Then, as an afterthought, he went back among the bodies and collected three rifles and a pistol to fortify his stronghold. Later he heard firing far down the ravine and concluded that the attacking force was continuing its sweep toward Garapan.

It was almost an hour after dark when he heard movement in the valley below him and the sound of whispered Japanese words. He made his way down the darkened trail until he could make out four figures, speaking softly among themselves. They turned, frightened, as he walked toward them.

"I am Captain Oba of the Eighteenth Regiment. Who are you?"

They identified themselves as members of the hapless artillery regiment, and Oba asked about other survivors of the attack.

"None that we know of, sir," one of them replied.

During the next two hours, seven more appeared, including five of those with whom he had breached the enemy lines nearly a week earlier: Privates Iwata, Sano, Hiraiwa, and Suzuki and Corporal Kuno, the only survivors, other than himself, of those who had sailed with him from Japan four months earlier.

"Where are the others?" he asked, thinking particularly of Sergeant Bito.

"They're dead," Kuno replied.

"Bito, too?"

"Sergeant Bito and the other seven ran directly into the fire of a machine gun as they tried to escape up the valley," the corporal said. "We were behind and below them. We swerved to the left when we saw them fall."

Gradually others filtered into the valley during the night until there were about twenty, mostly from the artillery regiment. Corporal Kuno, willing and anxious, immediately assumed the role that Bito had carried, and made his authority felt by Hiraiwa and Iwata.

"Go find your rifle!" he said gruffly to Hiraiwa, who had left it behind in the first panic-filled moments of the attack. "The next time, remember your rifle is a gift from the Emperor and treat it with the respect and honor it deserves!"

The private bowed. Darkness hid the chagrin on his face. He had no choice but to accept the rebuke. Of all his equipment, his rifle, entrusted to him by the Emperor, was the most sacred. And he had failed that trust by fleeing without it.

"Tell Hiraiwa and the others to collect every rifle and all the ammunition they can find!" Oba ordered the corporal. "We'll hide them near here and pick them up later."

He had no idea whether they would survive long enough to make use of the weapons, but he was determined to remain alive as long as possible and to continue to inflict casualties on the enemy until fate dictated otherwise.

As the men began searching the bodies in the clearing of the valley, and toward its upper end where Bito and the others had been killed, Oba heard a voice answering their whispered questions in a normal tone. Angry, he walked toward them to silence the fool who threatened their security.

"Shut up!" he ordered as he approached the figures. One of them, he could see, was sitting on the edge of the two-foot-deep dry wash that fed rainwater from the mountain to the sea.

"Who are you?" the sitting man asked, still in a normal tone of voice. As Oba drew closer he recognized the man sitting on the bank as the tattooed soldier who had demanded a cigarette.

He held a Nambu light machine gun on his lap.

"What are you doing with that weapon?" Oba snapped.

"I'm making a sling. I'm tired of being shot at without fighting back. I don't know about the rest of you, but I came here to kill the enemy. And from now on, that's exactly what I'm going to do!"

He went back to fashioning a belt from two rifle slings that would suspend the machine gun in a firing position from his shoulders.

"When did you return?" Oba asked, wondering why neither he nor the others had heard the man walk into the valley.

"I never left." Oba thought he saw the man smile. "I stayed right here," and he indicated a two-foot cut under the bank where the rushing water had dug into the rocky earth as it swung to follow the contours of the valley. "I lay down in the cut and watched them jump over me as they chased you," the man said matter-of-factly, then returned his attention to the improvised sling.

"We're collecting weapons to hide for use later on," Oba said. "Do you want to hide the machine gun, too?"

"No, thank you." He did not say "sir." "I decided today to kill one hundred Americans before I die. With dawn, I will begin. I will have need for this weapon then."

Oba knew better than to argue with a *yakuza*, especially one holding a machine gun. He turned with a grunt and walked back down the wash to where the others were stacking the weapons they had found, mortar and a box of mortar shells. Oba ordered two of the men to carry the machine gun and mortar, and two more to carry a box of shells. The rest of the armaments they hid in a small cave by placing rocks and bushes over its mouth.

"We are now as well armed as possible under the circumstances," he said to the sixteen soldiers who had survived from the artillery unit. "I have no idea what will happen from here on, but you may join us if you wish, or go your separate ways. I suggest, however, that we are stronger and have a better chance of survival by sticking together."

The entire group—trained in artillery and uncomfortable in the role of infantrymen—were grateful to join an officer and five soldiers who knew how to fight with small arms.

Before leaving, Oba walked to where the tattooed private still sat on the bank of the streambed. "What is your name?" he asked.

"Horiuchi," the man replied.

"You are welcome to join us."

"No thank you, Captain. You fight your way, and I'll fight mine."

Satisfied that he had made the offer and not surprised by the reply, Oba returned to where the other twenty-one waited and led them out of the ravine. He had no idea where they were going but was determined to put as much distance as possible between them and the valley before dawn.

The sky was still black when Oba, at the head of the group, heard a voice speaking in Japanese from the jungle ahead of them. "Halt! Who goes there?"

"Japanese soldiers. Hold your fire!" Oba replied.

The sentry ordered them forward, then saluted when Captain Oba identified himself. "Stay here until daylight," he told Oba, "then I will direct you to the others."

Oba spent the next hour conversing softly with the sentry

while his men slept. He learned they were at the foot of a hill known as Coffee Mountain, and that "the others" consisted of nearly two hundred Japanese who had been arriving in small groups during the past week.

"They're coming from all over the island," the enlisted man told him, "both soldiers and civilians. Most say they heard they were to gather at a point above Garapan and await further orders."

Who could have issued such an order? Oba asked himself. Was there a high-ranking officer still alive who planned to amass as many people as possible, then launch another suicide charge? Or did he intend to form a force that would remain in the jungle, harassing the enemy? Or, and just as likely, was it a rumor somehow started by the Americans in order to herd all surviving Japanese into a valley where they could be killed by a combined air, artillery, and infantry attack?

He eventually stretched out on the ground, but had only slept for a few minutes when the sentry shook him awake. The sun was almost to the horizon, and he could see they were on the edge of a wide valley with large trees whose interlocking foliage hid the valley floor from sunlight and aerial observation. In the pale predawn light, Oba could see activity beneath the trees as the two hundred soldiers and civilian men and women awoke to congratulate themselves on seeing the dawn of one more day. Cooking fires were already burning at several points in the camp, and Oba cursed himself for not bringing rice and dried rations from the artillery regiment supply.

The sentry had told Oba that there was no single officer in charge of the group, but that he had been posted there by a lieutenant from his original unit, the 135th Regiment.

Oba roused his men and, following directions provided by the sentry, moved into the valley until he found the lieutenant. Again he had to identify himself as a captain, and he saw the lieutenant's eyes record the absence of his insignia. But neither the eyes nor the manner of the younger man evidenced doubt, and his band was invited to share rations with the lieutenant's men.

"How many soldiers do you have?" Oba asked as they ate.

''Only seven from my original unit, but we've picked up more than a dozen stragglers from other regiments.''

Oba noticed that only a few of the lieutenant's force were armed. He considered telling him of the weapons they had hidden at Chikko no Sawa but decided to wait until he had learned more about this new group.

Later that morning, he walked among the people camped on the valley floor and confirmed there was no central leadership. Families, small groups of soldiers, and some individuals sat apart from each other, paying little attention to others. If it weren't for their unsmiling faces and somber attitudes, he thought, it could almost be a crowded picnic ground. Although calmer and slightly more organized than the refugees he had seen in China and Manchuria, they had the same despondency and submissiveness he had seen there.

Even the military men among them showed no sign of resolution or pride in being soldiers of Japan. What had happened? Did the spirit of Bushido exist only in victory? Could one defeat destroy a man's dedication to his Emperor? Why were they not as ready to fight and die for their country as they had been a month earlier? He thought again of the tattooed man who, with a light machine gun hanging from his shoulders, had declared his own private war on the enemy. Why had these people none of his spirit? What difference does it make, he thought, if a man surrenders to defeat instead of to the enemy? Disheartened, he wondered how long it would take his own men to slip into this lethargy. Or, for that matter, how long could he himself resist?

He walked toward the upper end of the valley. It narrowed and grew considerably steeper as it rose, but large trees continued to provide concealment. There were no sentries at this end of the valley, and Oba wondered what chances the group would have if the enemy swept down as they had done the previous afternoon at Chikko no Sawa.

He returned to where the young lieutenant—the only man he had met who seemed to remember he was a soldier—sat talking to his men. Oba told him of the food supply that had been left at Chikko no Sawa and showed the lieutenant on his map how to reach the valley, about two kilometers west of their position. He suggested, however, that no attempt be made to retrieve it until dark because the enemy might already have returned.

It was mid-afternoon when the sounds of rifle fire were heard by those whom Oba and his men had joined earlier in the day. Two hundred frightened faces turned toward the sound, which emanated from an area far below them. Families and soldiers alike exchanged concerned glances, then began to pack their meager belongings. Short bursts of automatic weapon fire could be heard among the rifle reports as the enemy flushed out hiding Japanese. It was apparent the enemy was moving up the valley, and a general exodus began in the opposite direction.

Oba and his men prepared to follow. He heard Suzuki berating Hiraiwa, who had been suffering from dysentery for several days, and who was obviously still ill. "You can't stay here," he was saying. "You've got to come with us."

The badly dehydrated soldier simply shook his head, but otherwise refused to move. Oba went over to where Hiraiwa lay. "On your feet!" he ordered.

"I'm sorry, Captain, I can't move," the soldier replied. The sound of shooting was growing louder.

"Suzuki!" Oba called. "Get a couple of men and move him to those rocks over there. Leave him there with his rifle!" Soon, he knew, his original group would be reduced to five: Kuno, Suzuki, Sano, Iwata, and himself.

Then, in an effort to set an example for the straggler soldiers who were retreating with no more spirit than the frightened civilians, Oba ordered his men to form two ranks and marched them in a military manner toward the upper end of the valley.

Again, I'm retreating, he thought. But this time is different. We are armed. We are in the hills that are ours. This time we will stand and fight from a position of our own choosing.

It sickened him to watch the disorganized mass fleeing blindly from the enemy.

The valley had narrowed to about twenty-five meters when they emerged from the trees and entered a gently sloping grassy area pocked with outcroppings of coral rock. Oba searched for a natural defensive position as he led his men and those who had not fled up the center of the cleared area. A hundred meters from the trees he saw a trench and foxholes that had been dug during the battle. The prepared positions, protected by a jagged two-foot ridge of protruding shale, were more than he had hoped for.

He positioned his men carefully, noting by the sound of American rifles that the enemy was moving more slowly up the valley than they. He turned to study the terrain below him. Soldiers and civilians stretched to the tree line. He considered stopping some of the soldiers who carried rifles, but let them pass because his own men occupied most of the foxholes.

He placed the light machine gun and mortar on his left flank, ordered half the men to take cover in the shallow foxholes, and assigned the remainder to the trench. Then a flash of color at the tree line caught his attention. A cadet officer wearing white trousers and brown boots emerged with two soldiers and began to climb the slope. The cadet spotted Oba and his men and headed directly for the entrenchment. He saluted as he reached the edge of the trench and identified himself and his men as members of a light weapons company.

"Can you handle a machine gun or mortar?"

"Yes, sir," the youth replied and glanced at the two weapons at the end of the trench. He indicated the bag that one of his men carried and added, "We've even got some extra mortar ammunition."

"All right, take over!" Oba ordered.

From the sound of the gunfire, Oba guessed that the enemy had reached the campsite. The increased volume of fire indicated a large number of the group had remained behind; either that, or the Americans were green troops who fired at every shadow. He wondered briefly if Hiraiwa's rifle was among those they heard, then turned to his men.

"Keep your heads below the rocks," he said. "We will wait until they get within twenty meters before we open fire. I will give the signal. Hold the mortar fire until we've broken their advance with the machine gun and rifles!"

Satisfied that his orders were understood, Oba stood behind a rocky projection from where he had a clear view of the tree line. The firing was still far below the line. He looked at his men. Each lay in readiness. Gone was the earlier passivity. Once again they were soldiers. All they had lacked was leadership and an opportunity to meet the enemy.

He removed three clips of ammunition from his pocket and laid them on a ledge from which he could reload his pistol quickly. As he searched his pocket for loose rounds, his fingers closed on two pieces of stiff cloth. He smiled, then withdrew the captain's stars he had removed nearly two weeks earlier. As he pinned them on his collar, he saw Suzuki grin and nod approvingly. Oba returned the smile.

The clearing was almost empty. A final group of twenty civilians struggled under bags of clothing and other personal belongings. Rather than veer off to the jungle on either side, they carried on straight toward the defensive position. As they drew closer, Oba could see they were mostly elderly couples. They stopped, winded, when they saw the soldiers lying in wait for the enemy.

"Get behind us!" Oba said brusquely. He was afraid the civilians would attract the attention of the still-advancing Americans. "You!" he pointed to one of the younger men. "Get everyone behind those rocks!" He indicated an outcropping twenty five meters above his defense. "Make sure they can't be seen!"

As he looked up at the rocks, he saw a stocky soldier leap lightly to the ground and walk directly toward him. The man's easy gait and the casual manner in which he carried his rifle indicated he was a seasoned soldier.

The man stopped at the edge of the stronghold and glanced professionally at the positioning of men and weapons. Oba could see the stars of a master sergeant pinned to his collar. The man saluted. "Master Sergeant Toshio Kitani," he said to Oba, "from the One-thirty-fifth Regiment."

Oba smiled and returned the salute. "You've come at a good time. We're expecting an enemy assault within minutes. Take a position and we'll talk later." If there is a later, he thought.

Nearly fifteen minutes passed before the first Americans emerged from the tree line. They came out of the trees slowly, spread across the entire twenty-five meters of valley floor, holding their rifles at port arms. Oba estimated there were about 150 of them approaching his position. The nearest were halfway up the cleared slope. He eased the safety off his pistol. Gradually they filled the lower half of the clearing. He glanced quickly at his twenty men. They were ready and waiting. The cadet was looking down the barrel of the machine gun. Oba selected a bush twenty meters down to his front. He would open fire when the first man reached that point.

Suddenly a long burst of fire shattered the silence.

"Damn!" The cadet had opened fire. Oba moved from the protection of the rock, standing in full view of the enemy and emptied his pistol as rapidly as he could find targets. Nearly a dozen of the enemy crumpled within the first five seconds. A few dropped to the ground to return the fire, but the rest turned and ran for the tree line.

Oba looked at the man with the mortar. He was already dropping the shells into the short tubular barrel and pulling the lanyard that sent the small missiles arcing toward the retreating enemy.

Those Americans who had returned their fire were now attempting to escape, some to the sides and some running zig-zaggedly toward the trees. Mortar shells exploded among them.

From his left, Oba saw the cadet and his two men run from their position. The young man was firing wildly with a pistol at the retreating enemy.

"Fool!" Oba said under his breath. The idiot was obviously filled with theory but had had little combat experience. In China, he too had charged after a retreating enemy. But this was not China. No books had yet been written about fighting the Americans.

A volley of fire rang out from behind the trees, and the young cadet fell face forward. His men tried to find cover but were thrown to the ground by a hail of bullets. The machine gun to his left answered the volley, raking the trees and the vulnerable spaces between them.

"Cease fire!" Oba shouted. In the ensuing silence, he watched for movement, either on the open slope or from within the trees. Five minutes passed. Then he gave the order to advance. Dodging from rock to rock, they moved down the slope. Oba counted seventeen bodies, including those of the cadet and his men, as they advanced to the tree line. Once under the trees, he ordered his men to move more quickly.

There had been no sign of the enemy by the time they reached the site of the earlier camp. Oba climbed one of the valley walls to a rocky promontory to study the canyon's lower end. Even without his binoculars, he could see the Americans in full retreat, most of them running toward the safety of Garapan.

As he returned to the valley floor, he wished that the soldiers who had fled with the civilians had been able to share this experience with him. At last he had proved the Americans were not invincible.

His exultation was dampened when he saw Suzuki and Iwata standing beside the body of Hiraiwa. The weakened soldier had placed the barrel of his rifle under his chin and pulled the trigger with his toe. His fear of being captured had forced him to take his own life before the Americans arrived.

Oba watched as Suzuki, who in spite of his frequent criticisms of Hiraiwa, had felt a close camaraderie with the slightly built soldier, gently moved the body to a rocky cleft and covered it with stones and bush. He, too, felt the loss. To share the closeness of death as many times as they had in the past weeks ties men's spirits with a lifelong bond. Their shared experiences would permanently etch Hiraiwa in Oba's memory.

He didn't live to see our first victory over the Americans, Oba thought with regret. Had he waited a few minutes, he might have remained undetected, and could have fired at them as they retreated instead of at himself. But there was no time to muse about his victory. Oba knew it was temporary. He suspected that the size of his group would be exaggerated by the Americans who had fled from his ambush, and that a retaliation in force could be expected within hours.

"Sergeant Kitani," he said to the sturdy little man who had joined them an hour earlier, "have the men gather all the enemy weapons and ammunition and prepare to move to another site."

As Kitani issued the order, Oba spread his map on a flat

rock and began to look for an area in which they could establish a base camp.

"Captain, sir." It was Kitani. He carried an officer's map case and was withdrawing a map of the central section of the island. "This one may be better." The detail of the new map gave a much better picture of the area.

"Where did you get this?"

"The officer who had it had no further use of it," the sergeant replied. "For the past three days I've been at Takoyama," Kitani said, pointing to a hill to their north east. "It is mostly covered by banyan trees that provide concealment, but with less jungle than in most places."

Oba could see from the contour lines that the hill rose to nearly a thousand feet. The western slope was gradual, while the eastern side was steeper with several deep ravines that knifed through the hills as they twisted their way to the sea. A number of printed trails crisscrossed the surface of the map, and Oba selected a route that would lead them to Takoyama.

The crash of the first volley of mortar shells reverberated throughout the valley and on the side of Coffee Mountain before they had gone five hundred meters. From the ridge on which they stood, Oba and the others watched as the explosions walked methodically from their original campsite to the cleared area of the ambush, then back again. They were near enough to hear the clunk of the mortars' propellant charges where the shells were being fired, only a few meters above their defensive position of two hours earlier.

Oba had outwitted the enemy. But in so doing, he had reopened the war. No longer would they be able to hide with relative security in the knowledge that the enemy was unaware of their existence. They had challenged the Americans and had underscored their challenge in American blood.

The Americans had given their first reply to the defiance with the mortar shells that could still be heard exploding in the valley. They would not rest, Oba was certain, until they had eradicated the last vestige of Japanese resistance. Or until the Imperial Navy returned to retake the island. And it would be his duty to keep himself and his men alive until that time.

Oba was caught between a desire to move as rapidly as he could from the valley under attack and his anticipation of possibly making contact with an enemy force moving to finish off any survivors of the mortar barrage. He sent Kitani and two others ahead to watch for signs of the enemy. An hour later they began to climb the gentle western slope of Takoyama. Huge banyan trees, standing on roots that joined their trunks a meter or more above ground, shielded them from the sky. The permanent shade had restricted the growth of jungle and underbrush. The roots of some of the trees, Oba noted, formed a space large enough for a man to take a defensive position, if necessary. He sent a soldier to call Kitani back to the main body of men.

"Have the men wait here," he said when the sergeant had returned. "You and I will check out the hill."

He watched the sergeant as they advanced up the slope. They exchanged no words, but Kitani's use of hand signals showed that he not only knew the terrain, but had a soldier's natural instinct for caution and survival.

An unexpected panorama of jungled hills and valleys, decreasing in size as they extended to the east, appeared as they topped the crest of Takoyama. Oba laid out the map that Kitani had given him and located the outstanding features of the lush landscape.

With his binoculars, he studied the flat plain inland from Magicienne Bay and was startled to see huge cleared areas on which thousands of tents and a few metal buildings in the shape of half gasoline drums had been erected. He drew a light penciled circle on the surface of the map to mark the area, which he estimated housed some twenty thousand enemy troops.

Directly below him, spiny, densely jungled ridges dropped sharply toward the plain. His map showed no trails within a half kilometer of their position. He concluded that an enemy attack from that direction would be almost impossible.

"Pick a site a hundred meters back in the trees," he told Kitani, "then have the men set up camp." He continued to study the lowland, making occasional notes on his map.

A few minutes later, he nodded approvingly at the area selected by Kitani. It was a level space that provided an excellent field of fire over the slope below them, and it was already taking on the appearance of a camp. Under Kitani's direction, emplacements on the edge overlooking the slope were being fortified by loose rocks. The machine gun was already mounted, and other defensive positions were under construction on the camp's perimeters.

He felt like a soldier again. He motioned for Kitani to join him. They discussed the years both had spent in China and their experiences since the invasion of Saipan.

"Were you at the Valley of Hell?"

"Yes, sir." Kitani gave Oba his account of the suicides of Generals Saito and Igeta and Admirals Nagumo and Yano, and of his own role in the suicide attack of July 7. "Since then, I've spent most of my time trying to stay alive, and the rest of the time wondering if I should kill myself. For the past week, I've been living with a group of civilians and military stragglers about half a kilometer north of here."

"How many soldiers?" Oba asked.

"More than fifty. But most are without weapons, and they're completely unorganized."

For a few moments Oba was silent. With every body counted, almost a seventy-man force, he thought. If they were organized, armed, and given the will to fight and win, they just might be able to resist until the Imperial Navy retook the island. The next morning, he decided, he would set out to find them. His thoughts were interrupted by Kitani.

"Are we going to fight, sir?"

"Yes, Sergeant, we're going to fight. But it will be a different kind of war from that we knew in China. And it will be different from the one we've fought on this island until now."

Kitani looked relieved. "That's good," he said. "I've been bothered by the way we collapsed so quickly before the enemy. I would be much more willing to die after having shown the Americans how well we can fight."

"Hopefully, they will be shown. But our mission will be to remain alive until the navy wins whatever battle it is fighting and returns, then to fight at the enemy's rear as our forces attack the shores. Meanwhile, we will collect information on American defensive positions and protect these hills from the enemy. We will strike them when necessary, but we will avoid any direct confrontation that could result in our defeat.'' Oba looked at the round, pockmarked face of the veteran soldier. There was complete acceptance of his proposal in the man's eyes and slightly crooked smile. ''It's good to have a man with your experience,'' Oba said. ''Now, let's post some sentries and see what we can do about food and water for the men.''

· 6 ·

AFTER COFFEE MOUNTAIN

In the fields of sugarcane that once fed the large refinery at Charan-Kanoa, before it had been reduced to a mass of twisted steel girders, U.S. Marines were cutting the cane with bayonets.

The battle had been won. The commanders of the 2d Marine Division had been hard put to find a way of keeping their twenty thousand young men occupied until someone had suggested that the several square miles of sugarcane on the island would take a year to cut with bayonets; the tips were sharp, but they made poor cutting tools.

George Pollard walked through a newly cleared area of Division Headquarters Company, where enlisted men were at work erecting octagonal tents; others were leveling the land, and spreading crushed coral. A man raking the sandy soil in front of a tent in an effort to make it appear more tidy jerked to attention and, holding the rake in his left hand, snapped a salute with his right.

"Good morning, sir."

"Good morning, son," Pollard said as he returned the salute. The boy's jacket was already dark green with perspiration, though the sun was barely twenty degrees above the horizon. The youth waited until Pollard had passed, then resumed his raking.

At thirty-six, Pollard's fatherly attitude toward the young men who made up the bulk of the 2d Division seemed natural. In civilian life he would have had little to do with boys just barely out of high school. But here, they—all twenty thousand of them—were the reason for his existence. And, to an extent, their existence depended upon him. It was he who determined where they fought, when they rested, and how they—or at least most of them—managed to survive. His decisions were, of course, subject to the approval of the division CO, but the old man rarely disagreed with him.

A large, rawboned man with short-cropped black hair, Pollard approached a tent where a Marine was placing a white signboard on which he had neatly printed 2d DIVISION PLANS AND OPERATIONS, D-3, under which appeared the name Col. George Pollard. He paused to read the sign, returned the salute of the sign painter, smiled, and said, "Good job, son."

As Pollard entered the tent, Maj. Herman Lewis turned from a map he had been studying and said, "Good morning, sir."

"Good morning, Herm," Pollard replied. "What are you doing here so early?"

"I hear scuttlebutt that we're going to get the job of clearing the mountain of stragglers. Is that right?"

"That's about the size it. The old man got the word last night. I don't think it'll be much of a job, though. They're probably mostly civilians, and when they get hungry enough, they'll be glad to give up." He tossed his garrison cap on the ornately carved "appropriated" table that served as his desk and reached for the coffeepot simmering over a small pressure stove.

"It's a helluva shame, though, that we have to make those kids run up and down those hills again in this heat. You'd think that after spending a month taking this damned island, then doing the same thing on Tinian, they'd give us a rest. You want some coffee?"

"No sir, I've already had a cup." The twenty-nine-year-old major still felt ill at ease with Colonel Pollard. Before he had been moved into the job of division intelligence officer two weeks earlier, Lewis had known Pollard only from a distance, as the man with the real brains running the war, at least as far as the 2d Division was concerned. Now, because he had been moved up to division level, he would be working daily with the man. It was rumored that Pollard was in line for a star, and that would mean Lewis would be transferred to an even more responsible position. But Lewis knew he wouldn't survive in his job for long if he appeared too subservient, so he took refuge behind his work, where he knew he was on solid ground.

"How do you plan to round them up, sir? I mean the stragglers, that is." He cursed himself for adding the last phrase, making it sound like the colonel didn't know what he was talking about.

"No big deal," Pollard said, easing into his chair and hefting his feet onto his desk. "There can't be too many of them, they're disorganized, scared, hungry, and they're limited to an area about three miles wide and five miles long. They gotta stick to the hills around Tapotchau because the country to the north, all the way to Marpi Point, is too open to give them concealment."

Lewis had studied advertising before volunteering for the Marine Corps. Now was the time to show that he could contribute to the plan.

"I don't think it'll be that easy, Colonel." Lewis was reluctant to contradict Pollard, but it was his job to know more about the enemy than others. "We found several food caches during the campaign, and for all we know, there may be dozens more. Besides, the ones that are still up there are there because they want to be. They had plenty of chances to surrender or to kill themselves or to die gloriously for the Emperor during the campaign. But they didn't. They're up there for some other reason . . . some other way of dying gloriously for their country."

Pollard stood, stretched, and turned to his open footlocker. "Well," he said, "we'll find out in a few days. The first patrols go up day after tomorrow."

Round one lost, Lewis thought. Or nearly. "Maybe," he offered, "we could turn out some leaflets that the patrols could scatter around up there, and . . ." He started to use the word *convince,* then changed his mind. "And make them realize how useless it is to hold out."

"Sure," Pollard said in a slightly patronizing tone. "Let's do that." With no more to say, Lewis left the tent and walked back to his own office, a similar structure, but lacking the crushed coral walkway and whitewashed rocks. He wondered if maybe Pollard was right; firepower could be more convincing than words. The Japanese still in the hills could have surrendered during the battle. In fact, all they had to do now was to walk out with their hands up. But many of them, he knew, were up there because they wanted to be, and like those they had fought from one end of Saipan to the other, most preferred to die rather than surrender.

And Pollard seemed willing to accommodate them.

Lewis's concern for his inability to impress Pollard gave way to a proud smile as he neared his tent and looked at a newly mounted sign bearing his name under the words DI-VISION INTELLIGENCE, D-2. He had been promoted to this position after his predecessor, who had been wounded in the fighting, was evacuated to Hawaii. Still smiling, he entered, walked to his desk, and picked up a message. "Shit," he muttered as a frown replaced the smile. He turned and strode back to Pollard's tent.

"Sir, we got a problem," he said as he entered. "Take a look at this."

Pollard read the single page rapidly, then tossed it on his desk. "Those bastards!" he said with emphasis on the second word. "What in the hell did you mean, Herm, when you said they were sitting up there waiting for an honorable death? Look at this report! Mortars, machine guns, and rifles, firing from dug-in positions. They turned back a patrol of a hundred and fifty men!"

"Yes, sir, I know. And that makes it a completely different ballgame."

Pollard picked up the message and walked to a large map of Saipan tacked to a piece of plywood. He checked the coordinates and located the site of the battle. He looked over his shoulder at the other officer.

"This is serious, Herm." He walked slowly back to his desk, thinking. Lewis took a seat at the side of the desk. "A bunch of raggedy-assed stragglers sitting around waiting to die—like that artillery regiment bunch the other day—is one thing, but an enemy that's shooting at us is another. Shit, I've already told Washington the island is secured. How's this report going to look?''

Lewis was staring at the message on Pollard's desk. ''Estimates from those involved say there were probably less than thirty of the enemy, and that they killed three.''

''That's not the point, goddamn it,'' Pollard exploded. ''We can't afford to have shoot-outs up there. Two weeks ago there were nothing but Marines and some army units on the island. A few skirmishes in the hills didn't particularly bother anyone. But now we've got noncombat support people coming in by the thousands. Hell, we've even got Red Cross doughnut dollies on shore. And if any of them get killed by Japs I told Washington don't exist, we're all in deep shit.''

Lewis watched Pollard light one of his cigars and gazed at the blue cloud of smoke that rose above them. ''Do you remember that artillery outfit last week, sir? They thought they had failed, so they were willing to die. They were just sitting there, waiting for us to kill them. Whoever is leading this outfit has not failed . . . at least in his own mind. He's going to continue fighting us until he does.'' He paused, and Pollard waited for him to continue. ''The best way to eliminate him, without a lotta our kids becoming casualties, is to convince him he has failed and that an honorable death is the only way out of his situation.''

''That Japanese psychology course you took may sound good in theory, Herm, but it's not worth doodley-shit in practice.'' Pollard looked at the map. ''There's only one way to clean out those hills, and that's to blast those people out. And until we do, I'm going to have one battalion up there every day, plus ambushes, night patrols, dogs, and spotter planes.''

That night, far from the Coffee Mountain site that Pollard had pinpointed on his map, Oba slept soundly in a natural shelter formed by the roots of a banyan tree. A light, warm rain awoke him at one point, but he readjusted his position so that the huge trunk provided more protection and immediately fell asleep again.

He awoke again later at the sound of voices. Quickly he rose and walked to the edge of the level area. Several of his men, including Kitani, were talking with about thirty strangers, some in uniform and some in civilian attire.

"Kitani!" he called in a voice barely loud enough to be heard. "What's going on? Tell them to be quiet! Come up here!"

The sergeant climbed the bank, and saluted. "They're part of the people I was living with last week," he explained. "They've heard of your victory over the Americans yesterday, and they want to join you. The civilians ask that you protect them from the enemy, and the soldiers want to fight with us."

So, Oba thought as he looked at the group below him. I won't have to go looking for them. They've come to me! The enormity of the responsibility he was assuming began to dawn on him. To increase his fighting strength was one thing, but to protect the lives of large numbers of civilians was more than he had expected or wanted.

Oba studied the group of men standing before him. All were unshaven and their clothing was ragged, even though most wore uniforms. "Tell the soldiers to move over there," he told Kitani as he indicated an opening among the trees to his left. "Send a leader of the civilians to me!"

A tall civilian, distinguished despite his tattered and blood-stained clothing, climbed the incline toward Oba, then bowed formally.

"Captain, sir," he said. "We are a hundred and twenty-four persons, including thirty-eight women and fourteen children under the age of fifteen. We have heard of how you can defeat the enemy. We have no wish to die or to become prisoners. We request that you protect us."

The speech sounded as if it had been rehearsed. Oba wondered how they had heard of the battle of the previous day. Then he remembered the civilians he had ordered to hide shortly before the ambush.

"What provisions do you have?" he asked.

"We have gathered food from a number of places where

it has been hidden. There is a spring near where we are camped, about two hundred meters from here," the man replied.

"Return to your camp and wait for me," Oba directed. "I will visit you later in the day."

Oba watched the group disappear and felt a sinking sensation in his stomach. He turned and walked up the hill until he reached the cliff overlooking the southern portion of the island. He settled himself in the niche of a rock, lighted a cigarette, and reflected on the position in which fate had placed him.

He gazed at the peaceful vista before him. The low-hanging sun cast a reddish orange glow on the sea and dotted the still-wet jungle below with sparkling reflections. Trucks and jeeps raised small clouds of white dust on the winding road in the distance. To his right, tendrils of smoke rose in the still air over the mess halls of American camps. He sniffed the air, as if to catch the smoke's aroma. It was too far away, but the action triggered a pang of hunger in his stomach.

Food. At least, the civilians have enough for the moment, he thought, but how can I keep them fed indefinitely? How can I protect them from enemy attacks? How can I control them? I'm not an administrator; I'm an infantry officer. And where do I obtain weapons? And ammunition? How can I do any of these things in a six-by-ten-kilometer area surrounded by maybe as many as a hundred thousand enemy?

For a moment he found it difficult to believe that the tranquil activity below him represented a threat, that any one of the men down there would kill him on sight.

He wished that more senior officers had survived, so they could assume some of the administrative responsibility and allow him to concentrate on the military aspects of their survival.

His attention was drawn to a tiny dot in the sky far to his right. As he watched, it was followed by another, then a third. They were rising from Asolito airport. As they came closer, he could make them out as low-winged aircraft. They were joined by others. Moments later they united in formation and flew past Oba slightly below his elevated position.

He counted twelve torpedo-bombers as they gained altitude and headed north.

Instinctively, his back straightened. He rose to his feet and stood defiantly, letting his eyes roam over the enemy activity below.

His duty was clear. He would fight, and he would remain alive. And so would his men. Together, they would feed and protect the men and women who sought his help. Fate had selected him for this role. Silently, with a determination of which he did not know he was capable, he swore an oath to continue the war and to make the Americans painfully aware that they had not yet captured Saipan.

· 7 ·

OBA TAKES
COMMAND

"Kitani!" Oba called when he had returned to where his men waited. "Get Kuno, Suzuki, Sano, and Iwata, and report up here immediately!" He sat on a rocky ledge near the tree he had slept under and waited until the men had assembled around him.

"As of this moment," he said, "Master Sergeant Kitani will be my next in command. The four of you"—he looked briefly at Corporal Kuno and Privates Suzuki, Sano, and Iwata—"will see that his orders are carried out by all, soldiers as well as civilians, and will report any violations to me. Suzuki, you will be in charge of weapons. Give me an account this afternoon of all weapons we have, and of ammunition on hand. Sano, I want the name and rank of every soldier with us."

The lantern jawed soldier snapped to attention, saluted, and said, "Captain, sir, we have nearly seventy more. They're with the civilians, but a lieutenant came over and said they all wanted to join us. He said they had heard about Coffee Mountain. He's waiting down below to talk to you."

The news came as a surprise to Oba, but he didn't show it. "All right, include them on your list. I'll talk to the lieutenant later."

"Iwata," he said to the young soldier from Osaka, who

met his gaze expectantly, "you come with Sergeant Kitani and me. After I meet the lieutenant, we're going over to talk with the civilians."

The lieutenant, who appeared to be about twenty-five years old, was slightly taller than Oba, but thin. He identified himself as Akio Nagata of the 316th Independent Infantry Battalion.

"How many men do you have?" Oba asked.

"Only two from my original unit, but there are nearly a hundred of us from various organizations living with the civilians."

"Have your men remain where they are for the moment," Oba instructed. "I'll talk with you later in the day."

The civilian camp was far better organized than Oba had expected. Canvas and other materials had been interwoven among the banyan tree roots to form crude shelters, oil drums had been converted into water containers, and a small aid station was being operated by a nurse.

The tall, muscular man who approached Oba from the civilian group identified himself as Yoshio Oshiro, and it was apparent from his accent that he was Okinawan.

"We have heard of you, Captain Oba. Welcome to our camp. We're not too well organized, but I believe we will be of more help to you than trouble."

The man seemed to be in his early thirties. Oba decided he could probably become a valuable ally. "It is my duty to protect and assist you to the best of our ability," he said. "I appreciate your offer to help. It is my intention to remain here until our forces retake the island. You and your civilians will be required to submit to my orders. Your security will be our security, and both will be my responsibility. Initially I would like you to prepare a list of all civilians, and then give me rosters of those who can be put on cooking detail, food gathering, sentry duty, and of those who are able and willing to fight with my soldiers."

"Yes, sir." Oshiro replied in a military manner. Then, after a slight hesitation, "I am told your men are without food. We would be pleased if they would share ours until we are able to show you where stocks have been hidden in the hills."

A slight smile replaced the stern, military look Oba had worn while laying down the conditions of joining forces. He felt a sense of relief; already the problems he had considered that morning were diminishing. "Thank you. You are very generous. Tomorrow we will assist you in gathering whatever supplies are available. What do you have in the way of medical supplies?"

"Very little at the moment, but we have a nurse from Garapan hospital who has told me she knows where a large stock was hidden just before the invasion."

"I have two wounded men. Could she return with us to treat them?"

Oshiro turned to a man standing nearby and said, "Call Aono the nurse."

A few minutes later, a tall, graceful woman in her mid-twenties returned with the man. She was followed by two children whom Oba recognized as belonging to Baba-san, the headmaster of the Garapan school in which he had been billeted for a few days after his arrival. He looked past the nurse to the children and asked, "Where's your father?"

The nine-year-old girl hid behind the nurse, but her younger brother stepped forward and said, "He's dead. And mother, too. The Americans killed them."

"I'm caring for them," the nurse interjected.

Oba turned his attention to the woman. She wore military trousers a size or two too large and a man's white shirt, which revealed occasional flashes of skin under the shirttails knotted at her waist. On her feet she wore American military shoes, and a sheathed American knife hung from her belt. She bowed to Oba, then glanced briefly at Kitani and Iwata. Kitani returned the bow and tried in vain to hold her glance.

"I have only those supplies that I've found on the bodies of medics," she said, "but I'll do my best to help your wounded." She did not smile, and her eyes met Oba's in a frank appraisal that was decidedly unladylike. Oba wondered if being born on an island so far from Japan could rob women of the feminine qualities of Japanese women. It was the first time he had seen a woman wear a knife in that manner. He remembered reading of the short two-edged knives worn inside the kimono by women in ancient times and wondered if this was simply a modern version.

"All right, let's go," he said. He led the way back in silence, contemplating this strange woman who seemed so unusually self-assured.

Oba was busy during the next few days, setting up a sentry system, collecting food from hidden caches, inventorying weapons—including those recovered from where they had been hidden after the attack on the artillery regiment—and organizing his growing force into a community.

Nearly forty more soldiers, arriving in groups of four or five, joined them during this period, most after hearing of the Coffee Mountain victory. The number of civilians continued to increase as well. Within a week there were close to 150 soldiers and slightly more than 160 civilians camped on Takoyama.

Fortunately, another captain was among the newcomers— a scholarly looking shipping engineer named Jimpuku. This captain was happy to assume administrative responsibility and equally pleased to leave the overall command and security problems in Oba's hands.

Food, Oba soon discovered, was not nearly the problem he had anticipated. Large caches of military rations had been hidden in caves by the high command before the invasion. The locations of many of these caves were known to the civilians who had been ordered to assist in transporting the food from Garapan.

The nurse Aono had led a group of Oba's men to the hidden medical supplies. The arrival of a trained enlisted medic further bolstered the group's health care, to the point where it was no longer a major consideration.

Oba's arsenal consisted of one machine gun, two mortars, thirty Japanese rifles, fifteen American M-1s, and about fifteen pistols. Although constantly deployed, the weapons had not yet been needed. Sentries had reported enemy patrols near Coffee Mountain and on the far side of Tapotchau, three kilometers distant, but none had approached Takoyama. They remained unmolested by the Americans throughout August and September, and Oba used the time to prepare for the inevitable.

Aono had stored the medical supplies in small coral caves on the side of Takoyama hill. As she was returning to the aid station from one of the caves during the week of Oba's arrival, she saw two soldiers deposit a barely conscious youth with a misshapen head and a badly stained army shirt. Aono shuddered at the infected wounds. Pus oozed from a scalp wound, matting the hair that lay partly inside the swollen wound. Another wound, marked by scabbed-over but weeping holes in the boy's shoulder and back, was less serious. A bullet had passed through him without striking any bones or, hopefully, his lungs.

"Put him here!" she ordered as she cleared an area next to her lean-to and spread a piece of canvas on the ground.

For the next hour she worked to clean the wounds, then sprinkled them with the hoarded supply of sulfa powder that had been removed from American first aid kits.

The boy remained conscious the entire time, wincing occasionally when her cautious fingers disturbed a nerve. She worked in silence. Several times her eyes caught his, and each time he smiled. She tried to return the smiles, but her suspicion that the boy was doomed prevented her from giving him the silent encouragement she knew he needed.

Absorbed with her task, she was startled by the voice of Kitani, behind her. "Hello, boy. Where's my helmet?"

The youth's gaze shifted to Kitani, and he smiled as he recognized the master sergeant. "It's back there," he managed to say.

"Do you know this boy?" Aono asked, turning to look up at Kitani.

"His name's Chiba. And he's not a boy. He's a good soldier. I saw him fight. Take care of him!" Kitani turned and walked away.

"All right, my young soldier," said Aono, "let's start getting well."

A few days later, Aono moved young Chiba to a cave closer to the civilian side of the hill to protect him from the heat and the flies that swarmed around her aid station. She visited him daily to change his bandages, which she boiled before putting them back on his wounds. Women from the civilian camp supplied the little food he consumed, and Kitani became a regular visitor.

His fondness for the spunky little soldier grew with each visit. Gradually, Chiba's awe of the master sergeant was replaced by admiration and trust. They began to develop a father-son relationship that led to long discussions. Kitani was constantly amused by the youth's deep bass voice that would have sounded more natural coming from a man twice the size of Chiba's five-foot, ninety-five-pound frame.

Chiba could only give a partial account of his escape after the suicide charge. He remembered hiding for a full day where he had been hit, then crawling deeper into the jungle that night. From then on, he had only spotty recollections of finding a half-filled American water can and dried rations, of stumbling through underbrush, and finally, of being discovered by Japanese soldiers.

"Last night I dreamed I was dying," he told Kitani during one of the visits. Then, turning his face away from the veteran soldier, he added, "And I was afraid. . . . I didn't want to die. . . ." Painfully, he turned his head to look once more at Kitani. "Am I a traitor? A coward? I know it's an honor to die for my country. Yet I don't want to die."

"No, son, you're not a coward. Nor a traitor. A true warrior fights to remain alive. That's why you're here now. That's why we're all here. Your fight is against infection. When you win that battle, you'll be able to join us against the other enemy."

"But it's taking so long," the youth complained. There were tears in his eyes. "I'm only a burden to everyone else. I lie all day in this cave while the rest of you risk your lives to find my food. Maybe it would be better if I did die. . . ." He turned away to hide the tears.

Kitani's voice took on the authoritative tone of his rank. "Now, you listen to me, soldier. You'll have your chance to risk your life. I'll personally see to it that you get twice as many food patrol assignments as anyone else. But your job right now is to get well." He rose and walked to the mouth of the cave, then turned and growled, "And that's an order!"

Gradually, as the days turned into weeks and the camp's daily activities became routine, Oba noticed signs of the same kind of lassitude that had gripped the artillery unit before they were wiped out. His force had grown to nearly 300 persons, and all were living on Takoyama.

On three occasions, sentries on food-gathering patrols had been spotted by the enemy, and on one of those occasions, survivors had reported the capture of two civilians by Americans. Although he had lectured soldiers and civilians alike on the importance of not revealing the location of their camp in the event of capture, he worried; a slip of the tongue could lead to their annihilation.

Rumors of other groups of by-passed Japanese soldiers hiding in the jungle near the peak of Mount Tapotchau and somewhere in the hills to the south had been brought to Takoyama by those who had joined Oba's band in recent days.

Perhaps a more senior officer existed in one of the camps, Oba speculated. He welcomed the prospect of being relieved of some of the responsibility for his rag-tag command.

One morning he announced a decision to Jimpuku and Nagata. "I'm taking Master Sergeant Kitani to reconnoiter enemy positions and to determine if there really are other units in the hills with which we might join forces. You two," he told the officers, "will remain here until we return."

He and Kitani followed major trails until they were on the upper slopes of Mount Tapotchau. They moved singly fifty meters at a time, one taking cover while the other advanced, thus protecting each other at all times. Oba carried his pistol with the safety off, ready to fire. He had left his heavy boots, which he had worn since the invasion, at camp, in favor of rubbersoled *tabi*-type shoes which enabled him to walk more quietly and surefootedly over the loose coral rocks.

Kitani, walking in the half crouch of a man expecting to come under enemy fire, was twenty meters ahead when he suddenly dropped to the ground. Oba watched, but neither man moved. Kitani raised the forward part of his body slowly, on his arms and looked ahead to his left. He remained motionless for nearly a minute before lowering his body. Then he turned and crawled to where Oba was waiting. "An enemy patrol moving up about two hundred meters down the hill," he whispered.

"How many?"

"I counted twenty-two, but it could be part of a larger unit."

Oba looked at the tangle of vines, tropical grass, and undergrowth that surrounded them. Making their way through it with a minimum of noise would be difficult, but they would have to, to avoid being discovered on the trail.

"This way!" he ordered, indicating a direction that would intercept the enemy. He doubted that the Americans would leave the larger trails unless they were fired upon, and he had no intention of revealing their presence. He did, however, want to observe their method of patrolling.

The two men made their way slowly through the undergrowth, stopping every few seconds to listen for the enemy. They were angling downward but had no idea at which point they would intercept the trail on which the Americans were moving upward.

It was difficult to estimate the direction or distance of the first muted clang of metal. But both men heard it and froze. Oba thought it might have been about a hundred meters to their left. He motioned to Kitani to follow as he shifted their direction slightly to the right and moved forward. Minutes later he edged around a tree, then almost fell on Kitani as he jumped back. He had nearly stepped onto a trail.

Both men lay flat on their stomachs and listened to the muffled sounds of the approaching Americans. They trudged past two meters away, their labored breathing clearly audible. Their dark green uniforms were wet with perspiration in the 110-degree heat. Most carried M-1 rifles slung over their shoulders. None glanced toward where the two Japanese lay.

Oba counted twenty-seven men. He waited a full minute after the last man had passed before moving cautiously to where he could see the trail in both directions. Then, with a smile, he signaled for Kitani to join him, and both began to follow the unsuspecting Americans.

Several times during the following thirty minutes, they were close enough to see the end of the patrol. The enemy never departed from the smooth and uninterrupted path and seemed content to verify that it alone was not occupied by Japanese.

The trail twisted upward and eventually brought them to a point just below the jagged rocks that tipped Tapotchau, where they stopped. As the Americans rested, Oba and Kitani moved to a thickly jungled point from which they could observe their enemy.

All had laid aside their weapons, and after drinking from their canteens, most were lying flat on their backs. Guards were not posted, and as far as Oba could see, no attempt had been made to protect them from attack. He was tempted to open fire but reminded himself of the rest of their mission, to seek other Japanese soldiers. There would be time for fighting later.

The Americans roused themselves after about twenty minutes and returned the way they had come. They would report, Oba presumed, that the sector had been cleared of Japanese. This complacency, he told himself, would permit his force to survive. If this was a typical enemy patrol, it would only be necessary to remain off major trails and out of sight to operate within and around them. And with an outlook system to alert them of approaching patrols, their security would be assured.

When the Americans were safely gone, the two men climbed to the tip of Tapotchau, from where they could see most of the island, the neighboring, flat expanse of Tinian, three miles south of Saipan, and 360 degrees of the horizon. They looked for a telltale waft of smoke that might reveal the location of other Japanese. Particularly, they examined the jungle immediately below them, because of a report that a camp existed not far from Tapotchau's peak.

"After seeing the way they patrol," Oba remarked, "it's possible there is a camp. Let's go down a hundred meters or so, then try to circle the mountain."

They descended by the trail the enemy had taken, then turned into the jungle, fairly confident that the crackling of twigs and rotting wood underfoot would not reach American ears. Twice, as they pushed their way through the tangled underbrush, they were forced to detour past steep fingers of rock that angled downward across their path.

"There's a trail!" Kitani had stopped and was pointing toward a barely visible path that followed the base of a rocky outcropping. The leaves of low-growing plants lay flattened and partially crushed.

"Let's go this way," Oba said, indicating the downward-sloping portion of the trail. "If there's nothing there, we'll try the other direction."

They walked carefully along the narrow path, watching for signs of recent passage. Through an opening ahead of them, they saw movement. Soundlessly, the two men dropped. For nearly a minute they lay unmoving. Then Oba gestured with his head, and they began to creep forward. Again they froze. An elderly civilian was walking toward them. He stood facing the jungle and urinated. They waited until he was about to turn, then Oba said in a loud whisper, "Oi, who are you?"

Startled, the man replied automatically, "I'm Oka." His eyes searched the greenery for the man who had spoken to him.

Oba looked back at Kitani and nodded, and the two men rose and pushed their way through the remaining jungle to the clearing.

"How many of you are here?" Oba asked as he replaced his pistol in its holster.

"About forty," replied Oka, visibly shaken. He was thin and old. His ragged clothing consisted of a once-white shirt and torn trousers. His black civilian shoes seemed oddly out of place. Oba wondered if the tremble of his hands was caused by fear or by age.

"Who's in charge?"

"Lieutenant Tanaka." The man glanced at Oba's rank insignia. "Do you want to meet him?"

"Yes, let's go."

They rounded a protruding edge of jungle and saw several lean-tos just below the crest of a slope. From the crest, they could see perhaps a dozen more. Seated under them were civilians and men in uniform; all regarded them with curiosity.

From below, a tall young man in a clean uniform walked toward them. As he neared, he saluted. "Lieutenant Kunio Tanaka, sir, of the Three Hundred and Seventeenth Independent Infantry Battalion."

Oba identified himself, and Kitani asked, "How long have you been here?"

"Ever since the island fell. There were only a few of us

then, but now we have fifteen soldiers and about twenty-five civilians. Are you hungry?''

Oba and Kitani exchanged smiles and accepted Tanaka's invitation. The camp, Oba noted, was in the shadow of a large domelike rock encrusted with stunted trees and vines. At its top, he could see a fortified outpost and two of Tanaka's soldiers.

"How's your security?" he questioned.

Tanaka smiled as he noticed Oba's gaze. "That's it. From there we watch the enemy as he walks to the top of the mountain almost every day. The trail is only a hundred and fifty meters away, but they never step off it. So far, we've had no trouble."

Later, as they ate army rations and sipped tea, Oba told him of his force at Takoyama. Tanaka was surprised. He had thought his was the only group on the island.

After learning of an easier access route to the camp, Oba said he would inform Tanaka if he and Kitani located additional Japanese. They filled their canteens from an ingenious rainfall diversion system on the side of the high dome and continued their search.

For nearly five hours they scouted the jungled hills and ravines that lay south of Mount Tapotchau and that gradually gave way to the slopes immediately above what were now American bases.

"This," Kitani said when they approached a ridge line that overlooked the beach where the enemy had blasted their way ashore months earlier, "was our second defense line. It was from here that we were to contain them on the beach if they made it that far." He looked at the flatland below them and at the enemy jeeps and trucks that moved along the widened beach road. There was bitterness in his voice. "But we only managed to hold them for one day."

By then, both were satisfied that there were no large encampments south of Tapotchau. As they returned, they skirted a ridge only three hundred meters from the second defense line, which was topped by a heavily wooded plateau of about an acre.

"This is so close to them that they might not patrol here," Oba observed when they had circled to its top. "The ridge is too steep for them to get here from the south, and once in the hills, they probably go north.'' Oba drew a crude map of the area and noted it on the larger map of the island that he carried.

They returned to Takoyama at dusk.

By mid-October, three camps under Oba's overall command had been established. Takoyama remained the headquarters with eighty-odd civilians and a roughly equal number of military personnel who had been organized into a unified body of resistance. Tanaka's camp near the peak of Tapotchau was augmented with additional soldiers and some civilians, and a third camp was eventually established on a lightly jungled ridge line near the second defense line, farther to the south, under the direct command of Lieutenant Nagata.

Oba spent at least one day every week in each of the camps, primarily to check the integrated security system, but also to settle problems of personnel, food supply, and assignments.

Lieutenant Tanaka had made great progress in housing the more than one hundred persons in his camp. He had supervised the construction of more than fifty shacks from the debris left by the enemy sweep through the island. His own shack, solidly built from lumber retrieved from a demolished farmhouse, was the largest of all, and even boasted a polished floor and a small fireplace suitable for boiling tea. During Captain Oba's visits, however, he deferred to rank and shared the quarters of a subordinate while his commanding officer occupied his.

Enemy patrols regularly visited the peak, but seemed more interested in the spectacular view than in looking for Japanese. They continued to come and go by the same trail. Tanaka's sentries grew accustomed to observing the enemy on this trail alone, and paid little attention to other possible approaches to the camp.

· 8 ·

STALEMATE
IN THE HILLS

A majority of the sixteen thousand civilians living on Saipan at the time of the invasion had been captured by American troops during the battle. The two thousand or so Chamorros, the original natives of the Mariana Islands, were relocated in the partially destroyed village of Charan-Kanoa on the southwest coast. The remainder of those captured, mostly Japanese, but including large numbers of Okinawans, Koreans, and Kanakas from other Pacific islands, were crowded into a large barbed-wire-enclosed area just north of Charan-Kanoa, known as the Susupe Compound. Bordered on the west by the beach and on the east by Lake Susupe and its surrounding marshland, the compound became a major headache for the U.S. military team responsible for feeding the roughly fourteen thousand people.

Debris from the demolished town of Garapan was transported to the compound and converted by the inhabitants into makeshift shelters. Wells were dug to provide a limited amount of water for drinking and bathing, and a hospital was established by the Navy adjacent to the compound, staffed by U.S. Navy and Japanese physicians, and Japanese nurses.

Daily American patrols in the hills surrounding Tapotchau during the months after the initial battle frequently captured small groups of the estimated one thousand Japanese, civilian

126

and military, who had managed to avoid death and capture during the campaign. All prisoners were taken first to the compound hospital. After a medical examination, they were placed either in the civilian compound or in a military POW camp at the northern end of the island.

Oba's first contact with this outside world came in October when a runner from the Second Line camp reported a large number of Japanese civilians clearing land a few hundred meters south of the camp. He left immediately to observe this.

From just within the jungle, barely fifty meters from the activity, Oba and Lieutenant Nagata watched the clearing operation. Armed American soldiers were stationed at fifty-meter intervals as nearly forty Japanese civilians chopped at the scrub growth on the almost level area. Other Americans manned small bulldozers with clawlike attachments that dragged the brush to where it was being burned.

"If they build a camp here, we'll have to move," Nagata declared, referring to the Second Line camp, which he commanded.

"Let's see if we can find out what they're planning," Oba suggested.

The two men lay watching for another hour, hoping one of the Japanese workers would come close enough to their position for them to attract his attention. Although several glanced occasionally toward the jungle, none came close enough for contact.

The following day they changed their tactic. Nagata changed his uniform for a pair of nondescript trousers and torn shirt and darkened the pale skin of his face, and they hid near similarly dressed civilians who were tending the burning brush. The shifting wind sent occasional heavy billows of blue-black smoke toward the nearby jungle where Oba, the lieutenant, and three armed soldiers hid. They waited until they were enveloped in a heavy cloud of smoke, then Oba tapped the lieutenant, who walked, unseen by the guards, to the fire.

"Keep working! Don't look at me!" he muttered to a civilian who reacted to his presence. "Tell the others to do the same!"

Nagata helped throw the next load of brush on the blazing pyre and turned to one of the men.

"What are you doing?"

"We're clearing the hillside for a farm. We're going to grow vegetables for the civilian compound," the man replied, continuing to work as he talked.

The prospect of fresh food brightened Nagata's features.

"When do you plant?"

"As soon as we clear and plow the land." The man had stopped working to talk.

"Well, get on with it, man. Hurry!" Nagata said good-naturedly as he moved downwind of the fire, waiting for a low cloud of smoke that would cover his retreat to the jungle.

Oba established a guard post near the work site to monitor the activity and report on developments. As the soldier on guard watched from a hidden vantage point the following day, he saw one of the workmen disappear into a cloud of smoke as Nagata had done previously. He hurried toward the point where the man had entered the jungle, and intercepted a wiry young man who, despite his ragged civilian clothing, had an unmistakable military bearing.

"I heard last night that you were up here," he explained to the guard, "so I changed places with one of the men assigned to the farm detail." He identified himself as Warrant Officer Tsuchiya of a military police unit. "I told them I was a civilian, because I have seen enough of prisons to know that I don't want to be in one," he explained.

After questioning the guard about Captain Oba and the size of his force, the lean young man said he would serve as a spy in the civilian compound and would keep Oba informed of developments there.

"If I can't get to you by posing as a farm worker, I'll slip out of the compound at night. Tell your Captain Oba that I'll visit him at Takoyama soon."

With that, he turned and walked back to the edge of the jungle, crouching until another cloud of smoke enabled him to resume his role as a civilian worker.

From that day on, Oba and his men waited anxiously for the food supply that would provide a welcome change to their diet of American canned goods stolen from the enemy storage points. In addition to being a dangerous means of acquiring food, the results were sometimes disappointing. Twice in the past two weeks, his men had returned with cases of what they thought was canned food. The first case contained cans of pepper, and the second, lubricating oil.

Of the forty-two women among the civilians, twelve remained at Takoyama. Three were with their husbands, and the others had selected companions from among the other civilians or from among Oba's soldiers. The single exception was Aono, the nurse.

Her only interests seemed to be in treating the ill and injured, in caring for the two orphaned Baba children, and in pestering Oba to allow her to carry a weapon when she went to visit one of the other camps. She had established a sleeping area on the edge of the military camp for herself and the two children, Emiko and Akira, and had built a medical aid shelter of canvas and tin, large enough to protect two persons from the frequent rains. Daily, she and the children carried water from the spring in the civilian camp for themselves and for any patients in her improvised aid station.

Emiko enjoyed the responsibility of helping treat the sick and spent most of her time trying to be of assistance to Aono.

Akira had selected Captain Oba as his hero and friend. Barefoot because his own shoes had fallen apart and those taken from American bodies were too large, the boy's feet had toughened to the point where he could scramble over the sharp coral as well as any of his shod comrades. The most cherished of his possessions was a deck of cards he had carried since fleeing his home in Garapan. Oba and the boy frequently whiled away hot afternoons playing *babanuki*, at which Akira showed surprising skill.

Although Aono was the only woman who had not formed a romantic attachment, the choice had been entirely hers. It was an open secret in the camp that Master Sergeant Kitani was smitten by her and that she refused to acknowledge him in any way other than to greet him, usually more formally than necessary. It amused Oba to see the burly sergeant acting like a bashful, love-struck teenager whenever he managed to say more to Aono than a simple greeting. But at the same time, it pained him to see Kitani continually rebuffed. When

Oba had reason to call Aono to his command post, he usually waited until Kitani was nearby before asking if someone would call the nurse. The master sergeant would always be the first to volunteer.

Frequently, Kitani would stop by the small cave to visit Chiba, who was recovering slowly from his wounds, but also hoping to see Aono. From a distance, Aono would watch Kitani depart from the cave. She waited until he was out of sight, then went to check on her young charge.

Oba came to know Aono better than the other women, because he sometimes took her with him when visiting the other camps. He had allowed her to carry a pistol on their first few trips and had noted that she, as he, carried it in her hand rather than in its holster. He had wished he had a camera to photograph her walking along the trail with her medical supplies in a backpack, pistol in hand, and the long sheathed knife hanging from her belt.

"Do you know how to use that pistol?" he had asked on their first trip.

"Enough to kill an enemy," she had replied.

Later that day, she had told him of how her parents and sister had been killed, and of her determination to avenge their deaths. "I would have happily died that day if I had known how to fire that machine gun and destroy those inhuman bastards who killed my family. Now, I know. Horiuchi-san was kind enough to teach me."

Oba had seen Horiuchi talking with Aono and young Emiko during one of the *yakuza*'s infrequent visits to the camp a few weeks earlier. He had been relieved that Kitani was absent at the time. A fight between those two would have ended with the death of one or both.

The tattooed *yakuza* visited Takoyama occasionally with the two men he had recruited over the months. Their combined firepower was formidable. His light machine gun was supported by two captured Browning automatic rifles. He boasted that he had never taken a step backward while attacking an enemy patrol, that he stood his ground until the Americans withdrew. Each week he drew closer to his goal of one hundred enemy lives.

His efforts to create a relationship with Aono, however, were rebuffed with the same coolness shown to Kitani.

It was on their return from a subsequent trip that Oba learned how serious Aono was about seeking revenge. They both heard the metallic voice of an enemy radio before they saw the Americans.

"Get off the trail!" he whispered as he pulled her into the concealment of the jungle. He led her several meters from the trail before selecting a spot from which they would have a limited view of the passing enemy. He kneeled behind a gnarled tree trunk and pushed Aono behind him.

Oba had counted ten passing Americans when Aono's pistol suddenly appeared beside his right arm, and he realized she was taking aim. Her finger was tightening on the trigger when he wrenched the weapon from her hand, turned, and mouthed the word "fool!" Even in his anger he saw that her eyes were calm and determined, and she glared back at him in silence.

The remainder of their walk back to Takoyama had been passed with Oba carrying her pistol tucked in his belt. He never again allowed her to have a weapon other than her knife.

At times, Oba considered seeking a companion from among the women, but always came to the conclusion that it would undermine his control over his men, only a few of whom had succeeded in establishing relationships with the women. Although she would never openly suggest it, the manner of a tall, thirty-two-year-old woman named Okuno Yoshiko had suggested that she would be more than willing to become Oba's mistress.

"It doesn't seem right," she had told him once, "that you should have to eat with your soldiers. You should have a woman to prepare your food." Her eyes and the slight upward turn at the corners of her mouth made it clear whom she had in mind for the job.

Oba had thanked her for her suggestion, and that night considered accepting the offer. He had little hope of returning to Japan and to Mineko-san, whom he had married seven years earlier. He had been a teacher of geography and judo at a secondary school in Gamagōri. By now, he reasoned, she had probably received the small white box that contained clippings of his hair and fingernails, the government's present to the families of soldiers killed in action. He was officially dead, and would probably be actually so within days or, with luck, a few months. And he had little doubt that if Mineko-san knew he was alive and knew the conditions under which he lived, she would urge him to live his remaining days as fully as possible.

But his prime responsibility was to the men of his little command. Any action of his that might sow seeds of dissension among them was to be avoided.

A month earlier, a fight had broken out between a civilian and one of the soldiers over the affections of a pretty eighteen-year-old girl in the Second Line camp. He had learned about it a few days later during a routine visit and had discovered that the soldier, who had won the fight but lost the girl, had threatened to kill the civilian. Oba had talked to all three, then settled the matter by ordering the soldier back to Takoyama and the civilian to the camp on Tapotchau.

No, he thought, unless the same opportunity is available to all of them, I can't accept. He fell asleep thinking of Mineko-san and their son, born while they were living in Manchuria, three years earlier.

The strain of living with the knowledge that each day might bring an attack that could destroy them all showed itself in many small ways throughout the camp. Two of Oba's men had joined Horiuchi in defecting from Oba's command and competing with each other to see how many of the enemy they could kill before they themselves were shot down.

Oba had not minded losing the two men, one of whom had taken with him a captured American Browning automatic rifle, but he had ordered them to pick their fights with the Americans at least two kilometers away from any of the three camps. He had seen Horiuchi seek out the enemy, open fire with his machine gun, then stubbornly refuse to retreat, waiting instead until the Americans broke and ran. He believed Horiuchi when he boasted he had already slain thirty-seven of the one hundred Americans he had sworn to kill. It was this demented obsession to kill, he speculated, that held a special attraction for Aono.

And although he could attribute her attitude in part to the strain under which they lived, her obsession to avenge the deaths of her family in American blood was not a normal one, especially for a woman dedicated to keeping others alive.

Many of the group, Oba noticed, had become withdrawn and would spend hours staring into the distance, apparently reliving happier experiences that they expected never to know again. Laughter, except from the two Baba children, had become rare, and petty arguments became more frequent.

The most pronounced change came in a thirty-seven-year-old former *shinkan*, a Shinto priest, Lance Corporal Ikegami. Oba had wondered how the quiet and aesthetic soldier had survived the battle. He was among those who had become distant and reflective, and on more than one occasion, Oba had speculated on what thoughts occupied his mind.

The answer came when he saw a small group of soldiers surrounding Ikegami late one afternoon. He walked toward the small cluster of men and was surprised to hear Ikegami praising him in a voice reminiscent of that used by Shinto priests when praying in a temple.

"You will follow Captain Oba's words because through me, he will carry the word of God," the lance corporal was saying. "Together, God, he, and I will deliver you from this situation, and together, we will defeat the barbarian heretics who surround and threaten us."

Oba walked back to his command post. That evening he sent for Ikegami.

"What were you telling the men this afternoon?" he asked.

"Only that God has approved of you as our leader," Ikegami replied.

"How do you know that?"

"Because God speaks to me and has directed that I inform the men of His pleasure in you and of His promise to help you defeat the enemy."

Oba was tempted to smile but remained serious. He looked into the bespectacled eyes of the lance corporal and saw only candor. As long as the man's innocent ramblings did nothing to threaten his control or their collective security, he thought, they represented no danger. "Thank you," he said, dismissing the deranged soldier.

Ikegami, who had been kneeling before him, rose with his hands clasped, bowed in the manner of a priest, and walked to his sleeping quarters.

During the next several days, Oba kept an eye on the man and noticed he had begun to build a structure on a high, flat rock close to the civilian camp. Gradually Ikegami acquired pieces of tin, canvas, and boards and daily added them to his dwelling. Oba ordered him taken off sentry duty and placed him on the camp cleanup squad in order to keep a closer watch on him. He worked obediently, but his every spare moment was spent in improving and enlarging his abode.

The first indication of trouble occurred a week after his first conversation with Ikegami, when Aono came to Oba with her dark eyes flashing in anger.

"I want you to do something about that crazy old fool Ikegami," she stormed. "He told me to stop trying to treat people, because he was taking over as the camp healer."

Oba heard her out, then advised her to humor him as much as possible, explaining that the man was ill in a way none of them could treat. Her anger gradually dissolved, and she agreed to ignore him if Oba would promise to keep him away from her aid station. "I don't have much medicine left," she admitted, "but I can certainly do more for our people than that crazy old goat!"

The following day Aono returned, as angry as the day before. "Captain, come with me, please. There's something I want you to see." Together, they walked toward the bottom side of the camp, where a line of some ten civilians and military stood or sat waiting to be treated by Ikegami.

He had fashioned various pieces of cloth into a kind of priest's robe and was mumbling prayers as he placed his hands on the swollen and ulcerated leg of an elderly man.

"And what's worse," Aono whispered in a voice trembling with anger, "he's got about half the camp, including some of your soldiers, believing that he can heal by touching them. I try to keep their cuts clean, and he places his dirty hands on their open wounds."

Oba was already aware that perhaps more than half of both

camps believed Ikegami was a mystic with supernatural pow-
ers. "My mistake," he told Aono as they walked back to the
command post, "was in pretending to believe him, or at least
in not denouncing him as mentally ill. Those who saw me
listening to him and nodding to humor him thought that I was
agreeing with him."

"Will you tell them now that he's sick?" she asked.

"We're all in need of hope, of assurance. We want to know
that we will triumph over this situation. Ikegami has offered
this hope, and the people are hungry to accept it. For me to
destroy their new confidence, no matter how unfounded,
would do more harm than good. Our survival depends upon
our remaining together. I can't afford a confrontation that
might split us."

That afternoon Oba received a written summons to visit
Ikegami at his "temple." The wording of the note was in the
form of a command, which piqued the captain. But, setting
his pride aside and restraining his anger, he walked to the
rock atop which Ikegami had built the shack he called his
"temple."

Oba could hear mumbled prayers from inside as he mounted
the rock. He pulled back the canvas that served as a door,
and in the dim light, furnished by a single candle on a stone,
he could see Ikegami, sitting cross-legged like an emaciated
Buddha.

With his eyes closed and moving only his lips, Ikegami
addressed Oba in the same tone of voice he had used in his
prayers: "Captain Oba, you have done well. We are pleased.
From now on, with our help, you will do even better. But
since I speak with the voice of God, there is one change you
must make. As the voice of God," he continued with his
eyes still closed, "we feel it is unfitting that I continue with
the rank of lance corporal. We recognize your position as our
leader, and we do not desire that I be elevated to an officer's
grade. We do believe, however, that I should be given the
rank of master sergeant and request that you announce this
promotion to both the military and civilian camps today."

Oba had to suppress a smile in spite of the misgivings he
felt. "Lance Corporal Ikegami, you are from the Forty-third
Division, and I from the Eighteenth Regiment. As you know,

only your own company commander may recommend you for promotion. Even if I wanted to, it would be impossible to promote you to master sergeant."

"In that case, I shall give you until tomorrow to make the announcement," Ikegami intoned.

Oba started to reply in anger but thought better of it and backed out through the narrow canvas door.

Gradually it became apparent, even to those who had initially believed Ikegami's proclamations, that he was ill. One of his more obvious mistakes was to claim he was a *tengo*, a character from ancient Japanese mythology reputed to have the power to leap great distances. In attempting to prove his ability to doubters, Ikegami had fallen while trying to jump an impossible distance between two rocks and bruised himself severely.

The climax of his illusions had been his claim that by drawing an imaginary *X* in the air—part of a prayer game played by children—he could prevent the enemy from entering their camp. Oba watched with pity as the deluded man walked solemnly around the camp's circumference, gesturing large *X*'s. The next day, however, when he learned Ikegami had descended in daylight to a point just outside an American camp—to make his protective sign to prevent the enemy from leaving the camp—Oba ordered the man put under guard.

By the following morning, Ikegami realized that he had endangered the camp's security, and retired to his temple to listen for further instructions from the voice of God.

He seemed to be improving, until about a month later, when an approaching enemy patrol forced Ikegami and others to hide in the jungle alongside a major trail. As the Americans approached, a broadly grinning Ikegami stepped onto the trail and bowed deeply from the waist. Unaware that ten other Japanese watched the mini-drama from cover of the jungle, the American troops frisked, then marched, the still-smiling but confused soldier away.

In December, the Americans, using civilians from the compound, began a systematic search for food stored in caches throughout the mountains. Those that Oba had used as a reserve, or on which his people had depended for periodic supplies, were destroyed by fire or taken to the civilian compound at Susupe. Within two weeks the mountain had been swept clear of food.

By the following week the camp's supply had been exhausted, and their only food was unappetizing breadfruit, papaya, and the large snails that thrived in the jungle. Almost three inches in height, the slow-moving, repulsive creatures left a trail of sticky and repugnant mucus as they inched across rotting leaves and decaying logs. One of his soldiers had died from eating them raw, but Oba discovered that the snails could be made edible by boiling them thoroughly.

More and more they were forced to rely on foodstuffs stolen from the enemy. Almost every night, patrols were sent to scout the American camps on the western side of the island, where security was less tight than in the eastern areas where the Marines were based.

Oba frequently led the patrols which, in time, became a deadly game of attempting to outwit the American guards. The reward for victory was much-needed food; the penalty for a mistake could be death. Yet the men frequently smiled with boyish delight as they wormed their way under a barbed-wire fence or purposely distracted the attention of a guard while a nearby confederate gained entrance to a food dump.

On one such patrol, Oba and Suzuki were well within an enemy camp at about four o'clock in the morning when through the lighted window of a small building they could see two Americans, attired in white aprons, working inside. The aroma of freshly baked bread told them of the prize that awaited them.

From a position well beyond the glare from the lighted interior, they watched for several minutes. Hot loaves from the oven were being placed on a cooling board just inside the window. Except when they turned to the window to lay the loaves on the board, the men faced in the other direction.

After a whispered consultation, Suzuki remained where he could observe the room's interior, and Oba walked to the building, crouching under the window with his eyes on Suzuki. At Suzuki's signal, Oba popped up, grabbed a loaf, and, bouncing it in his burning fingers, suppressed a laugh as he made his way back to his partner. They watched as a baker placed another batch on the board, absentmindedly filling the gap with another loaf.

"Let's get another," Oba whispered, and moved to his position beneath the window. Following the same procedure, Oba waited for the signal, but this time scooped up three loaves and scurried, laughing, back to Suzuki.

A few moments later, when one of the bakers turned toward the window, they heard his exclamation. Shaking with silent laughter, they watched as he backed slowly away from the window, looking frightened and confused.

Still chuckling, they shared their bread and related their experience to Lieutenant Tanaka and his men at the Tapotchau camp an hour later. Several cans of salted meat, acquired by one of Tanaka's patrols, provided a welcome change from their normal diet of fruit and snails.

By nine o'clock the next morning, the heat was already oppressive. Most of those who had spent the night foraging for food were asleep in their crude shacks. Others looked for activities that would help pass another uneventful day. Some added wood or tin to their flimsy shacks. The women carried water from the barrel at the foot of a spout that caught rain water from a ten-meter rock that formed the eastern wall of their settlement.

Oba stirred restlessly on the mat spread on the polished floor of Tanaka's hut, located at the bottom of the slope. From there he could see most of the shacks extending to the top of the ridge, as well as those erected along the lower reaches of the slope to his left, out of sight from the top of the ridge.

· 9 ·

THE AMERICANS MOVE

About a thousand meters to the east, where Fox Company of the 2d Battalion, 2d Marines, was setting up a command post, Capt. Edward Atwood studied a map spread on a rock. Around him, each with a similar map, were the four lieutenant platoon leaders of the company. To each, in turn, he indicated the area to be patrolled.

For the past two weeks, companies of the 2d Regiment, 2d Division, had been on rotating patrol duty. This was the first for Fox Company. If they were lucky, they might pick up some of the stragglers still hiding in the hills. Several had been taken prisoner by other companies, and most were so hungry and ill that they had offered little resistance. Once the platoons had been dispatched to their assigned areas, Atwood settled down to wait for the radio checks that each would make every twenty minutes.

The first platoon, led by 2d Lt. Paul Lang, moved up a ravine that slashed directly south from Tapotchau. The lush jungle muffled their sound and hid them from the outpost Tanaka had stationed two hundred yards south of this camp. Unseen and unheard by the two guards, who were finding it difficult to remain alert in the heat, the patrol followed a dry gully that led them directly toward the camp. Eventually the defile ended in a steep embankment which required the Marines to use vines and tree trunks to pull themselves to the top. Lang checked his map at the crest, then signaled his men along a trail that passed the base of a sheer rock cliff.

The patrol was reduced to single file as it passed between the cliff on its left and a jumble of rocks and undergrowth on its right. Lang had gone three steps outside the narrow passage when he stopped. It took him several seconds to realize that the shack of tin, plywood, and canvas directly in front of him was not a figment of his imagination. Still unmoving, his eyes swept to the left, where he could see ten or fifteen similar structures. Two men emerged from one of the shacks, shocking him into action. He fired three rounds from his carbine and dove behind a rock. Those behind him squeezed through the narrow gap, firing at the surprised Japanese who darted from the shacks for safety.

Oba snapped awake at the first sound of rifle fire from the top of the slope. Bolting from the door, he ran up the slope at a crouch until he was close enough to see what was happening. The Americans were hidden just inside the east entrance of the camp and were firing from concealing positions. Oba glanced around him and could see several of Tanaka's soldiers returning the fire from protected positions.

Ahead of him, two civilians burst from a shack only a few meters from where the Americans were firing. The first pirouetted in the air as a slug ripped through his shoulder, then slammed against a boulder and bounced back. Before he hit the ground, the top of his head disappeared in a brief pink cloud of blood. The second man had taken only three steps when he doubled forward, then fell back into a sitting position, holding his stomach. He toppled to his left and lay still.

Others, who had managed to reach the safety of a rock or tree trunk, returned the enemy fire, preventing the Americans from breaking through the narrow passageway. Moving with Oba from tree to rock to tree, the Japanese soon amassed sufficient firepower to keep the Americans pinned down. The civilians of his group, meanwhile, retreated into the jungle that covered the embankment on the other side of the camp.

Oba suspected that his group far outnumbered the American patrol, but he had no intention of fighting to the finish unless it was under conditions of his choosing. Once the main body of his people were safe, he motioned for a slow withdrawal to the jungle on the far embankment.

Lieutenant Lang suspected that he was outnumbered. From his position he could see a dozen shacks near the crest of the ridge and estimated he was receiving fire from at least twenty rifles. He signaled to his radioman who crawled to his side. He reached for the microphone and pressed the button.

"Hello, Rainbow. This is Rainbow Two. We have engaged about thirty of the enemy and are under fire. Over."

The voice of Atwood's radioman answered a moment later. "Roger, Rainbow Two. What is your position?"

Lang looked at his map and read the coordinates into the microphone. "Roger, Rainbow Two. This is Rainbow. Hold your position."

Atwood checked the coordinates with his scout, then called the other three platoons and told them to hold their positions and stand by to assist 1st Platoon if necessary.

"C'mon, Jones, let's go," he said to the scout, a nineteen-year-old corporal. It took the two men nearly twenty minutes to traverse the thousand yards to the spot Jones had marked on the map. As they approached, Lang and his platoon were returning from Oba's camp.

"They disappeared, sir," Lang told the captain. "We got four or five of 'em, and we figure there were about thirty more."

While the two officers talked, Jones eyed the souvenirs carried by the men of Lang's platoon. The young corporal had a theory about war. "First, you fight for your ass," he had said many times, "then you fight for souvenirs." And the prizes of battle he was admiring at the moment represented those he wanted most. Two of the men carried decorated samurai swords, one had an ornate dagger, and another a Japanese pistol.

"Okay, Jones, let's go!" Atwood and his scout moved toward the scene of the firefight while Lang and his men continued in the other direction.

Jones doubted the wisdom of walking into an enemy camp but dutifully followed the captain. As they passed through the narrow entrance, they could see that Lang and his men had torn down the first two shacks. Four bodies sprawled grotesquely on the ground near them.

Feeling that they had to make some contribution to the day's activities, the two men ripped a third shack apart. Atwood, spotting two five-gallon cans of uncooked rice, said, "Cover me!"

Jones watched as the captain, with a pixieish grin on his face, poured the contents of both cans on the ground, unzipped his fly, and urinated on the white mound of rice. "Okay," Jones said when the officer had buttoned his trousers, "Now cover me," and followed Atwood's example.

"Konchikisho!" Oba muttered from the far bank of the ravine as he watched the two men foul a portion of their scant rice supply. They deserved to die. He was tempted to kill them where they stood, but he wasn't ready to start a major battle. He watched from his vantage point as the two Americans turned and retraced their steps through the narrow rock entrance.

After Fox Company had returned to their octagon tents halfway between Tapotchau and Magicienne Bay, Corporal Jones decided he would waste no time putting his theory into effect. He had been too busy "fighting for his ass" during the earlier month-long campaign to acquire the souvenirs he wanted. But if today's patrol was an example, the cream of the crop was to be had at that Japanese campsite.

After stowing his rifle, helmet, pack, and other gear on his bunk, Jones went to the battalion intelligence section tent, where his boss, Captain "Mo" Morgan, was in a meeting with Captain Atwood.

Atwood had just finished telling the battalion intelligence officer of his platoon's encounter that morning. Both men turned toward the young corporal as he entered.

"Excuse me, sir," Jones said. "It occurred to me that Easy Company has patrol duty tomorrow, and they may have trouble finding the Japs we saw today. If you want, I could go along and lead 'em there."

"Good idea," Morgan replied. "I'll inform Captain Rall.

You stand by to join E Company at oh seven hundred tomorrow.''

A self-satisfied smile spread over Jones's face as he walked back to his tent. He would be sure he was one of the first to go through the shacks that remained and would have first crack at the pistols and swords he was certain would be there.

The next morning, Capt. Bob Rall announced that Easy Company's CP would be established on the northern slopes of Tapotchau and that only one platoon would be dispatched to the site of the previous day's firefight on the southern side of the mountain. The captain assumed the Japanese who had been there were probably still running. Jones was even happier. With only a platoon—thirty-six men—there would be less competition for souvenirs.

Three hours later, Jones knew he had missed the small trail that should have led him and the platoon to the campsite. ''Why don't you hold the platoon here, Lieutenant, while I go back and look for the trail?'' he said.

The young officer readily agreed. His uniform, like those of the thirty-five men he led, was drenched with perspiration. Jones moved back down the trail while the others slumped to the ground and reached for their canteens of lukewarm water.

Within three hundred yards, Jones located the nearly invisible trail he had been searching for. He moved cautiously along the poorly defined path until he emerged from the underbrush within ten feet of the shack he and Atwood had destroyed the day before. Jones dropped to one knee, pushed off the safety of his rifle, and surveyed the scene. The four bodies were still there but were covered by straw mats. The rice was untouched. He remained motionless for nearly a minute but heard no sound and saw no movement. Quietly, he backed several steps, then turned and walked rapidly to the waiting platoon.

''They've split, sir,'' he reported to the young lieutenant. ''I don't think it's necessary to take the whole platoon back. It'll only take a squad to check the place out.'' Twelve men, he figured, would lessen the competition even more and increase his booty.

The lieutenant, to the joy of three-fourths of his platoon, agreed. When the fourteen men arrived at the crest of the campsite, the young lieutenant ordered them to spread out and start moving down the slope.

Jones was on the extreme left flank, looking at the blackened base of the rock cliff, which had been the cooking area, when two rifle explosions sent him to the deck in an automatic reaction.

"There's another one," someone shouted, and a volley of fire burst from Jones's right.

"Everybody back to the top," the lieutenant yelled. Jones, with the others, backed toward the crest, watching for movement among the shacks.

None of the squad was sure they had hit the men who ran from one of the shacks into the jungle, but several confirmed that they had fired at two Japanese.

"Okay, we'll hold here until we get the rest of the platoon," the lieutenant said. He looked at the jungle-covered slope on the opposite side of the ravine. "They may be sitting up there waiting to ambush us."

"Oh, bullshit. I mean, sir . . . Lieutenant," Jones exploded when he saw his chance at the souvenirs being diminished, "those two were probably just a couple that didn't get the word."

Six of those around Jones shared his desire to check out—and clean out—the shacks, and took his side in the discussion. The lieutenant relented. "Okay, I'll give you guys thirty minutes to get down there and back."

After going through a few huts, Jones realized the Japanese had returned to remove everything of value before vacating the area. In one shack he found a rusty bayonet, which he threw down in disgust.

The seven young men descended cautiously, not only because of the possibility of additional stragglers lurking in the shacks, but because of the many small puddles of human excrement which indicated an epidemic of diarrhea had swept the camp. Methodically, they examined the interior of every shack.

Jones approached the largest and most well constructed of the shacks. It was located near the bottom of the ravine, from where he could see another forty or fifty shacks extending along the base of the slope to his left.

With rising hopes, he stepped inside onto the polished wood of the floor. Everything of value had been removed. With a snort of disgust, he pulled a bunch of bananas from a hook in a corner and stuffed them inside his shirt. As he did, he heard the lieutenant call from the slope's crest: "Hey Jones, your half hour is up!"

Stepping to the door of the shack, Jones shouted back, "Okay, we're coming up."

As if he had given a command to fire, the jungled slope, which now loomed above them from its base only thirty feet away, exploded in rifle fire that tore through the shack. Jones dived through the doorway and landed behind a rock with a jar that sent his helmet rolling into the open. Frantically, he pulled the squashed bananas from his shirt in an effort to get closer to the ground. The souvenirs were forgotten. He was back to worrying about his ass.

The barrage of rifle fire kicked up dirt around him and broke twigs off trees above him. He cursed himself for volunteering to lead Easy Company to the campsite. He looked up the slope at the trees and shacks and the wide open spaces between them, through which he and the others would have to maneuver to reach safety.

The Japanese firing at them were invisible behind the thick jungle that covered their side of the ravine.

"Oh, shit," he muttered, more frightened than he had been in a long time.

Then someone above yelled for him to get ready to move as they gave covering fire. When he heard the crack of five rifles and the automatic fire of a Browning, he crawled to where his helmet lay, then used his elbows and a snaking motion of his hips to move upward, taking advantage of any objects that offered cover or concealment. As he rounded a large rock, he hesitated when he saw a puddle of excrement directly in his path. But his hesitation was only momentary. He moved on, with momentary amazement at what fear can make a man do. Eventually he reached a position near the topmost of the six men. Kneeling behind a tree trunk, he joined the others in firing at the opposite slope while the next lowest man moved up. Leapfrogging in this manner, and supported by the rifles and BARs of those at the top of the ridge, the seven men made their way out of an ambush that more seasoned Marines would never have walked into.

High on the slope opposite them, Captain Oba smiled as he watched the frightened Marines withdraw. He had known they would return after the previous day's encounter and had been ready for them. Now he would have another twenty-four hours to resettle his people and to plan his defense. Unsure of what they were facing, the enemy would require time to plan a counterattack. They would return tomorrow in force, he knew, but they would find no one.

Oba motioned to Tanaka, who was still crouched with his weapon at the ready. "Bring the men to where we left the civilians. Then assemble the entire group. I want to talk to them." He turned and began climbing the ridge toward the trail that led to where the others of Tanaka's command had been told to wait.

The forty-odd civilians of Tanaka's force were huddled in a ravine two hundred meters from their campsite. The sounds of the battle had been frightening, but not as frightening as the silence that had followed while they waited to see the nationality of the troops about to enter the ravine.

Oba called them from their hiding places. "You will all move today to Takoyama to join forces with us there. Bring with you what supplies you can carry, and we'll return later for the rest."

He turned to Tanaka. "Lieutenant, you will be my second in command," he said loud enough to be heard by the others. "Get your people under way as quickly as possible. We're reasonably safe for the rest of the day. The Americans aren't likely to react until tomorrow. I will return to Takoyama immediately to announce your arrival."

Oba and Suzuki followed one of the lesser-used trails from Tapotchau west toward Takoyama. Although confident that the Americans would have to report today's battle before a countermeasure could be launched, he was wary of a chance encounter with a training patrol or with souvenir hunters.

His main concern, though, was with how the Americans would react on the following day and in the days to come. Again, he had reopened full-scale war. After three months of relative quiet, he had challenged the Americans' right to be on Saipan. He had demonstrated his strength in a manner they could not ignore. He knew that from that day onward, his small force would be the object of daily searches by the enemy, until—and he paused as the word *if* slipped into his thoughts—the navy returned.

Later, when the civilians and military from Tapotchau had been integrated into the Takoyama camp, he shared his last cigarette with Tanaka. "From now on," he confided, "security will be our main problem. We can expect an attack at any time, from any direction." He laid the map he had received from Kitani before them and drew small *X*'s on the hilltops in all four directions from Takoyama.

"I want sentries posted at each of these points at all times," he said. "Two men to a post. One will be designated as a runner who will report enemy activity the moment it is observed. Use civilians as runners, but be sure they know the fastest trails from their posts to Takoyama. Work out the details, and see that the posts are manned tomorrow morning."

Then he called Kitani and directed him to strengthen the defense around the camp and to prepare an escape trail leading down one of the steep ravines that cut into the eastern side of Takoyama. "It would be too difficult for them to launch an attack from that side," he explained, "and it offers an excellent means of withdrawal."

Next he sent for Oshiro and told him to have the civilians ready to vacate the camp on a moment's notice, and to keep them that way. He did not mention the proposed evacuation route to the east because if the enemy were to learn of it from a captured civilian, it could turn into a death trap.

Early the following morning, before Tanaka had dispatched his sentries, Oba assembled the nearly 150 soldiers of the camp. They squatted in a semicircle around the rise on which he stood.

"Fate has given us the responsibility of maintaining a Japanese military presence on this island," he told them. "Despite overwhelming odds, we have managed, so far, to survive in the midst of the enemy. From this day on, however, our task will become more difficult. We have not only our own lives to protect, but those of more than one hundred civilians.

"Yesterday, once again, we bloodied and humiliated the

enemy. We will continue to attack him whenever the opportunity arises. But we can expect that he will increase his efforts to destroy us. Today, we will initiate a new security system that will place tremendous responsibility on each of you. You will become the eyes and the ears of all of us. I know that I can depend on you.''

Col. George Pollard leaned back in his chair until it balanced on two legs with its back against the wall. His tent had been replaced by one of the dozens of Quonset huts that housed offices and mess halls throughout the 2d Marine Division area.

Maj. Herman Lewis stood uneasily before him, perspiring from nervousness and from his hurried walk from his office. He had worked with the colonel long enough to know that his relaxed manner was at times an affectation to hide an anger seething inside. He had a feeling this was one of those times.

"Now let me get this straight, Herm. You say a platoon of the 2d Battalion fired on about thirty-five Japs . . .'' He rose and walked to a large wall map of Saipan. "Just south of the peak of Tapotchau yesterday, and you didn't know about it until today?''

"Yes, sir. It was in the morning report.''

"And today,'' Pollard sat down and leaned his chair back again, "elements of another company went there and were ambushed by rifles and automatic weapons?''

"That's right, sir.'' Lewis shifted his weight from one foot to the other.

"What about casualties?''

"None. We don't know about theirs. By the time the platoon got back to the rest of the company, it was too late to check the area out.''

"Why in the hell weren't we notified last night?'' Pollard got to his feet and walked back to the wall map. "If there's an organized group of Japs up there, I want 'em out! I've already reported this island as secure, and I don't want a bunch of raggedy-assed Japs changing my report. Where's the lieutenant involved in today's fiasco?''

"He's outside, sir.'' Lewis was glad he had thought of

calling the lieutenant to division headquarters immediately after learning of the ambush. He felt a little sorry for the young man. He had had a rough day. Some of his men had almost been killed in an ambush, and now the wrath of Colonel Pollard awaited him.

"Get him in here!" Pollard barked.

Lewis opened the door and signaled for the frightened lieutenant to enter. He stood aside as the crew-cut youth walked up to Pollard's desk, removed his cap, and stood at attention.

"Second Lieutenant John Meyers reporting as ordered, sir."

"Meyers, Major Lewis informs me you allowed your men to walk into an ambush today. Is that true?"

"Uh, yes, sir. But we didn't know they were there, sir."

"How many were there?"

"I don't rightly know, sir, but there musta been about twenty rifles and a couple of automatic weapons . . ."

"And according to this report"—he indicated a paper lying on his desk—"you let the men walk into it looking for souvenirs?"

Meyers swallowed hard. "We were checking out the area, sir." He stared straight ahead at the wall above the sitting colonel's head.

Pollard pulled a cigar from his pocket, bit off the tip, rolled it between his lips, and lighted it leisurely before replying.

"All right, Lieutenant, go on back to your unit. I hope you learned something from this. You're just lucky I don't have your ass up for a court-martial."

The young man muttered, "Thank you, sir," executed a sharp about-face, and strode from the building.

Pollard turned to look at Lewis. "What do you think of it, Herm?"

"Colonel, we've been taking Japs out of those hills every week for the past three months. But always in ones and twos. None of the prisoners ever mentioned an organized group."

"You intelligence people give me a pain in the ass, Herm. Just because nobody ever told you they were up there . . ." Pollard got up and went again to the map. For several moments he studied it, then said, "Tomorrow, I want four companies to converge on that area. Three companies will hold lines here, here, and here, and the fourth will move up from here, with its flanks in contact with the side companies.''

With his hands, Pollard indicated three sides of a box, with the fourth side moving up toward the top. He turned back to Lewis.

''You got that?''

''Yes, sir.''

''All right, tell operations to get on it immediately!''

''Right, sir.''

Pollard ground out his cigar and threw it at a wastebasket. He missed. ''Damn!'' he growled.

At 6:00 A.M. the following morning, three companies of the 1st Battalion and one from the 2d stood on the dusty road that ran between sugarcane fields in the 2d Regiment area. Lt. Col. James Thornton was briefing his company commanders.

''You'll be transported to your respective jump-off positions by truck. From there, you will move to the coordinates indicated on your maps to form the box. Make all the noise you can. Fire a few rounds occasionally to let 'em know you're coming. We want to flush 'em out and get 'em on the run. Be careful when Charley Company passes in front of you. Have your men hold their fire unless some Japs try to go through your lines.'' He glanced toward a convoy of trucks. ''Okay, let's load up.''

He walked toward the jeep that led the trucks and saluted as he recognized Colonel Pollard. ''Good morning, sir,'' Thornton said. ''We're ready to roll.''

''Good morning, Jim,'' Pollard said with a casual salute. ''Herman and I thought we'd tag along as observers. Do you mind?''

''Glad to have you, sir. I plan to set up an OP at the peak of Tapotchau. Would you like to join me there?''

''Sounds good, but first I want to be with George Company when they clean out the site of yesterday's ambush.''

''Right, sir. I'll tell the CO.''

The narrow road winding toward Tapotchau was little more than a trail. Branches and underbrush scraped the sides of their jeep as they made their way up the mountain. Pollard rode in the front seat with the driver, and Lewis, in the rear with the radio. Lewis pressed the butterfly switch on the set's microphone.

"Hello, Redbird, this is Eagle. What's happening?"

He waited a moment until the slightly garbled voice replied, "Hello, Eagle. This is Redbird. Nothing yet. We've found some land mines, which we'll detonate, but no sign of any Japs."

Lewis spread his map on top of the radio and said, "What are your coordinates?"

"We're at fourteen-point-three, six-point-seven. We're approaching the site of yesterday's ambush."

"Roger, out."

Pollard, who was sitting half-turned, listening to the radio conversation, asked, "How close can we get to the ambush site?"

Lewis studied the map, then replied, "About two hundred yards. We'll pass through George Company on the way."

"Let's go, son," Pollard said to the driver, and the jeep began to crawl forward. Within minutes they saw the men of George Company who were closest to the trail. The jeep halted as a young lieutenant approached. "We're almost there, sir," he said as he saluted. "The ambush site should be just over that ridge . . ." He was interrupted by the voice of the company radioman.

"Hello, Eagle. This is Redbird. We're at the site. No sign of the enemy, but we can see about fifty shacks."

"Okay, let's go," Pollard said as he swung his legs over the side of the jeep. The two men cut diagonally through the jungle to where the forward elements of the company had found the Japanese bivouac area.

"God almighty! Look at 'em!" Pollard exclaimed as they stepped between the rocks at the top of the ridge above the now-deserted shacks on the slope.

"Lieutenant," he said to the platoon leader. "Get me an exact count of those shacks!" He looked toward the jungled bank on the opposite side of the ravine. "Send a company up to check out that slope. Then continue your sweep," he told the lieutenant. He and Lewis returned to the jeep to wait for all four companies to reach their assigned positions for the day's operation.

At 9:00 A.M., the order was given for Charley Company to begin moving upward, closing the box formed by the other three units. Pollard and Lewis joined Colonel Thornton at the tip of Tapotchau, which overlooked the interior of the box.

"Keep your heads down," Thornton warned the men with him. "If Charley Company opens fire, their rounds may come this way. And hold your fire unless some Japs try to get through us!"

The hot sun blazed on the exposed rocks of the mountaintop, but no one sought the protection of trees a few meters away. Everyone wanted to witness the closing of the trap. Some firing was heard far below them, but there was no sign of enemy activity in the broad, grassy areas that extended nearly five hundred meters to their immediate front.

"Where in the hell are they?" Pollard muttered to Lewis, who sat beside him. They were seated behind a jutting rock formation for protection.

"It's a big area up here, and we're only covering a small part of it," Lewis replied. "If they bugged out, they could be anywhere now."

They listened to the occasional radio conversation between the companies as they confirmed positions to avoid firing into friendly forces. Only Able Company saw anything worth reporting—the capture of an elderly Japanese couple.

The tension eased as the next hour passed, and when the line of Charley Company's Marines appeared on the grassy slope below them, it became apparent that the trap had failed.

"Tell everyone to secure," Pollard told the battalion commander, "and proceed on foot to their areas."

The civilian couple, the only ones caught in Pollard's "box," were taken to the hospital operated by the U.S. Navy, adjacent to the sprawling but crowded camp where civilians were interned. The husband required treatment for an ulcerous infection on his leg. His frightened wife, certain she would be killed by the Americans, was allowed to remain at the hospital during her husband's two-day hospitalization. Her fears were eventually calmed by one of the Japanese nurse-trainees, who assured her that the Americans neither raped nor killed civilian prisoners. Comforted, but still nervous and in need of someone to talk to, the woman began to tell the nurse of her experiences in the hills and of the group commanded by Captain Oba. Surprised that the girl had never heard of him, she elaborated on his abilities as a fighter and spoke with pride of his victory at Coffee Mountain. The young nurse-trainee was impressed and passed the account to other nurses and Japanese employees of the hospital. Before the day was over, however, a U.S. Navy doctor was among those who had heard the story.

That evening, Maj. Herman Lewis walked rapidly between rows of the octagonal tents of the officers of division headquarters until he came to George Pollard's.

"Colonel," he said, "I think I've got a line on that group of Japs."

Pollard, who had been lying on his cot, reading by the light of a lantern, propped himself on an elbow and said, "What kind of a line?"

"One of those civilians we picked up yesterday says there's a Japanese captain up there with over three hundred people, half of them military. She was with them until yesterday, but couldn't keep up because of her husband's lame leg."

"Holy shit!" Pollard murmured. "Three hundred! Why in the hell didn't we know about this before? Does she know where they are now?"

"I don't know. No one has interrogated her yet. We got the story from a doctor at the Susupe hospital who heard it from a nurse."

"She may be dreaming, but it's worth checking out. Now you'll get a chance to use that Japanese you studied. We'll drive down there tomorrow morning."

· 10 ·

GET OBA!

The morning heat was just beginning as the two men drove past the civilian compound. Pollard, whose duties rarely brought him to this part of the island, was amazed at its size and crowded conditions.

"Holy Christ! How many people they got in there?"

"About fourteen thousand," Lewis replied. "Then there are about two thousand Chamorros at Charan-Kanoa."

"That four-strand barbed-wire fence is about as useless as tits on a boar." The colonel pointed to the barrier that surrounded the compound.

"Yeah," agreed Lewis, "but where is there for them to go?"

"Nowhere, I thought until last night. But now I'm not so sure."

Lewis, who had attended a crash course at a Japanese-language school at Boulder, Colorado, obtained little more information from the woman than they already knew. She had remembered the lecture Captain Oba had given them about not revealing their location in the event they were captured. Relieved that she had at least not done that, she told Lewis in more truth than deceit that she was completely lost all the time she was in the hills and had no idea where they were. But she seemed to have a maternal affection for Captain Oba

154

and willingly described him and the manner in which he had organized and defended them. It wasn't his fault, she said, that she and her husband had to drop out when the group was moving to another location. The captain had to think of the safety of the group. When Lewis asked her if she knew where the group planned to go she replied no. She was pleased to be following Oba's instructions, even though she actually had no idea of their destination.

Jeeps with markings of the three infantry regiments that made up the 2d Marine Division—the 2d, the 6th, and the 8th—crowded the small parking area next to the Division Plans and Operations office, the Quonset hut office of Colonel Pollard.

Pollard waited until all regimental commanding officers and their subordinates were seated before entering the building.

"Ten-hut!" shouted Lewis, who was seated at a table facing the dozen or so officers in the room. They rose as one and stood at attention while Pollard strode past them to the table.

"At ease," he said as he took his place. "Be seated, gentlemen." He waited until the sound of shuffling feet and chairs had subsided, then said, "We have a problem, gentlemen. Major Lewis informs me our problem's name is Oba, and he's a captain in the Japanese army. He's got some three hundred people in the hills, at least half of them armed, and he's shooting at our people. Headquarters in Washington is already asking why we declared Saipan secure three months ago if an armed force is operating there. The island will not be secure until Oba and his mob are gone. And that, gentlemen, is your job!"

Pollard walked to the wall map, to which a transparent plastic overlay had been attached. A red line on the overlay circumscribed an area of central Saipan that roughly covered the jungle hills surrounding Tapotchau. Other lines and figures showed areas of operation for all three regiments, including the three battalions of each.

"Oba is limited to this area, about five miles long and three miles wide," Pollard continued. "That's a pretty small area in which to hide three hundred people. So we're going to find them. I want a full division sweep of the area. I want a line three miles long, with Marines moving at arm's length, to cover every inch of those five miles. The sweep will be launched in five days. D-3 is working on your orders. You'll have them in two days. Elements from each of your regiments will be on the line. The rest of your men will be held in reserve. And in one week from today, gentlemen, I want Oba and every Jap up there to be in a prison compound or in a grave. I'll confer with each of you after you receive your orders. Any questions? All right, that's all gentlemen. Thank you.''

As the men left the building for their vehicles, Pollard looked at Lewis, who nodded his head in approval, and started to open an envelope containing leaflets written in Japanese, with accompanying translations. ''Do you want to take a look at these, sir? They're some leaflets our language section worked up. We figure that if we airdrop them all over the hills, we'll get some of those people down.''

Pollard waved them off with a grin. ''Too late, Herm. We don't need 'em. In five days we'll have all those people down, one way or another. C'mon, let's go get some chow.''

Word of the planned assault was met with mixed reaction among the twenty thousand men of the 2d Marine Division. Those whose task it had been to patrol the rugged hills each day saw it only as more sweat, flies, and exhaustion. Others, who had been kept busy cutting sugarcane with bayonets, welcomed a change in their schedule of useless activities.

Although intended to be kept secret, rumors of the planned sweep soon spread throughout the island. Even Tsuchiya, the army warrant officer who masqueraded as a civilian in the Susupe Compound, learned of the attack.

The following morning, he changed places with one of the laborers assigned to the farm near Second Line camp. He trudged to the farm with the others. With no difficulty, he slipped into the jungle. Within minutes, he was explaining to Lieutenant Nagata what he had heard. ''It's scheduled for tomorrow. I don't know where they plan to start the attack, but it will be big. Tell Captain Oba to prepare.''

He had no details. Nor did he have much time. Periodically, the guards who accompanied the farmers made a routine head count. If he were discovered missing, he would be unable to rejoin them without detection.

"If possible, I'll return tomorrow morning to keep you informed," he told Nagata as he started back.

Within an hour Oba learned of the scheduled assault on his mountain redoubt. He sent for Nagata and Tanaka and ordered Kitani to find Horiuchi, whom he had heard was based with two others on Gakeyama, just east of Garapan. The two officers arrived at Takoyama by mid-afternoon. Horiuchi and Kitani walked into camp an hour later.

"We have two choices," he told them. "We can try to elude them as we've done in the past, by fighting a united battle that will lead them away from the civilians, and then vanishing into the hills, or we can make a final stand that will probably result in our deaths."

The bearded *yakuza* was the first to offer his opinion. He paid no deference to the military rank of those around him. He no longer wore a uniform. He was garbed in a strange mixture of American combat boots, tattered trousers that revealed the artistic tattoos extending into his shoes, and a dirty khaki shirt, open nearly to the waist. A scowling Kabuki-style tattoo glared out from his bared chest, just below his beard.

"You people are still afraid to fight. Alone, I have already killed almost half the one hundred enemy I swore to kill. You fight only when you're forced to. And then, only until you can escape."

Oba looked at the faces around him. Kitani's eyes reflected his anger. Nagata looked toward Oba for some sign as to how he should react. Tanaka stared at Horiuchi. None made an attempt to reply.

"We have the lives of nearly two hundred civilians to consider," Oba said finally. "We must not sacrifice ourselves or them, as long as we have hope of the navy returning to recapture the island. I agree with you that now is the time to fight. But not as a single unit. The enemy does not know our numbers. A single battle, whether we win or lose, may make them believe they've encountered our main force. We will remain as separate companies. Nagata, you at Second Line, and I will remain here with Tanaka at Takoyama. Whichever camp is hit will fight with the strength of all of us. One of us, hopefully will convince the enemy that they've found the force they seek, and the other camp may escape the attack.''

All five men now gave their attention to Oba. He spoke quietly and firmly. ''Prepare your men to attack at the first sight of the enemy. If they should approach both camps, we will all have the opportunity to give our lives for our country.''

He looked at Horiuchi. The bearded renegade squatted on his heels and smiled. ''And I,'' he said, ''will be waiting for them on Gakeyama. If they come that way, there may not be enough left to bother you.''

The two officers and the *yakuza* left Takoyama shortly after nightfall. Oba had given Nagata instructions to notify him immediately if Tsuchiya passed on any new information the following day.

It required nearly three hours to line up five thousand Marines from the edge of the 2d Division area, near Magicienne Bay, westward across the ravines, ridges, and dense jungled areas to the coastal plains on the other side of the island. Convoys of trucks deposited companies as close to the departure line as possible, then returned to pick up more loads.

Company commanders, each of whom had been assigned a three-hundred-yard front, checked to be sure they were tied in with units on each flank. Overhead, a light observation plane dipped and circled over the line.

Marines sat or lay on the ground, already sweating in the hot sun. And they complained.

''Another fuckin' wild goose chase. I'm getting tired of crawlin' all over these damn mountains,'' a young Marine said to no one in particular as he lay with his head resting on his helmet, his eyes closed.

''Shit,'' a voice replied. ''There's nothin' up there but a few lousy stragglers. I say forget 'em.''

A runner reached Oba shortly after 9:00 A.M. the next morning to report the activity to the south of the Second Line camp. With Kitani and Kuno, Oba climbed to the rocky peak that jutted up from the top of Takoyama and scanned the area to the south. Even in the limited area that was visible, he could see convoys of trucks shuttling between the Marine area and the southernmost foothills of Mount Tapotchau.

"They're coming by the hundreds!" Kuno exclaimed in a high voice.

"Shut up!" Oba ordered, without taking his eyes from the binoculars.

A voice from below shouted for Oba. A soldier was making his way up to the pinnacle where Oba and the others stood.

"They're coming, sir," he said between deep breaths. "They're lined up clear across the island. Thousands of them."

"Who are you?" Oba demanded.

"Private Hayashi, sir. Lieutenant Nagata told me to tell you."

Oba looked past the soldier to the group that stood at the base of the jutting rock, at the people who depended on him to make the decisions that would determine whether they lived or died.

This was the moment he had dreaded. It was even worse than he had imagined. He could meet and possibly survive an attack, even if he were grossly outnumbered, from any direction that allowed him an avenue of escape. But a solid line of troops, moving methodically from one end of the island to the other . . . Not even a solitary man could escape detection. Whether they attacked or fled, they were doomed.

"What do you think, Kitani?" He turned to the only man whose experience equalled his own.

"If we were a few, we might attack and break through. But with three hundred, mostly civilians, we'd never make it. We can't hide, and we have no place to run."

Oba nodded. "We have no choice," he said. "We must stick to our original plan. Within an hour of their advance they'll hit Second Line. Two hours later it will be our turn."

He knew the end had come. And it was an anticlimactic one. He had hoped it would be in a situation of his own choosing. But now, with his force scattered, he would have to wait for the enemy to find him.

He thought of the many times he had allowed American patrols to pass unmolested and cursed the chances he had missed to strike at the hated enemy. Perhaps Horiuchi had been right all along: kill as many as possible before they get you.

He was thinking of a platoon-sized patrol he had watched from a cliff only a few days earlier. They . . . He straightened with a sudden realization. "I've got it!" he shouted. "We'll get above them." Excitedly, he turned back to Kitani. "They always patrol looking straight ahead, don't they? They never look up! All we have to do is get above them!"

A plan rapidly formed in Oba's mind. "Kitani, go to Second Line. Tell Nagata to return here as quickly as possible with all his people." He turned to Kuno. "Go tell Horiuchi that we need him here. Under no circumstances is he to attack the Americans. Tell him the safety of the entire group depends on his following my orders!"

Then he called to one of those standing at the base of the rock. "Sergeant Iwama. Go find Oshiro at the civilian camp. Tell him to join me at the top of the cliff on the south side of the mountain."

Oba cimbed down from his rocky perch and walked swiftly to the southern side of Takoyama, still only half-convinced that his new plan could succeed. But it was the only one he had that gave them a chance of survival.

His pace increased as he approached the abrupt drop where, a millennium ago, part of the mountain had slipped away to become an indistinguishable part of the valley floor. Ignoring the fact that he made a likely target for any enemy that might be lurking below, Oba walked along the edge of the thirty-meter-high cliff, stopping occasionally to examine irregularities in its stone face.

"Captain Oba!" He heard his name called from behind. Oshiro, with Sergeant Iwama, was walking toward him.

Rapidly Oba explained his plan and his reasoning. He pointed to the narrow ledges that crisscrossed the face of the cliff. "There's room on those ledges"—and he hoped he was right—"for everybody to stand."

Oshiro leaned over to see the narrow, broken mantels that ranged in width from half a meter to a few inches. He accidently dislodged a small stone that bounced from one ledge to another until it disappeared in the jungle below.

"But even if they could get onto the ledges," he said incredulously to Oba, "there's no concealment. They would be seen by anyone who looks up."

"The enemy doesn't look up. They look at the jungle around them, but they never look up. Besides, it's our only chance." Oba explained about the unbroken line of enemy soldiers that was sweeping the island. They were all doomed, he said, unless everyone, civilians and soldiers alike, could cling to the cliff while the enemy passed below.

"All right, I understand," Oshiro said without hesitation. "I'll get my people ready." He turned and trotted toward the civilian camp.

From the south, the sound of a light airplane grew until Oba was able to see a high-wing monoplane skim the treetops, then rise to several hundred meters and swing gracefully back to the south. Americans don't look up, he thought, but I hope some of them don't look down.

Fifteen hundred meters to the southwest, a sweat-soaked Corporal Kuno climbed the rounded side of Gakeyama, whose northern extremity also ended in a sheer cliff. He had run all the way from Takoyama, fearing that at any moment he would come face-to-face with the six-kilometer-long line of American Marines.

He had rehearsed what he would say to Horiuchi. After all, Horiuchi was only a private, and he was a corporal, a noncommissioned officer on a mission that could determine whether three hundred persons, himself included, lived or died. He would conduct himself in a manner befitting his rank.

He reached the top of the mountain, paused a minute or two to regain his composure and his breath, then set off toward an outlook point where he hoped he would find Horiuchi or one of the two men who fought with him.

All three were busy building emplacements when he spotted them. He stopped by a tree to call to Horiuchi. He wanted something to hide behind in case the short-tempered and quick triggered *yakuza* answered his call with a burst of machine-gun fire before he was recognized. He suddenly remembered Oba's description of Horiuchi: "He's no longer a soldier. He's an independent killer."

Kuno mustered his courage and called out in a voice just loud enough to be heard: "Private Horiuchi!" All three men stopped working and turned toward him. Horiuchi was glowering.

No, Kuno thought, that was wrong. He doesn't consider himself a soldier. He took another breath. "Horiuchi!" Horiuchi continued to glare at him. Once more: "Mr. Horiuchi," he said in the most congenial tone he could manage. Then he bowed and added, "Excuse me, please."

"What do you want?" the bearded killer said, hefting his machine gun.

"I have an urgent message from Captain Oba." Less fearful now, Kuno walked toward the three men.

"Sorry to bother you, but the plans have been changed. Captain Oba wants you to return to Takoyama. He says you are not to attack the enemy." Again he bowed. "I am sorry . . ."

"Don't be a fool," growled Horiuchi. "Haven't you seen them? They're lined up like ducks in a shooting gallery. I'm not only going to get a hundred, I may get a thousand today."

"That may be, but . . ." Kuno carefully and politely explained Oba's plan to evade the approaching line of enemy. When he had finished, Horiuchi spat on the ground.

"No, I'm staying. This is the best chance we've had." His normally angry countenance grew darker, and he turned back to piling rocks on his half-finished emplacement.

Frustrated, Kuno began once more. "He says the lives of all three hundred depend on your cooperation . . ."

"That's enough!" barked Horiuchi. "I understand! Just tell Oba I understand!"

"Yes," Kuno said as he unconsciously bowed again. He managed to catch himself before adding a "sir." He made an effort to walk like he felt a noncommissioned officer should as he returned to Takoyama.

Oshiro had divided the civilians into groups of ten, each with one man in charge. He had called the group leaders aside to explain Oba's plan and the reason for it.

"Have your people destroy as much evidence as possible of our having lived here," he told them. "Have them bury or hide everything except what they're wearing. They can retrieve it later.'' He glanced at his watch. "I want everyone to be at the cliff side of the mountain in thirty minutes.''

Kuno hurried toward Takoyama with a sick feeling in the pit of his stomach. He had failed to return with Horiuchi. Everyone would die, and it would be his fault. And almost as bad, he had disgraced his rank. He, a corporal, had bowed and said "please" to a private. He had failed in the most important mission of his military career. How could he face Captain Oba? What would he say?

The light plane flew over the hills three kilometers south of Tapotchau. Col. George Pollard sat in the front seat, directing the pilot through an intercom microphone in one hand, while in the other he held a microphone connected with a radio tuned to the division network.

"Hello, Bluebird. This is Eagle. Do you read me?''

"Hello, Eagle. This is Bluebird. Read you loud and clear, over.''

"Are all units ready to move out? Over.''

"That's affirmative, over.''

"All right. Pass the word to move out. I'm going to move ahead of the line to see if we're getting any action. Over.''

"Roger, Eagle, Wilco. Bluebird out.''

Radios up and down the five-thousand-meter line of men relayed the order to advance.

· 11 ·

5,000 MARINES OUTWITTED

Thirty minutes after Oshiro had left the cliff to organize his civilians, Oba returned with the entire military unit of Takoyama. He bristled when he saw the civilians sitting in small groups near the cliff edge.

"They're afraid to go down," Oshiro hurried to explain. Oba brushed past the civilian leader, strode to the center of his people, and fought to control his temper.

"You people," he began, "once asked me for protection. I agreed to provide it only if you accepted my orders. The only way you can hope to survive this day is to follow the orders I've given you through Oshiro-san. I want you all"— and his voice rose to emphasize his command—"to climb down on those ledges and to remain there, without making a sound, until the enemy has passed!"

Hesitantly, the civilians began to comply.

Oba heard a familiar feminine voice at his shoulder: "Captain Oba." He turned, and his attitude softened. Yoshiko Okuno, the woman who had offered to become his mistress, bowed.

"My mother"—and she indicated the elderly and lame woman beside her—"cannot walk on the ledges. And there are others who also are too old or unsure of their footing. And," she added, "what about Kagata-san?" She nodded

164

toward a woman who held a baby in her arms and a small child by the hand. "How can she keep her children quiet for such a long time?"

Oba looked around him at the elderly and at the other women with small children. "You're right."

His experiences with farmers from the civilian compound had altered, to a degree, his opinion of the enemy. He had learned the Americans did not kill civilians and had been surprised to hear that they even had a voice in governing the compound at Susupe.

"Yoshiko-san, collect all those who cannot join the others on the ledges. We will have someone guide them to . . ." —and he tried to think of a location where they could be "captured" safely—"to the valley near Second Line."

When she had gathered the sixteen civilians, including her mother, Yoshiko returned to Oba. "I cannot leave my mother. I'm going with them." Her eyes met his for a long moment.

"I'll miss you," he said finally. He saw the tears in her eyes and wanted to say more. "Good luck," he said softly, then abruptly turned his attention to those who were descending the treacherous trails to the ledges below.

Minutes later, at shortly after 9:00 A.M., Kitani reached Takoyama with Nagata and the soldiers who had been at Second Line. Shortly thereafter, Kuno returned and said only that Horiuchi had replied that he understood Oba's message.

"Where is he?" Oba demanded.

"I don't know, sir. He's coming, I think. . . . I hope . . ." Oba ordered his troops to the ledges and put them next to civilians where possible to prevent panic, which would betray their presence. When Aono's turn came, Kitani took a step toward the ledge, then looked toward Oba. The captain shook his head slightly. "I want you with the men." Aono, who recognized Kitani's gesture, raised her eyes to his and bowed slightly in gratitude.

"What about Chiba?" Oba asked the nurse.

"He's safe. We have hidden him well," she replied.

During the next several minutes, the thirty-meter cliff took on the appearance of a surrealistic painting as more than 250 human beings anchored themselves on its white face. Many were unable to sit or crouch because of the narrowness of the platforms on which they stood.

Oba had received word that the five-thousand-man line had begun its advance shortly before 10:00 A.M. He calculated they would reach Second Line an hour later, Tapotchau camp by noon, and would pass beneath, and probably on top of, Takoyama's cliff before 2:00 P.M.

At thirty minutes past noon, his people were in place. Oba, together with Kitani, Kuno, Sergeant Iwama, and two other soldiers, descended to the bottom of the cliff. The overhead foliage hid most of the cliff, but there were openings in it that revealed much more of the white stone wall and its human occupants than he had anticipated. He began to doubt the wisdom of his decision. What if he had misjudged the enemy? If only one were to glance up through an opening, or if one of those who covered the top of Takoyama were to peer over the edge of the cliff . . .

Shutting his mind to the possibility, Oba ordered those with him to climb to the lower ledges of the rock wall. Inching their way along the narrow, jutting stone face, the six men separated themselves on six- to eight-inch ledges only a few meters above the valley floor. Oba took the lowest position, at only three meters' elevation. If he had made a mistake, he would be the first to die.

The time was nearly 1:00 P.M. He did not know exactly when the sweeping Americans would reach Takoyama but felt it could be at any time in the next ninety minutes.

He was forced to stand with his face against the cliff, with the fingers of his outstretched hands clutching irregularities in the rock wall to maintain his balance. He could look to the left or right, but always at the risk of moving too far back from the cliff.

The whining sound of the light aircraft broke the silence of the valley, and Oba tried to look up. The plane, hidden by the cliff to his front and the trees to his rear, approached to within a few hundred meters of Takoyama before swinging back to the south.

Col. George Pollard tried to see through the solid mass of greenery below him but detected no sign of enemy activity.

He directed the pilot to return to where he could see portions of the human line moving slowly northward.

"Hello, Bluebird. This is Eagle. Do you read me?"

"Go ahead, Eagle," his headphones crackled, "this is Bluebird."

"No sign of enemy activity yet. What's happening down there? Over."

"The Third Battalion just passed through a deserted camp area at coordinates H-62, B-7, but no enemy contact. Over."

"Roger, Bluebird. I'll take a look. Eagle out."

Checking the map he held in his lap, Pollard directed the pilot until they flew over the area of the now-deserted Second Line camp. Pulling back on the throttle, the pilot lowered the plane to a few meters above the highest trees and skimmed the jungle at slightly over stalling speed.

Pollard's eyes swept the areas to his left and right. "Shit," he muttered. "Where the hell are they?"

Wheeling back to the north, the plane banked to the left as it approached Tapotchau, then dropped its nose again, heading for the west coast.

"Hey, what's that?" Pollard shouted over the intercom as he pointed toward the ground to his left. The pilot dropped the left wing and began a slow descending turn. Some fifteen persons were emerging into a clearing. The two men passed over them at an altitude of less than three hundred feet. Pollard could see their upturned faces, and his sphincter muscle contracted as he waited for rifle fire. Sensing the same fear, the pilot swung quickly to the right and pushed his throttle forward to gain a safer altitude.

"Didja see that?" Pollard said to him. "They didn't fire on us or try to run. Let's make another pass."

The light monoplane swooped down toward the group. This time Pollard could see that they were seated in a group within the clearing. He spotted several women, including one or two with babies, as the plane flashed over them.

"Hello, Bluebird," he said excitedly into his hand microphone, "this is Eagle. Come in!"

"Go ahead, Eagle. This is Bluebird, over," came the reply.

"I've located fifteen or twenty of the enemy. They look

like civilians. They're sitting in a clearing at coordinates"
—he hesitated and checked his map—"L-19, R-47. Do you
read me? Over."

"Roger, Eagle, that position is about five hundred yards
north of First Batallion elements. The line should arrive there
in thirty minutes. Can you observe until then? Over."

Pollard looked over his shoulder to the pilot, who had monitored the conversation. The man glanced at his instruments,
then shook his head.

"Negative, Bluebird. We'll remain above them as long as
possible, but we'll have to refuel within the next few minutes.
Eagle out."

Oba could still hear the plane, somewhere to the south.
That meant the line was at least a kilometer away. Possibly
another hour to wait. Somewhere overhead, a dislodged rock
clattered down the side of the cliff and fell into the jungle.

His fingers began to tremble as he realized his mistake. He
should have used scouts to report on the enemy advance and
moved his people into position shortly before their arrival. In
a moment of cold clarity he realized there was no possibility
that three hundred people could maintain their precarious
footing for another hour. And when the Americans did come,
it would take only a cough or a falling stone to betray them.

We'll die like the Christ of their religion, he told himself,
crucified to this cliff. Then his thoughts turned to his own
religion. Please, he prayed, make them come quickly, and
keep everyone silent until they've passed. He continued to
pray silently and fervently. Droplets of sweat rolled down his
forehead and their salt stung his eyes.

He kept his head turned to the right, from where they would
come, but his field of vision was limited to what he could see
over his shoulder. A wild thrashing in the undergrowth made
him strain to the right. From the corner of his eye, he saw
two Japanese start up the narrow trail to the top of the hill.

"Hold it!" he called. They stopped and glanced upward,
then reacted as they saw the cliff studded with humans.

"Where shall we go?" one asked.

"There's no room on the cliff," Oba replied. "Climb a
tree!"

Moments later, Oba saw them in the upper branches of a tall tree, just within his line of sight.

Time dragged by. Although his hands were again firm, Oba's legs trembled from muscle fatigue. Soon they would begin to fall, he knew.

He heard them before he saw them. They were advancing as if on an animal hunt, flushing their game before them. Shouts, some nearby and others more distant, made it apparent they had no fear of their quarry.

A camouflaged helmet suddenly appeared ten meters away. Oba strained his eyes and could see three more, all within two meters of each other and moving slowly forward. Their rifles were directed to their front, as were their eyes.

But they moved so slowly.

He looked up to where Kuno was clinging in the same crucified position. Helpless targets, he anguished. No defense, no escape. He closed his eyes and waited for the shout of discovery that would precede a barrage of fire, the moment that would climax with failure his effort to keep this group alive.

Slowly he opened his eyes. The enemy seemed to be exactly where they had been earlier. He knew he had failed. After months of resistance, he had led these people into a trap of his own making. He and he alone would be responsible for their deaths.

More shouts, and once again they were moving. Breathlessly, he watched a helmet approach until it was directly below him. From a crouching position he could have kicked it. For a brief second, he considered trying to—a futile and final gesture of opposition.

Minutes passed. The sound of voices receded. He began to turn his head to the left. As his nose brushed the cliff, the strength drained from his legs, and he almost lost his balance. Something was touching his back! He froze, unable to see and afraid to move. He felt the movement again, but this time he realized it was the tremor of a protesting back muscle.

He slowly exhaled in relief and continued to turn his head. The scrape of a boot above him caused him to start, and he watched unbelievingly as Sergeant Iwama climbed to a higher ledge in order to see in the direction the Americans had taken.

"You fool!" Oba whispered. As he watched, the sergeant cringed in fright. Then, in a panic, he grabbed a fist-sized rock and threw it toward the jungle. Its sharp crack against a tree trunk beyond where three Marines stood talking brought an immediate reaction. Rifles and automatic weapons poured their bullets toward the sound.

Iwama quickly climbed down to his original perch and looked in terror at Oba. The enraged captain could only glare back. He knew that all was lost. He shifted his position for the necessary footing to jump the three meters to the ground. If he were to die here and now, better to do it with a pistol or sword in his hand.

His movement was arrested by a new sound of automatic weapon fire, higher pitched and more rapid than the enemy's. A Nambu 99!

Horiuchi!

Bullets from the light machine gun ripped into the jungle below Oba. He inched his feet around until his back was to the cliff. He pulled his pistol, then glanced up to where Kitani and the others were also shifting their positions.

For a moment he was undecided. Should they attack while the enemy was occupied with Horiuchi's machine gun? Should they try to escape to the top of Takoyama? Surely the line had covered the top of the mountain. But what if they were still there? What if the sound of the shooting caused them to look down at the face of the cliff? But in any case, the entire line would return within minutes, they would be discovered, and they would die. Better, he decided, to die fighting.

He hesitated before jumping to locate the sounds of the battle. The rapid reports of the Nambu were clearly distinguishable among the heavier explosions of M-1 and Browning automatic rifles. But—and he waited to be sure—the sounds were growing more distant.

Horiuchi was drawing them away from the cliff! He was still fighting his own war, disregarding others. He had seen Oba's people perched as defenseless targets on the cliff, and then taken a position nearby with his two BAR-armed men. He had not given up his goal of destroying one hundred of the enemy, but he had placed the safety of the three hundred above his own desires. How fortunate, Oba mused, he had not followed orders this day. His arrogance was saving the lives of all of them.

Oba leaped to the valley floor and signaled Kitani, Kuno, and the others to follow. Then they ran to the broken trail to the top of Takoyama.

"Climb back to the top," he told those on the cliff within earshot. "Pass the word. Everyone to the top."

Oba watched as the frightened civilians scrambled to the crest. He listened to the now distant sounds of Horiuchi's withdrawal. He was pulling them toward Gakeyama. Hopefully he would elude them there. Or would the temptation to reach his goal of one hundred lives lead him to stand and die?

Kitani stood near where those coming to the crest made their final step. A soldier was helping them keep their balance. The master sergeant waited until Aono neared the top, then stepped in front of the soldier and held her arm until she was safely on top. Again, wordlessly, she bowed her thanks.

"Tanaka!" Oba called to the young lieutenant. "Take everyone to the valley just east of here. Keep them hidden until I return." He felt sure that having once swept the area, the Americans would not soon return to the mountain.

Horiuchi was still fighting. How, he wasn't sure, but he had to help him. "Kitani, let's go!" he said to the master sergeant. The sergeant smiled, plucked a bandoleer of ammunition from a nearby soldier, and without a word started down the trail to the base of the hill with Oba. The two men trotted southward in a direction that would lead them around Gakeyama where, Oba hoped, they could join Horiuchi.

Midway to the hoped-for rendezvous, the sound of gunfire ceased. The two men stopped to listen. "It's over," Oba said in a voice just above a whisper. "I hope he's still alive."

"He's a bastard, but we owe our lives to him," Kitani said. "If I see him again, I'll tell him. . . ." Both men listened intently. "If I see him again."

"Seventeen scared civilians!" Pollard snorted as he looked at the D-2 report Lewis had handed him a moment before. "The sonofabitch outwitted us. Slipped right through our fingers! He's making us look like fools, Herm!"

Lewis did not reply immediately. He knew Pollard had

more than a professional interest in getting Oba. The colonel had hoped to be on the promotion list that had been radioed from Washington the day before. Now he blamed Oba because he had not been given his brigadier general star.

"We've got to find another way of getting to him."

"How about getting to work on some new leaflets?" Lewis volunteered.

"I can't think of anything better at the moment. Let's try it."

Oba returned to Takoyama, where they had lived undiscovered before the sweep. Evidence of camp had been well disguised, and the enemy apparently had not discovered it. The same was not true, however, of the camps at Tapotchau and Second Line, which continued to be visited frequently by American patrols. So he gathered his entire force at Takoyama.

The following day, Horiuchi walked into the camp. His machine gun and a bandoleer of ammunition hung from his shoulders. With him was one of the two men who had joined him. The man carried two American BARs, one on each shoulder.

Oba greeted the *yakuza* warmly. "I'm glad to see you're alive. We owe our lives to you. Thank you for drawing the enemy away from us." Then he noted the two weapons carried by the other man. He looked questioningly at Horiuchi. "Noguchi . . . ?"

"He's dead."

The man's hard, round eyes took in the soldiers who had grouped around them. "I have a weapon for a man who isn't afraid to use it." Three of Oba's soldiers stepped forward. "You!" he said.

Without a word, the man accepted the American weapon, and the three turned and walked away.

Lewis's leaflets had far from the desired effect among Oba's men. They were angered at what they believed to be the enemy's lies and used the leaflets as toilet paper.

Oba, however, was less certain than the others and studied the alleged photographs of reconnaissance flights over burned out sections of major Japanese cities.

"Sano," he said one afternoon to the young private who had been with him since the invasion, "You come from Tokyo. Look at this photograph and see if you can recognize any part of the city." The photograph was of several square miles of what the leaflet claimed was Tokyo, and showed only smoking ruins. An occasional concrete building remained standing, but what had apparently been a residential section of the capital had been reduced to ashes. Only the streets stood out as white lines crisscrossing the blackened area.

The young soldier looked at the leaflet. With his finger, he traced two faint lines.

"These could be Odakyu and Keio-sen railway lines," he ventured, "and if they are, this area would be near Shinjuku. But there's no way of being sure. Do you think they really are bombing Japan, Captain?"

"I don't know. But if they are, we're lost. The navy will never return."

In addition to Kitani, whose thinking paralleled his own in so many ways, Oba had developed a special camaraderie with five other men of his command: Corporal Kuno, a twenty-two-year-old whom he had first met when the destroyer had plucked them from the chilling water off Formosa, and Privates Suzuki, Sano, and Iwata, all of whom had survived with him the bloody charge through American lines and the artillery camp attack that took the lives of Banno and Bito, and Private Shimizo, a former draftsman on whom Oba frequently called to sketch drawings and maps of enemy installations, to be used when the time came to retake Saipan.

With these people he shared his thoughts and his food. The rest of his command had similarly divided themselves into small groups who used common cooking fires and thought of each other as friends rather than simply as fellow soldiers.

Oba spoke more openly to those of his small band than to the others. He knew his discussions with them were never repeated, and he valued their opinions.

More and more, their conversations had dealt with speculation on the war's progress. Three times in the past month they had been heartened by the appearance of Japanese aircraft that had swept in from the north to bomb and strafe enemy aircraft at Asolito, far to the south. Oba had witnessed the second attack during a visit to the camp near the peak of Tapotchau.

"It's started," he had said gleefully to Lieutenant Tanaka as they watched from a vantage point that gave them a view of most of the island. "They're destroying the enemy's air power so that the navy can return unopposed."

"Do you suppose they're coming from navy carriers?" queried Tanaka.

"Either that, or from Iwo Jima," Oba searched the sky in the north for the additional waves of bombers or fighters he expected would join the approximately half dozen Zeros sweeping over the enemy airfield.

Additional planes soon were in the air, but they were the stubby fighters and the odd-looking two-engined planes with dual fuselages that arose from Asolito to meet the Japanese assault.

Spellbound, Oba, Tanaka, and the others had watched as the planes swept below their mountain lookout or became tiny specks forming contrails thousands of feet above them locked in mortal combat. Three times that day, planes either exploded in the air or fell, trailing smoke behind them. Each time, Oba and the others cheered, confident that it was a Japanese victory.

But after the third air raid from the north a few days later, the attacks had ceased. His efforts to obtain news from the farmers who toiled south of Second Line had produced little information on the war's progress. Tanaka, in his ragged masquerade as a civilian, had grown adept at moving from the jungle to the farmers, but they could tell him nothing.

He did, however, manage to loosen several floorboards of the small shack where they stored the garden tools at night, and he arranged for the farmers to hide food, clothing, and other needed items during the day. Oba's men visited the shack each night and returned with supplies, but never any information about the war's progress.

There must, Oba reasoned, be some in the camp who knew more than the farmers. He began working on a plan. He lay staring at the stars, waiting for dawn. Sleep had been pushed aside by his newly hatched plan to find out what was happening beyond their isolated mountain.

"Private Sano," he called to the enlisted man sleeping nearby. Sano lifted his head. "Find Captain Jimpuku and ask him to come here." Sano disappeared and returned a minute later with the somewhat sleepy-looking captain.

"I'm going to the civilian compound," Oba told him. "You will be in charge until I return."

"But how can you?" the shocked officer asked. "If you try to return with the farmers, you'll be recognized. They'll spot you immediately."

"I'm going tonight."

"But how? We don't even know where it is. And what about the enemy camps between here and there?"

Oba had no answers. He knew only that the compound lay somewhere between the large body of brackish water known as Lake Susupe and the western shore of the island. From the jungle's edge near Second Line he had seen the many tents and rounded buildings that looked like halves of oil drums clustered in the three kilometers between him and the lake.

"Don't worry. I'll make it," he said with more confidence than he felt.

Later that morning he briefed Kitani and the others.

"Let me go instead," Kitani protested. "We need you here."

"No, you remain here with Captain Jimpuku!"

He knew the mild-mannered captain could rely on the knowledge and experience of the war-hardened master sergeant if, for some reason, he did not return.

· 12 ·

IN THE ENEMY CAMP

Oba packed and stored his sword with his clean uniform, Lieutenant Banno's thumb, and the intelligence data he had collected on American defense positions before leaving that night. He timed his departure so he'd reach the farm shortly before dawn. He paused at the edge of the jungle overlooking the tilled area and, although he saw no signs of the enemy, decided to pass to the west of it and follow the jungle line leading almost to the enemy camp area.

He emerged from the jungle a hundred meters from a highway, which already had some traffic. Light from lanterns shone in the windows of several buildings on the far side of the road. He crouched for several minutes behind a clump of bushes, studying the area before him. It was the first time he had ventured alone to the flatland occupied by the Americans. For a moment, he doubted the wisdom of his decision.

He paused at the edge of the road until no vehicle could be seen in either direction, then darted across. The white crushed-coral strip seemed to mark the ultimate boundary between his hills and the country of the enemy. He began walking to the left, away from the lighted buildings. The night was moonless, and a recent rain had softened the dirt of a trail he had found.

He froze at the sound of voices. But the glow of cigarettes

directly ahead prompted him into action. There was no place
to run, so he dropped to the ground a meter off the trail,
lying on his side with his pistol trained on the approaching
men. He counted thirty black American soldiers as they strode
by talking and laughing. Secure in their own camp area, they
had no reason to suspect that a Japanese would have penetrated it.

Oba got up and walked southward. The soft dirt turned to
mud, then to clinging muck that made a sucking sound each
time he raised a foot. Ahead was the marsh grass that ringed
the lake. To the left was higher ground, but to go there would
place the lake between him and his objective.

He turned west toward the lighted buildings. Curiosity led
him to the nearest one. He saw it was one of the half-circle,
corrugated steel structures he had seen from afar. It had several windows along the side. He crept to the nearest window
and raised his head to look inside. He looked directly into
the eyes of an American who sat holding a book on the far
side of the room.

For two full seconds they seemed to stare at each other.
Oba considered firing his pistol at the man but knew the report would result in his death before he could escape.

He lowered his head slowly and as silently as possible and
tiptoed away, waiting for the American to give alarm as he
passed the other buildings. But he heard nothing and wondered if the soldier had returned to his book.

He kept to the northern edge of the swamp, eventually turning south when he came to a rutted dirt road. He followed it
for about four hundred meters, glancing frequently at the first
indications of dawn in the eastern sky. Large four-engined
planes passed overhead and were silhouetted briefly against
the pale light of the east before landing at the airfield on the
far side of the lake.

Three large breadfruit trees loomed ahead of him. He noted
them as a landmark for future reference, then discovered that
one was being used as a cornerpost for a barbed-wire fence.
Beyond the fence he could see a hodgepodge of tin and
wooden shacks. He was sure it was the compound.

Even in the dim light, he could discern that those moving
among the shacks were Japanese. He turned and looked be-

hind him for guards. None was visible. Should he crawl through the fence? Would the people inside help him before word of his presence spread to enemy ears? He continued on.

A hundred meters ahead, a woman walked to the fence and began to remove clothing that had been hung to dry. She looked up as he approached. Then, in a loud whisper, she called, "Captain, Captain, this way!"

Startled at hearing himself addressed by his rank, Oba hurried toward the woman. Okuno-san! She had not been killed during the sweep! Some quirk of fate had led her, among the fourteen thousand persons of the compound, to be the one to discover him.

"Yoshiko-san," he said in astonishment.

"Through here, quickly," she said as she separated two strands of the wire. Oba squeezed through, then grasped both her hands and said simply, "Thank you."

"This way," she said, holding one of his hands and pulling him toward a nearby shack of rough boards and roofing tin.

As they entered, Oba could see by the dim predawn light that there were about ten people sprawled in sleep in the small room. With her fingers before her lips for silence, Okuno stepped carefully over several figures, leading him to a curtained-off anteroom enclosed by mosquito netting. She raised the netting and indicated a futon. "Rest here," she said.

Still shocked at finding her here, Oba nodded. As she turned to leave, he pulled her toward him. For the first time, he felt her arms cling to his back and the comforting feeling of her head pressed to his shoulder. Her body melted against his. Then she pushed him away.

"Not now. First you sleep. I will awaken you later."

She stepped outside the netting and closed the curtain that hid Oba from the other rooms. For a long moment he stared after her, almost unable to believe what had happened. Then he placed his pistol under the edge of the futon, lay down, and in moments was asleep.

He was awakened in mid-morning by the sound of excited voices in the next room. He withdrew his pistol and listened. He could hear Okuno telling someone that the captain was resting and should not be disturbed. Male voices replied in Japanese, saying it was important they see him.

Oba replaced his pistol, raised the mosquito net, and stepped beyond the curtain into the room. The conversation ceased, and eight pairs of eyes were on him. Stiffly and with only a slight motion from the waist, Oba bowed to the seven men who stared at him. "Oba Sakae, army captain," he said softly. As one, they returned his bow. Each mumbled his own name. Okuno moved to stand beside Oba.

"Welcome, Captain Oba. We are honored by your presence," one of them, a portly and partially bald man, said formally. "For what reason are you here?"

It was apparent from the man's demeanor that he was concerned about the island's most wanted man being in their midst. "I have come to learn what I can about the progress of the war. The Americans, through their propaganda leaflets, are spreading many rumors in the hills. It is my hope that I can learn the truth from you."

Most of the others in the room were dismissed by the portly man. Oba later learned that his name was Motoyama and that he was the unofficial leader of the Japanese in the compound. "But don't any of you," he cautioned as the men left, "mention that we have a special guest!"

Among those who remained was young Tsuchiya, the warrant officer who had warned them of the enemy sweep two months earlier.

"He wanted to meet you," Motoyama explained, "because he has a plan to escape from Saipan and wants you, as the ranking officer, to accompany him."

They discussed Tsuchiya's escape plan. He had managed to be assigned to one of the two fishing boats that had been made seaworthy after the battle and were now used to supply the compound with food.

"At least one of them," he assured Oba, "could be sailed to Iwo Jima, and from there we could fly to Japan, where you could convince the high command to retake Saipan as quickly as possible."

"How could we take it to sea?" Oba asked, excited by the idea.

"They go to sea every day to supply the compound with fish. I meet them each evening to help unload the catch."

"Aren't they guarded?"

"Each carries an armed sailor," Tsuchiya replied, "but he could easily be overcome. We could capture the boat late in the day, then have all night to sail north without the possibility of being detected. In two days we'd be at Iwo Jima."

For a moment, the prospect filled Oba with hope, and he was tempted to agree. But the reality of the situation kept him from expressing his thoughts. If, in the six months since the invasion, the Imperial Navy had not returned, he would not be able to convince it to do so. Although impressed with the daring of the young warrant officer's scheme, Oba realized it would be futile.

"Let me think about it," he said, knowing the plan could not compete with his responsibility for those in the hills who depended upon him.

Dinner consisted of fish provided by one of the boats Tsuchiya wanted to take north and rice that had been removed from the mountain food caches on which Oba had once depended.

Throughout the evening, Oba, Motoyama, Tsuchiya, and three or four others discussed the war and Japan's prospects for winning it. The large silver planes he had watched landing that morning, he was told, were called B-29s. The Americans claimed they were making daily bombing raids on Japan. Oba fished into his pocket and produced two leaflets with photographs claiming to be of bombed-out portions of Tokyo.

"They're lies!" Tsuchiya said immediately. "There is no airplane that can fly from here to Japan and back without refueling."

Oba thought of the road he had marveled at in July, less than two weeks after the Americans had captured the central portion of the island. But he said nothing. He was there to learn, not to argue or teach.

"Tsuchiya-san is right," Motoyama asserted. "Our navy is busy repelling the Americans on other fronts, and when they are victorious there, they will return to liberate Saipan!"

"That is my reason for being," Oba declared. "My soldiers and I will lead the fight from behind the enemy's lines, and I hope you, too, will disrupt his attempts to defend the island.''

Okuno interrupted with cups of weak, but hot tea, which she replenished several times. While she served, Oba reflected on what he had just said, and realized, with a sudden sadness, that his words expressed more conviction that he felt in his heart.

It was well after dark when Motoyama and Tsuchiya departed. Oba removed his uniform and, in a borrowed *yukata*, went with Okuno-san to the bath, where he washed with real soap for the first time in months.

He tried not to notice Okuno's lithe form as she soaped her body next to him. Several others had selected the same hour for bathing, but they paid no attention to Oba or Okuno-san. The water was tepid but as enjoyable as any in which he had ever bathed. Okuno-san ladled the water over Oba's head and back, giggling as he expressed his pleasure with exaggerated sighs.

Tsuchiya was waiting when they returned.

''They know you're here,'' he said excitedly. ''You've got to leave.''

''How do you know?'' Oba asked.

''I saw several soldiers around the camp office, and Motoyama-san was told to report there immediately.''

Oba spoke quietly to Okuno, and she nodded.

''It's still too early for me to leave,'' he told Tsuchiya. ''Go watch the office, and tell me if they begin to search!''

Okuno, meanwhile, had changed her thin *yakuta* for a blouse and *mampe* and had stepped out into the narrow alley.

Oba looked for his clothing and discovered that someone had washed his uniform and hung it in the curtained-off area to dry. Fairly confident he was not in danger of immediate discovery, he lay down on the futon in the small room and dozed off. For the first time in months he fell asleep without the fear of waking to the sound of an enemy attack.

Still, the touch of a hand on his cheek was enough to awake him. ''It's all right,'' Okuno whispered in the darkness. ''They're not looking for you. They were assembling men to lay a water pipe tomorrow. You can sleep until morning.''

Oba heard the light rustle of cloth as Okuno removed her

yukata, then felt the warmth of her body as she slipped under the light coverlet and pressed herself against him.

Two hours later he gently removed her arm from across his chest and sat up. "What's the matter?" she asked, suddenly awake.

"I must go. I've learned all I can. To remain longer would not only endanger you and the others, but might prevent me from returning."

Okuno nodded, her eyes downcast, and handed him his still damp clothing. Then she produced a small packet containing a razor with honing stone, soap, and medicines and gave it to him.

The moisture in his clothing chilled him slightly as they stepped into the night air. Okuno held open the strands of wire, and he stepped through the fence. "Be careful," she said.

"Thank you." He turned and left the compound. He decided not to take the road leading to the American camp he had taken the previous evening, but walked instead toward the lake. He stopped at an abandoned shack on its shore and removed a loosely hinged door. He dragged it to the edge of the water and tested its buoyancy, then launched it as a raft and eased himself on top. Paddling as if on a surfboard, he directed it toward the far side of the lake, where he hoped there would be fewer of the enemy.

Halfway across the lake, he heard the roar of heavy planes as they raced down the runway of the airfield and lifted into the sky, shooting short streams of burning gas into the darkened void.

Was it true? he wondered. Were they really flying to Japan? If so, how could they penetrate the defenses of the Japanese air force? He counted the planes as they lifted off and had reached forty-four before the airfield became quiet. He paddled on in silence. Soon he encountered the marsh grass of the far shore and carefully edged off the door until his feet touched the soft lake bottom. Pushing his improvised raft ahead of him, he slowly made his way to solid ground.

As he had hoped, there was no sign of the enemy, and he walked unmolested all the way to Takoyama.

• • •

Private Suzuki and a civilian named Taneguchi had spent the morning at their sentry post watching activity in and around Tanapag Harbor, about two kilometers distant. Small landing craft shuttled back and forth between the docks and the twenty-odd ships that rode at anchor outside the harbor. Lines of bulldozers were attacking the huge piles of rubble that had once been the city of Garapan, gradually forcing it into the sea.

Trucks and jeeps created a constant haze of coral dust over the coastal highway, and communities of Quonset huts had sprung up in the past weeks where there had been only jungle.

Far below them and still unseen, two sailors from the S.S. *Sabik,* one of the cargo ships stationed offshore, followed a trail from a Navy rest area into the jungled foothills of Tapotchau. One carried an M-1, and the other a .45 slung low on his hip, the way cowboys wore them in Westerns.

"Hell, we won't find anything here on this main trail, man. We gotta look where nobody else has been," the pistol-packing sailor complained to his friend, a lanky man well over six feet tall.

"Well, shit, we can't just go bustin' through this jungle. Let's go on up till we find some smaller trails."

The two young men approached the observation post of Suzuki and Taneguchi. One of them had found a rusted Japanese army helmet. By the time they had progressed to within two hundred meters of the Japanese who were watching them, the taller sailor was ready to turn back.

"Hey, how much farther you want us to walk? This heat is killing me."

"Aw, c'mon. Just because you found a helmet, you wanna quit. Let's check out that hill over there."

As they began to climb the slope from whose top the two Japanese watched them, Suzuki whispered to Taneguchi to return to Gakeyama and report the sailors' presence. The sentry started down the slope toward a trail that would lead him to the camp. He ran across an open area as the sailors emerged from the trees 150 meters below.

The smaller man pulled his .45 and began firing at the Japanese, who dived for safety at the sound of the first shot.

"I think I got 'em! Come on, let's get some fresh souvenirs!" His friend looked around at the jungle that surrounded them, then, holding his rifle at the ready, moved to join his companion, already several meters ahead.

Taneguchi watched them approach with growing fright. Unarmed and with only a bush for cover, he lay directly in their path. In near panic, he wormed his way backward, keeping the bush between him and the Americans. Then he rose and dashed into the thick of the jungle.

"There he is." The taller American raised his rifle and fired at the civilian, now only a few meters from him. A second shot rang out immediately, and the sailor, with an unbelieving look on his young face, crumpled to the ground.

His friend looked toward the hilltop, sobbing, "Oh, God, no!" He opened fire blindly in the direction of the sentry tower. Suzuki lined him up in the sights of his Sampachi and squeezed the trigger.

Oba had heard the firing and was halfway to the outpost with Kitani and several others when they met Taneguchi. Together they returned to Suzuki's observation post. The bodies of the two Americans lay where they had fallen.

Oba ordered crude stretchers to be made and had the bodies carried back to the main trail near the Navy rest area so as not to attract attention to their observation post. He watched as his men took the sailors' weapons and searched the bodies for additional ammunition.

While trying to fall asleep that night, Oba wondered if any of the unit from the field medical station had survived and were still hiding in the northern part of the island. He decided to revisit the area the following evening.

Suzuki, Kuno, Sano, and Iwata offered to accompany him, but Oba declined. Although all were acquainted with the trails and enemy camps on the southern part of the island, none had been north in more than eight months.

Armed with his pistol and sword, and with a supply of food sufficient for three days packed in his gas mask bag, Oba headed north shortly after nightfall. A full moon provided sufficient illumination for him to move silently. As always, he walked with his pistol in hand, ready to fire. He moved slowly through the unfamiliar valley, avoiding areas he thought might be occupied by Americans. It was too dark to consult his map, so he was never sure of his location except when he crossed the wide road where he and the others had eaten the chicken months ago.

Several minutes after crossing the road, Oba stopped suddenly at the sound of dripping water. Other than the steady drip, no sound could be heard. One measured step at a time, he approached the sound until he could see a shadowy structure three meters high that supported a container two meters long. He could see silver beads of light, reflections of the moon's glow in the water that dripped from the container. Oba examined the structure boldly. He saw a rope hanging from the container. Beneath it was a crude floor with gaps between the boards. Tentatively he pulled the rope, and a stream of water drenched his clothing. Although he had read of Western showers, he had never seen one. Quickly, he scouted a circle around the structure. Satisfied the enemy was not in the immediate vicinity, he removed his clothing, stepped under the container, and smiled as the rope released a stream of water, still warm from the afternoon sun.

Refreshed and re-dressed, Oba followed a narrow road northward from the shower. He moved as cautiously as before, but with a much lighter spirit. Thinking about the shower, he realized it had been a reckless act, but it gave him a sense of heady satisfaction to know he had gotten away with it.

He had gone no more than a hundred meters when the reflection of the moon in three globular objects just off the road stopped him in his tracks. Unmoving, he studied them. He had come to the conclusion that they were watermelons, when one of the objects shifted its position, and he recognized it as an enemy helmet. They were less than ten meters from him but apparently looking in the other direction. Another step, either forward or backward, might attract their attention.

His spirit of audacity had stayed with him since the shower, and he broke into a run, emptying his pistol at the figures as he ran past them, passing within two meters. Suddenly he was laughing, like a boy who had pulled a practical joke.

Bullets cracked by him as he ran, but he was still laughing as he veered off the road into the shelter of the jungle.

He quickly reloaded his pistol and crouched in the undergrowth. After several minutes passed and there was no sign of pursuit, he crossed the road and moved through the jungle away from whatever the three soldiers had been guarding. Occasionally, he chuckled silently.

The luminous hands of his watch stood at midnight when he reached the ridge overlooking the site of his former field hospital. Even in the dim light, he could see nothing remained. There was no sign of the shelter he had used to house his men nor, fortunately, was there any indication of enemy presence.

He descended and walked through the area, making his way toward where he had hidden a spare uniform, his company money, and an extra pistol before setting out to breach the American lines on July 7. The small niche into which he had stuffed his belongings had been discovered by the enemy. The pistol and the money were gone. His uniform, however, had been stuffed back inside, where it had been protected from the sun and frequent rains. He rolled the shirt and trousers as tightly as possible and stuffed them into his gas mask bag with the dried rations he had brought with him.

He rested there until the sky began to lighten, then moved up the valley, passing the door he had used as a desk for his improvised command post, to the hill from which he had seen the approaching tanks. He chose another that offered a view to the north and climbed to its peak.

Except for another new road and some buildings at the base of Marpi Point, the mostly open field that swept upward toward Marpi seemed unchanged. He selected a level spot between two outcroppings of rock, pulled some branches from nearby trees over himself for protection from the sun, and slept.

A chilling rain roused him an hour later, and he moved to the protection of a rocky overhang, where he ate some of his rations and watched the peaceful scene below him. The heavy clouds passed, and once again the sun returned with its oppressive heat.

After studying his map, Oba decided to cross to the east

as far as possible, then angle back toward Tapotchau. He picked his way down the steep eastern face of the hill until he saw a trail which skirted the base and led eastward. Large trees shaded the path, and the damp, soft earth was much easier to walk on than the sharp coral strewn on the trails near Takoyama.

He was suddenly aware of another set of footprints in the soft ground. He knelt to study them and realized they had been made since the rain an hour earlier. The deep, squared indentations of the sole told him they were made by an American shoe, but, he reasoned, Americans did not walk alone in the hills. He followed the footprints.

The tracks turned north on a small trail, which made them more difficult to follow. Oba persisted, stopping frequently to listen. After about two hundred meters he saw movement and stepped quickly into the jungle beside the trail. Oba could see eight Japanese sitting near a hut they had fashioned from bamboo and broad leaves. One tended a fire. He watched them for several minutes from his concealed position. He saw no weapons, but to play safe, he called out, saying, "Hey, I am a Japanese. Hold your fire!"

The startled Japanese stared dumbfounded as Oba stepped into view. The closest had identified Oba's rank insignia and jumped to his feet and saluted.

"I'm Captain Oba of the Eighteenth Regiment. Who are you?" All eight were from the 25th Engineers Regiment and had been hiding in this spot since their headquarters, near Marpi Point, had been overrun.

"Who's in charge?" Oba asked.

A corporal stepped forward and said he had assumed command upon the death of their CO, Lieutenant Yoneya, two weeks earlier. They invited him to join them for lunch, and Oba saw they had a large stock of Japanese rations and some American canned food. Lieutenant Yoneya had ordered them to hide the rations in caves at the time of the invasion, the corporal explained, so they had no immediate worry about food.

Still concerned about the fate of those from his field hospital, Oba questioned them about other survivors in the area. They replied that until his arrival, they had thought themselves the only Japanese on the island. They seemed relatively indifferent to being discovered by the enemy. Between the eight, there were two rifles. They had never needed them, they said, because the Americans never patrolled this part of the island.

Oba considered moving a portion of his group to the area but dismissed the thought because the small and scattered clumps of trees would not provide concealment for a group as large as his.

He remained with the engineers for two days, then returned to Takoyama.

· 13 ·

SURRENDER
OF THE CIVILIANS

Maj. Herman Lewis's fingers drummed nervously on Colonel Pollard's desk as the plans and operations officer read translations of the most recent batch of propaganda leaflets produced by the 2d Division's language section. He had anticipated Pollard's reaction and was prepared for it.

"Herm," the colonel said finally, leaning back in his chair, "you've been dropping crap like this in the hills for the past month. What good has it done? As far as I know, not a single Jap has come down."

"Okay, George, I grant you that the leaflets haven't worked. And you know why? Because they didn't communicate. There was no two-way communication."

"What do you want to do, give 'em a telephone?"

"I'm serious, George. Think about it. How are we going to change somebody's mind without an exchange of thoughts? Now, listen to this. I know how we can communicate with Captain Oba. And maybe get him down."

"Okay, smart guy, tell me."

"I've got two prisoners. One's a soldier who used to know Oba. The other, who speaks some English, was the principal of the middle school in Garapan. He knows him, too, because Oba was quartered at the school last year. The principal recently heard that his two kids, whom he thought were dead, are in Oba's camp. He asked us if he could go up to get them.

"So," Pollard said when Lewis paused to allow him to digest the facts, "How does that get Oba to give up?"

"Both these guys know Japan is losing the war, and they're both willing to go into the hills to find Oba and try to talk him into surrendering. I think it will work." Then, to give an official note to his proposal, he added "Sir."

"Herm, you're a nice guy, but I think you and your D-2 games are full of shit!"

He paused to light a cigar and to give himself time to consider the idea. He took a couple of puffs, then, exhaling a cloud of blue smoke toward the ceiling, said, "But what the hell, nothing else has worked. Let's give it a try!"

Corporal Kunihara was proud that he had served briefly under Captain Oba during the last, hectic days of the campaign. He had been wounded and captured during their attempt to break through the enemy's lines on July 7. In an effort to share the fame that had been built around Oba, Kunihara had told and retold his experiences with the captain, elaborating a little more each time he told the story. Sgt. Sam Buren, the POW compound interpreter, had mentioned the story to Major Lewis during one of his routine visits.

A few hundred meters away, in the more relaxed atmosphere of the civilian compound, Makoto Baba, the thirty-year-old former Garapan middle school principal, sat on a straight chair inside the camp's administration office. He had been called there to await the arrival of a major and hoped it was in response to his plea to be allowed to go into the hills to find his two children Emiko and Akira. A former neighbor, who had recently been captured, had sought him out to tell him that the children were with Captain Oba.

He watched with curiosity as the young lieutenant seated at the desk in the room jumped to his feet and saluted the officer who had entered. He understood the words "good morning," but the rest of their conversation was too rapid for his comprehension. The lieutenant had pointed at him, and the officer had asked several questions while studying him. Baba wondered uncomfortably what they were saying.

The major turned and strode toward Baba, then stood, legs apart and clenched fists on his hips. He stared at the Japanese several seconds before he spoke.

Baba tried to recall the English he had learned in school years ago and steeled himself to understand what the man was about to say. The major was halfway through the sentence before Baba's frantic mind recognized that Lewis was speaking in heavily accented Japanese.

"Who told you your children were with Captain Oba?"

Baba explained. Several times during the subsequent interrogation he had to fight an impulse to smile at the major's simple Japanese. Twice the major turned from him to speak to the young lieutenant, and once Baba heard the word *tomorrow*.

When Lewis had departed, the camp interpreter explained that Baba's request to see his children had been granted. He bowed gratefully to the interpreter and to the lieutenant, then was dismissed from the office.

Early the following day, Baba was taken to a point halfway up the slope of Mount Tapotchau. With him was Corporal Kunihara from the POW compound. An armed guard sat beside him in the vehicle's rear seat. In a second jeep rode the major of the previous day's meeting and another officer.

Before leaving the compound, the major had given him photographs of American planes bombing Japan. He had promised to show them to Captain Oba and try to persuade Oba that it was useless to remain in the hills. The major had explained in his difficult-to-understand Japanese that Oba and his men would be well treated if they surrendered.

They stopped near the edge of a clearing, and the major walked to their jeep. "From here, you two go alone. And remember, if he won't come down, try to get him to meet me under a flag of truce. Tell him I would like to talk to him, man to man." The major spoke slowly so that Baba could understand. He and Pollard watched the two Japanese walk across the clearing and disappear into the jungle.

"Let's keep our fingers crossed," Lewis said as they got back in their jeep.

"Yeah," replied Pollard. "But you know? This is just nutty enough to work."

• • •

A runner hurried toward the camp at Takoyama with word of the two Japanese. He and another sentry had watched them arrive in an American jeep.

Baba and Kunihara pushed straight up the hill toward Tapotchau, skirting the jungle as much as possible. They had gone no farther than three hundred meters when a stern "Halt" froze them in their tracks.

Oba knew, when the runner described the men as spies, that the first inclination of Tanaka's sentries would be to kill them. But spies, he reasoned, would not come halfway up the mountain in an American vehicle. He was curious. They might be killed later, but he wanted to talk to them first.

He called Corporal Kuno and ordered him to return with the runner to where the two strangers were being held. "You stay with the two and bring them to me, but send the runner back ahead with a report of what they have said since their capture."

It was nearly an hour before the runner returned.

"Both men say they know you, sir. One, who claims to be a corporal, says he served under you when you attacked the American lines in July. The other says he was principal of the Garapan middle school and knows you from there. He says he has come to get his two children."

Oba reacted immediately. "Go to the aid station and tell the nurse to report here at once!"

When Aono appeared, Oba told her to take the two children to the civilian camp and to stay with them there until he called for them. "I'm told a man who claims to be their father has come here to take them down. I don't want him to see them until I've talked to him, and I don't want the children to know that he's here." He watched her collect the children and lead them to the other side of the hill.

The two "spies" arrived blindfolded, with their hands bound. They were accompanied by Kuno and a half dozen soldiers. The civilian dropped to his knees and pleaded for his children. "Honorable Captain. We are not spies as your soldiers accuse us. I am here for my children. I have been told they are with you. Please allow them to return with me."

Oba ordered their blindfolds and bonds removed and recognized the man as principal of the school in which he had been billeted during his first three weeks on Saipan. It embarrassed him that the dignified scholar should be groveling on his knees before him.

The other man, who claimed to be a corporal, he did not recognize. The man had saluted and now stood at attention. He was dressed in the blue denim of a POW.

"They were brought to the hills by Americans," Kuno told him. "They should be shot for the spies they are."

"How do you know they are spies?" Oba asked.

"Because they carried enemy propaganda." Kuno produced some American newspapers and copies of the leaflets they had seen for the past several weeks. The soldiers who had gathered around them voiced their agreement.

"Silence!" ordered Oba. "Kuno! Send your men and the rest away. You remain with me and the prisoners! Baba-san! Stand up! Act like a man instead of like a maid-servant! Why did the enemy allow you to come into the hills? Why did this man come with you?"

The man got to his feet. "We are to ask you to come down to the Americans," he stuttered. "They say Japan is losing the war and that you will be well treated."

Oba could feel the hairs rise on the back of his neck. What kind of a Japanese was this, who would side with the enemy to the point where he would ask a soldier of Japan to surrender? Had he come only for his children, Oba would have been inclined to accommodate him. But to ask a soldier of Japan to betray his country . . . He considered turning the man over to the soldiers who demanded his life.

"You, Corporal!" Oba said, turning to Kunihara. "Is what this man said true?"

None of the men at the command post paid any attention as Aono approached and stood beside a tree, listening to the conversation.

"Yes, sir," Kunihara replied. "The Americans asked me to show you photographs of their planes bombing Japan. They say the war will soon be over and that you should end your resistance in the hills."

"You lie!" The high-pitched scream turned everyone's attention to the rushing form of Aono, who lunged at the frightened soldier, sinking her knife into his chest with the momentum of her attack. "You're a lying traitor!" she shouted, and plunged her knife once more into the falling man before Oba could react. Oba was the first to reach her and backhanded her with a blow that lifted her from her feet and sprawled her on the ground.

"You fool!" he shouted. "Call Watanabe-san. Attend to this man!"

Frothy blood bubbled from the corporal's lips. He tried to speak but managed only to cough. Then he lay silent, his eyes pleading for help.

Aono got to her feet and walked forward until she stood over the dying man. Then she turned and walked toward the civilian camp. She stopped Watanabe, who was hurrying to the scene with their almost empty first aid kit. Aono snatched it from his hands. "Don't waste this on him," she hissed. "He's a traitor!"

The medic tried to stem the flow of blood from the man's chest but could do nothing about the internal hemorrhage that was drowning the corporal in his own blood.

Oba ordered his men to bury Kunihara, then tried to explain to Baba that he considered it too dangerous to allow the children to leave the hills. "They're too young to keep our location a secret," he said. "The Americans could trick them into revealing something about this area that would tell them where we are. Our food supply is already short, and eventually we will be forced to send all the civilians down. You may remain here until then."

"Let me see my children first," Baba answered. "Then I will decide."

"I can't do that. It would be unfair to the children if you were to leave. And I warn you that that, too, would be dangerous. Although I can have you escorted to the edge of the jungle, there are men among us who believe you, too, should die and may ambush you before you reach the Americans."

"Tell me at least, how my children are," the man pleaded.

Oba smiled slightly. He sympathized with the man, but he had to place the group's security above all. "They're both fine," he said, and wondered for a moment about the welfare of his own son, Kazohiro, in Gamagōri. "Emiko is learning to be a nurse, and Akira sometimes beats me at *babanuki*. But now"—and he grew serious—"you must make your decision. Will you remain with us, or do you insist upon returning to the civilian compound?"

"I gave my word. . . ."

"All right." Then to Kuno, "Lead him to where you found him. See that he is not harmed."

He knew Baba did not understand the reasons for his decision, but he also knew it would be impossible to convince the man it was better that his children did not know he had come. It would be equally difficult, he knew, to discipline Aono. He sent for her and sat down to wait, pondering the action he should take.

Her usually tightly wrapped hair was loose and hanging to her shoulders when she appeared before Oba. Like a defiant child that knows it is to be chastised, she looked him squarely in the eye. "You sent for me?"

"Sit down."

Her defiant stance was broken by the simple act of sitting, but her high cheekbones remained flushed in preparation of her defense.

Oba indicated the empty sheath that hung from her belt. "Give that to me," he said. "You will no longer carry a knife. I know that you're here because of what the enemy did to your family. But your personal desire for revenge cannot be allowed to endanger the security of the rest, nor to violate the rules under which we must live and fight.

"We'll never know whether the man you killed today was a traitor. If I were certain he was not . . ." and he left the sentence unfinished. "As long as you remain with us, your mission will be to save lives, not to take them."

Aono slipped the sheath from her belt and handed it to Oba. "He was a traitor," she said with finality. "His lies will be proven when we retake the island. I try to keep your soldiers healthy for that day, so they can help destroy Americans. And when that day does come, I will join them, not just as a nurse, but as a soldier."

"And on that day"—Oba glanced at the sheath—"I will return your knife."

• • •

Food was rapidly becoming a major problem. The caches on which they had once relied had been swept clean by the Americans. Fruit in the hills was becoming increasingly difficult to find. And security around the civilian farm had been tightened since the discovery of Second Line camp during the sweep. Oba still sent raiding parties to the farm every few days, but it was becoming more difficult for them to evade the troops who guarded it. Food patrols into enemy camps had become their principal sources of supplies, and the increased number of patrols took its toll in lost lives.

Aono had told Oba that the incidence of skin infections, caused by malnutrition, had risen alarmingly, and that she no longer had the drugs to combat it.

The problems of survival assailed his mind, and Oba was unable to sleep. He rose from his canvas spread under the roots of a banyan tree. He was unsure of what he would do, even as he strapped on his sword and checked his pistol, but he felt the need to do something. He remembered that Nagata had led a farm-raiding patrol earlier in the evening, and for no reason other than a sudden need for activity, walked out of camp in the direction of the farm.

Alone, he followed the familiar trail that skirted the eastern slope of Tapotchau's peak, then dipped into a valley before winding through a pass that led to the former Second Line Camp. A half-moon that passed behind broken clouds faintly illuminated open portions of the footpath, and Oba's sense of caution guided him almost noiselessly through the darker portions of the trail. He walked slowly, alert to signs of the enemy and noises that might indicate an ambush.

Descending into the valley just south of Tapotchau, he stopped and crouched. The silence of the blackness was unbroken, but something inside him warned of danger. A mosquito lighted on his arm. Slowly, without a rustle of clothing, Oba moved his other hand to dislodge the insect. He kept his eyes trained on the valley ahead. He lowered his pistol to rest it on one leg while kneeling on the other and remained motionless for several minutes. Then he arose and backtracked several meters until he found a small path that followed the tree line of the open valley. The detour, he knew, would cost him an additional thirty minutes, but he rarely failed to follow the inexplicable urges to change his route when they raised a red flag of caution within him. Too many of his group, especially civilians, had been cut down at night by bursts of gunfire from a concealed and waiting enemy as they trod the more traveled trails. The night ambushes had taken a much higher toll than the easily spotted day patrols, which were well monitored by sentry posts from the moment they entered the hills. Several times while flanking the valley, Oba stopped in an effort to obtain confirmation of his inner warning, but detected nothing.

When he was within a hundred meters of the former Second Line camp, from where his food patrols usually operated, he turned to his right and moved slowly in a large circle that carried him completely around the camp. He knew that since he could easily avoid detection by sentries at night, the enemy also was capable of surrounding a camp, from where they could wait for dawn to open fire. Circling a camp before entering it had become a habit that, like so many other precautionary actions, had helped him stay alive. Finally he selected a grassy area some hundred meters from the camp and lay down to await the daylight which would permit him to enter safely.

A blast of automatic weapon fire jerked him from near sleep to full awareness. He knew by its sound that it was a Browning. He estimated its position at several hundred meters to the south. The garden, he thought. Although anxious to know what had happened, he was reluctant to move now that his patrol and the enemy were alert and nervous. He settled back in the grass to await the dawn.

Several minutes later, he heard the movement from the direction of the farm. Men were moving stealthily through the undergrowth toward where he lay. He waited, unmoving, to see whether it was Nagata and his patrol or the enemy. He waited until they had passed, then fell in behind them as they followed a trail leading north toward Tapotchau. Soon he was close enough to see by the faint moonlight that they carried bags over their shoulders. "Oi!" he whispered, "Wait up!"

Nagata, who led the four men laden with bags of potatoes and other booty from the garden, walked toward him from the head of the patrol.

"What happened?" Oba demanded.

"They got Ohara-san. He stood up with his bag before he was clear of the garden, and they shot him." Nagata hesitated, then added "I don't think they killed him, because I saw them carry him away."

Oba considered the problem only a moment. Another civilian, who might or might not reveal the location of Takoyama, was in the hands of the enemy. The lives of 120 civilians and about 80 military would be forfeited if he were tricked by the Americans into talking of the camp.

"Let's go!" he ordered. "Immediately!"

Oba followed Nagata and his patrol as it moved single file along the most direct trails to Takoyama. He was so engrossed in his new problem that he failed to exercise his usual caution. He had tripled the population of Takoyama and was cut off, at the same time, from a principal source of food. More and more now, they would have to rely on raids of American supply dumps, increasing the danger of capture and disclosure. He had decided on the only viable course of action by the time they reached Takoyama.

"Tell Oshiro to report to me immediately," he instructed Kitani. "You come back here with him."

"Tomorrow morning," he told the two men when they arrived, "Oshiro-san will lead all civilians out of the mountains to join the other civilians at Susupe. You will carry a white flag and will make every effort to see that there is no shooting and no casualties. All civilians will join you."

Oshiro, who had been a strong leader and a better fighter than many of Oba's soldiers, understood without being told the reasons for the exodus. He simply bowed slightly and said, "Yes, sir."

While Oshiro relayed the order to the civilian camp, Oba walked to the aid station. Aono was talking to the two children.

"We don't want to go!" they said almost in unison when they saw Oba approaching. Young Akira ran to where he stood. "I'm almost old enough to be a soldier. Please make me a soldier so I can stay."

Oba tousled the boy's unkempt hair, then sat near Aono

and Emiko, who watched him expectantly. "There's someone else who wants to see you," he said to the children, who had long since accepted the fact that their parents had been killed during the invasion. "Your father is at the compound, and he is waiting for you to join him."

The smiles and excited reaction of both children assured him that another problem had been solved. Aono waited until the children were occupied in their discussion of the news, then said, "I'm told that I am to leave with the others, Captain. I would prefer to remain where I can be of assistance. I have no desire to become a prisoner."

Oba looked for a long moment at this woman who had proved to be as brave as any of his soldiers. She was, after all, the only person of his command who had the medical knowledge they required.

"I won't go!" Aono said bluntly. "I'll kill myself first."

Oba knew she spoke the truth. His decision was not difficult. "It's not a matter of surrendering," he replied. "It's a matter of survival. You may stay because we will need the help that you can give us."

The 120-odd civilians, accompanied by several soldiers, began their march with the first light of day. Some of the elderly sick were carried by Oba's men. The trails were clear of enemy activity, and the group moved as rapidly as possible until they had reached a point just north of the farm area, where Oba ordered a halt.

Oshiro fastened a borrowed white chemise to a branch hacked from a tree, then, with two others, walked to the garden and stepped into the open. The three stood for a full minute waiting to be challenged or shot at. Then, with a backward glance and a nod to Oba and Kitani, who watched from the jungle's edge, they walked straight toward the road several hundred meters away. Their white flag could be seen long after the three men had diminished in size to unrecognizable figures.

A truck stopped as they approached the road, then a jeep, followed by several other vehicles that braked to a stop to gape at the three Japanese and their strange white flag. With his binoculars, Oba watched a crowd of American soldiers surround the civilians, then saw the three Japanese board a vehicle which sped away.

"They're taking them away," Kitani said as he saw the flag disappear into one of the jeeps. "What do we do about the rest?"

"We'll just have to wait and see. How many men did we bring with us?"

"About fifteen."

"Post them around the camp. Have them report immediately on any enemy troop movement. Then return here."

Oba had been lying just inside the jungle line for nearly thirty minutes, when Kitani returned. They watched the road below them and occasionally Oba scanned the surrounding terrain with his binoculars. A small caravan of jeeps commanded his attention as it pulled to the side of the road near where he had last seen Oshiro. He smiled as he saw the tall civilian, still holding the white chemise, climb from one of the jeeps. "They're back," he said to Kitani without taking his eyes from the glasses.

Within moments, a small detachment of uniformed Americans, with Oshiro in their midst, started up the hill toward the garden. About half the Americans carried rifles, but most had them slung over their shoulders rather than in combat-ready positions.

Oba continued to study them until they reached the far side of the garden, about two hundred meters distant. There they stopped, conferred briefly, and remained, while Oshiro, still holding his flag, walked alone.

"Keep watching the Americans," Oba said as he handed his glasses to Kitani. He waited until Oshiro entered the jungle and could no longer be seen by the enemy before intercepting him.

"What happened?" he demanded.

"They've ordered trucks to carry us to the compound," Oshiro said, smiling. "I told them we would be at the road in thirty minutes."

Oba walked to where the civilians stood. He was tense with fear of what would happen to them once they fell into enemy hands, but the fear was tempered with a tinge of relief that their long ordeal in the hills was about to end. The eyes of every man and woman in the group followed him as he walked to the edge of the assembly.

"My friends," he said in a soft and emotionless voice that barely traveled to those on the far side of the group. "Arrangements have been made to transport you to the compound in which some fourteen thousand of your former neighbors and friends—and possibly family members—are living. Your departure from the hills, where you have honorably resisted the efforts of the enemy to kill or capture you, is a sad event for all of us. I hope your country will remember your determination to live as unconquered Japanese. I know that I will not only remember you, but always be proud to have been part of your resistance. You all know of the conditions that have forced us to request your transfer to the compound at Susupe. You are not surrendering. You are making it possible for us, those who have sworn to uphold the honor of Japan until victory or death, to continue our resistance until our forces return to liberate Saipan from the enemy. Our ability to do this will rest in your hands. The Americans will try to trick you into talking about the number of soldiers still in the hills or about our location. You are to tell them you know of no soldiers in the hills"—he paused to allow this statement to be well understood—"and you are to tell them you do not know the location of the camp in which you have been living. Our lives"—and he paused again—"depend upon your secrecy."

Again he paused while his eyes scanned the attentive faces before him. Then, slowly, he bowed from the waist. "I salute you."

The men, as one, returned the bow, while the women dropped to their knees, lowering their heads to their hands, flat on the ground before them. A gentle murmuring of gratitude arose.

"Oshiro-san, please lead them to the road," he said to the civilian leader.

Oba watched as the long line re-formed and the men, women, and children he had helped keep alive for nine months ended an unforgettable chapter of their lives.

"Captain-san." Oba looked down at the soprano-voiced

source of the words. Akira Baba, barefoot as usual but seemingly taller than a day earlier, formally bowed and said, "Thank you, very much." Oba straightened his own back and, in an equally formal manner, returned the bow.

"Remember me to your father."

· 14 ·

THE FINAL ROUND

After the civilian exodus, three days of heavy rains dampened the spirits of Oba and his men as well as the jungle.
The sudden absence of the civilians—especially for those who
had made romantic attachments—left the camp with an air of
loneliness. Sergeant Kitani alone was undisturbed by the
evacuation, because the woman he loved—albeit without much
hope of its being requited—remained in the camp.

Even Horiuchi and his followers joined the men as they
huddled under makeshift shelters to ward off the rain. He
complained about the steady downpour, because it kept the
enemy out of the hills and prevented him from increasing the
number of Americans who fell before his bullets. He claimed
thirty-seven so far, sixty-three short of his goal, but swore he
would not die until he reached it.

They ate well during the three days because the civilians
had presented their hoarded food before leaving. Some had
even produced small bags of rice which Oba had thought long
exhausted.

The hot rice with *tsukemono*, dried fish, and some canned
American C rations, filled Oba, Kitani, and the others with
an inner warmth despite the chilling rain that had fallen most
of the day. Gradually clearing skies promised an end to the
storm. One of the men produced a small bottle of *yashizake*,

made from the fermented juice of a fruit that grew in the jungle.

Emboldened by the mildly alcoholic drink they shared, Kitani prepared a plate of leftovers and walked to where Aono was preparing a less elaborate meal near her now deserted aid station. The absence of a steady stream of civilian patients, added to the loss of the two Baba children, had created a void difficult to overcome. For weeks she had been busy with her responsibilities as a nurse. At times, she had almost forgotten her reason for remaining in the hills. Now, the only woman among seventy-two men, she kept to herself and refused to eat or socialize with the soldiers.

Kitani's usual fluid, slightly rolling gait was suddenly awkward and stilted as he carried the tin dish toward Aono's aid station.

"This was left over," he said with unusual gruffness. "It's for you."

"Thank you. You are very kind." Aono bowed slightly as she accepted the dish.

Kitani waited for an invitation to join her, but Aono returned her attention to the pot she stirred over a small fire. To hide his embarrassment, Kitani coughed. "I think I'm getting a cold. Do you have anything for it?"

Aono laid aside the stick she had been using to stir, rummaged in a canvas bag, and produced two small white pills. "These are only aspirin, but perhaps they'll help." She handed them to the embarrassed noncom, then turned back to her pot.

"Thank you." Kitani hesitated a moment more, then turned and walked back to the command post.

Horiuchi, who lounged under a shelter of American ponchos strung between trees, smiled in contempt as he watched the rebuff. He was too far away to hear the exchange of words, but Kitani's apparent uneasiness and his abrupt dismissal by the nurse left no doubt of her message.

The fourth morning brought clear skies and a searing sun that quickly dried the sodden jungle. Oba ordered the men to get ready to move out. He was concerned that one of the civilians might have inadvertently disclosed the location of their camp, and wanted to move all his men to a new site before the enemy might react. He had selected Gakeyama as the most desirable location. The enemy had frequently patrolled that area for a month following their escape through the American sweep in November, but there had been no activity there since.

He called Captain Jimpuku and Lieutenant Nagata to explain his reasons for the move to Gakeyama. "Now that we no longer have civilians to protect, we will reform into three units. Two will go to Gakeyama, and the third, under Lieutenant Nagata, to a ridge overlooking the former camp at Second Line."

The two officers exchanged glances at the mention of Gakeyama. "Isn't that dangerous?" Nagata asked. "We were almost trapped there."

"That was at the base of the hill in a ravine," Oba interrupted. "Our campsite will be at the top, and the ravines will provide separate avenues of escape in case of emergency." He and Kitani had scouted the hill the previous week when he had decided to make the move.

"We can evade the enemy in any one of three directions," he continued. "There are numerous trails leading in this direction, east to Tapotchau, and west toward Flame Tree Hill." He pointed to the landmarks on his map as he spoke. "Get the men ready to move in an hour."

Oba packed his few belongings in a knapsack. Within the folds of his spare uniform he placed the dried thumb of Lieutenant Banno. On top of that he packed his maps and sketches showing enemy installations. Placing his second pistol uppermost in the pack, Oba was ready, by midday, to begin the one-kilometer walk to Gakeyama.

He turned to observe the final preparations of his men and saw Aono hurrying toward him. "Captain, Chiba is gone. He's not in the cave."

"Well, find him! He can't have gone far. Kitani," he called to the sergeant who had watched the nurse's arrival, "go with Aono and find that young fool Chiba!"

"Why did he pick this time to disappear?" Aono asked as they looked for some sign of him around the cave. "I'm sure his skull was fractured, and walking around now could kill him.''

''I don't think he wanted to be found,'' Kitani replied. ''I think he's decided he would rather die than be carried to Gakeyama. And maybe he is right.''

They spent as much time as possible searching the abandoned civilian camp area and the fringes of the adjacent jungle before returning to the others.

Nagata and his twenty-one-man platoon took a separate trail to the south. With Horiuchi and his two friends, Oba's contingent consisted of fifty-one men and Aono. Horiuchi, his machine gun hanging by its sling from his shoulders, followed ten meters behind the others, as if to make it clear he was not really a member of the force.

They were no more than five hundred meters from camp when Takoyama seemed to explode in a series of blasts that sent clouds of smoke billowing into the air. A barrage of mortars rained on their campsite, hurling jagged hunks of hot shrapnel into the banyan trees under which they had lived for four months. They had escaped by only a few minutes.

Kitani, who was usually the last man of any patrol, as Oba was the first, walked forward to where Aono watched the bombardment with wide-eyed shock. ''It was his choice,'' he said. ''It was what he wanted.''*

Aono nodded, then turned away. Kitani returned to his position at the end of the line.

One of the civilians, either out of treachery or by being tricked, had pinpointed their camp for the Americans. The civilians were gone now, but the danger still existed that one of his own men, if wounded or captured, could reveal their locations. True to their training, his men would prefer death to being taken prisoner. And since surrender was out of the question, any instruction in what to say and what to conceal in the event of capture had not been part of their training. Furthermore, the family of a captured Japanese soldier would

*Author's note: Chiba was captured after returning to his cave. He was sent to the United States, where he was hospitalized for nearly a year, then spent another year working as a cook at a military base. He now lives in Tokyo.

onsider him dead, as would the rest of society, eliminating
ny hope of his ever returning to Japan. In this traumatic
tate, Japanese soldiers, Oba knew, were frequently willing
o divulge any information their captors desired.

Oba considered these facts as they wound their way through
ne jungle toward Gakeyama. His thoughts detracted little
rom the caution that had become second nature. As usual,
e walked at the head of the group, his pistol in hand. They
ollowed the most direct trail, hoping the enemy would wait
full day before sending up a patrol after the rain.

Jack Grince, the twenty-seven-year-old captain who com-
nanded King Company, 3d Battalion of the 2d Regiment,
vas on his first patrol. Until a month earlier, he had been the
xecutive officer of the Marine Corps training depot in San
Diego, California. He had had every reason to believe that if
e stayed out of trouble, he would spend the rest of the war
nere. His transfer orders to the 2d Regiment had come as a
hock. He had arrived on Saipan just a week earlier and had
aken over K Company three days later.

The first Japanese he had ever seen were those tending a
vegetable farm that his company had passed through as they
tarted their patrol an hour earlier. He had been unimpressed.
f those stunted, bowlegged creatures were an example of the
nemy, he had thought, they could be no match for American
Marines.

His orders were to scout the area immediately south of
Tapotchau for signs of enemy activity and to capture or kill
ny enemy he encountered.

Things had not gone well during the first hour. He had
een surprised at the oppressive heat. With the rains of the
ast few days, a thick slime had grown on the rocks and
otted vegetation of the jungle. To his embarrassment, he had
lipped and fallen twice. He had ordered the company to
dvance on a platoon-wide front but soon discovered that the
olling green foliage he had seen from a distance concealed
reacherous cliffs, ravines, and areas of impenetrable jungle
hat made this impossible. He had been forced to settle for a
ingle file column that followed a narrow trail northward.

More experienced officers of the regiment had told him the

patrol would probably be no more than a conditioning exer
cise, because they had not encountered an armed Japanese i
the hills for several weeks. Grince had hoped they wer
wrong. As long as he had been transferred to a combat unit
he thought, he might as well become a hero. He hoped tha
somehow, something would happen on his first patrol tha
would be the talk of the division and maybe even earn him
medal.

His three-man point maintained a lead of fifty yards ove
the next element of the company. Although the book calle
for him to keep at least one platoon in advance of his com
mand post, Grince was with the lead platoon. His radioma
was tuned to the frequency used by the other platoons, bu
so far, there had been no reason for any of them to transmit

Two hundred meters to the east of King Company, a lon
line of the enemy Grince considered no match for the Amer
icans was strung out on a parallel course. At an intersectin
trail, Oba checked his map, then gave a hand signal that the
were to turn west toward Gakeyama. The trail he had selecte
cut through a clearing at the base of a steep hill whose side
became more and more precipitous until they formed a ver
tical cliff of exposed volcanic rock.

Another half kilometer, he thought, and they could begi
setting up their primary defenses at the rugged top of Gake
yama. He passed a small ravine on their right which divide
the jungle-covered hill and the cliff. Directly behind him
some thirty men followed the same trail, with Jimpuku an
the rest of the soldiers behind them. Horiuchi and his tw
friends continued to trail several meters behind the last o
Jimpuku's men.

The first of Captain Grince's three point men pushe
through a clump of undergrowth and dropped to the ground
The two men behind him, although they had seen nothing
followed suit. The first man pointed toward the base of a cli
to his left and whispered, "Something moved over there.
think someone just walked . . ."

He did not finish. To his right, Japanese soldiers entere
the small clearing he could see from his concealed position.

All three men opened fire and continued pouring bullets
into the seven or eight men they could see, as rapidly as their
M-1 rifles would explode and throw new rounds into the
weapons' chambers. Fortunately for the last two Japanese, all
three Americans concentrated their fire on the first five men
in line. The last two, who were just entering the enemy's
view, were able to duck out of sight while American bullets
struck down their comrades.

Captain Grince and the first platoon that accompanied him
hit the ground in unison. Grince waved to a white-faced corporal lying near him. "Take your men and see what the hell
is going on! Everyone else hold your position!" The squad
leader and a dozen soldiers began inching their way forward,
using their elbows to propel their bodies over the rotten undergrowth.

To another corporal, he ordered: "Tell Second Platoon to
move up on our left and Third Platoon to the right. Then have
Fourth Platoon join us here." The corporal ran to the rear to
convey the orders.

An increase in the volume of fire told him the squads he
had sent forward had found targets. Enemy bullets began to
rip through the foliage above him, accompanied by the high-
pitched crack of the .25-caliber missiles. Most of the enemy
fire came from their right.

"All right, let's go!" he shouted to the remainder of 1st
Platoon, hearing his voice as though the words were spoken
by another. It was against all his principles of self-preserva-
tion to be leading men directly into enemy fire. "But keep
your asses down!" he added, still in the voice of another.
Hugging the ground to stay below the cracking death above
him, he began elbowing his way to his right, toward an enemy he was unable to see.

From his left, he heard the reports of rifles of 2d Platoon,
followed by the explosions of hand grenades. Fear began to
form a knot in his chest, and he was aware that he was breathing rapidly through his mouth. There were shouted orders
from somewhere, and he wished he could understand, or at
least recognize, the voice. It wasn't fair, he thought in growing panic, to be forced to fight like this with men he hadn't
had time to get to know.

The shouts had come from a young lieutenant who commanded the 2d Platoon. He had been ordering his men to spread out and fire on a group of Japanese who had taken cover at the base of a rocky cliff twenty meters to their front. The enemy was unable to move from their concealed positions behind the jumble of rocks that had fallen from the cliff, and he knew it was only a matter of time until they would be annihilated. He lobbed one of his three grenades toward the cliff, then ducked until he heard it explode.

Grince estimated he and those with him had advanced about eight meters. The sound of enemy rifles was closer, but the dense undergrowth prevented him from seeing anything farther than a few yards away.

Captain Jimpuku's body had been thrown against a rock by the impact of American bullets. The left side of his neck had been blown away, and his head hung in a grotesque, unnatural way on his right shoulder. Near him lay the bodies of four others, either crumpled or sprawled in unmistakable positions of violent death. The survivors of his platoon had sought the protection of rocks, tree trunks, or any rise in the ground, from which some returned the fire of a growing number of enemy. Gradually, those who were unable to see the Americans began to move back along the trail.

"Fools!" They heard the snarling voice of Horiuchi. "This way, quickly!" The tattooed renegade, his blue arms pointing his machine gun at them, motioned for them to move into the jungle. Relieved to have someone to tell them what to do, seven or eight men followed Horiuchi into the jungle, then swung to their right, directly toward the sound of enemy weapons.

Horiuchi did not bother to conceal their advance. He pushed through the entangling vines as rapidly as possible, heedless of the noise he and the others made. An instinctive fighter, the former *yakuza* moved to flank his opponents while their attention was directed at those trapped on the trail.

Suddenly he saw seven or eight Americans crawling through the jungle on their stomachs toward the trail. Not one looked in his direction. He opened fire, automatically counting the bodies into which the bullets of his light machine gun thudded.

Capt. Jack Grince heard the first burst of a machine gun and rolled on his left side to see a man with strange blue-colored arms standing five meters away, grinning savagely as the machine gun that hung from his neck spit death at him and his men. It was the last impression Grince's mind recorded before he changed from a human being into a statistic of war.

"Oh God, the captain's . . . I'm hit!" a fear-filled voice screamed directly behind the captain's body. Others turned to shoot the apparition that was killing them with methodical bursts of fire. Some, mesmerized by the sadistic grin and tattooed arms, simply held out their hands in an unthinking effort to deflect the bullets.

There were no Americans left to kill when those following Horiuchi reached him. They heard him say "forty-five," then grunt, "Let's go!"

Capt. Sakae Oba, twenty-nine-year-old veteran of Japanese victories in Manchuria and China, lay flat behind a pile of loose rocks and cursed his stupidity. He had led his entire force into a death trap. Behind them, a sheer wall of rock held them at the mercy of the enemy. Escape along the trail was impossible. He fired through an opening in the rocks at the muzzle blasts of enemy weapons until his pistol was empty, then tried to pull out his spare pistol without exposing himself to the bullets that chipped the rock in front of him.

To his left, Sano lay in a pool of blood. The top of his head had been blown away. His rifle lay on the trail in front of him. Oba could not see farther down the trail.

Am I alone? he wondered. He could see no others. Lying on his side, he groped at his pack until his hand closed on the second pistol and a small bag of loose ammunition. Hurriedly, he loaded the gun, then gathered his legs under him to spring forward. He did not think about dying, only about firing as many of the bullets as possible into the enemy. Blood dripped from one hand; he had cut it on the sharp rocks.

The high staccato of a Nambu light machine gun stopped his forward movement. Horiuchi was still alive!

The young lieutenant of 2d Platoon heard the machine-gun fire from his right rear and recognized the bark of a Nambu. "They're coming in from behind us," he shouted. "Stop 'em!" His men shifted positions to meet the new threat. Some began firing into the almost solid wall of green in the direction of the machine gun. When a rifle-bearing Japanese soldier suddenly appeared only a few yards away, twenty rifles and a BAR almost shredded his body before it hit the ground.

Oba sensed what had happened. He rose to his feet, a pistol in each hand, still undecided. He looked to his left and, from his elevated position, could see several faces watching him from behind other piles of rocks. He waved a pistol in a sign for them to join him and was surprised to see men appear from hiding places all along the base of the cliff. He stooped to pick up Sano's rifle, then turned and began trotting along the trail away from the momentarily distracted enemy.

The heavy automatic fire of BARs reverberated through the jungle with the reports of M-1 rifles as the 3d and 4th platoons advanced to join the battle. They surprised the small group of Japanese who had been firing on the 2d Platoon and killed three before the others withdrew toward the hill. The Americans advanced in short one-man rushes that were covered by the fire of those around them. Their progress was stopped eventually by an open area at the base of the hill. Enemy fire was being directed from the narrow ravine that separated the jungled portion of the hill from a steep cliff of rock.

"Keep firing at the upper end of that ravine!" a sergeant yelled at a machine-gun squad that had set up an air-cooled .30-caliber weapon at the edge of the clearing. "Keep 'em bottled up!"

The two American squads were restricted in their movement by the light Japanese machine gun firing from a well-protected position halfway up the right side of the ravine.

''Get that sonofabitch with the machine gun,'' someone yelled.

''Miller! Take your squad up the reverse side of that slope and get that bastard!'' another voice shouted.

For ten minutes the Americans remained behind protective cover as the machine gunner fired short bursts at their slightest movement. Enemy rifle fire had ceased, and the Americans waited long minutes for the squad to get above the machine-gun position.

A small cloud of smoke accompanied the explosion of a hand grenade and marked a black spot on the side of the ravine. Sixty seconds passed without a sound from the ravine. A few Americans rose cautiously to their feet and began to advance. A burst of machine-gun fire sent them diving for cover.

Another grenade exploded, throwing ricocheting shrapnel among the Americans, who instinctively lowered their heads. They raised their eyes to behold a sight none would ever forget: a bloodied figure, with one of his strange blue arms hanging at his side, stepped into the open. Balancing a machine gun on a looping vine, the man fired randomly with his good arm at the jungle below him.

Weapons in the hands of more than twenty Americans poured bullets into the tattooed figure. The man fell backward with his weapon caught on the vine, his finger frozen on the trigger. The gun's bullets continued to spew into the air long after the man was dead.

Oba ordered Corporal Kuno to escort the survivors to the top of Gakeyama. He and Kitani then circled the hill in front of which they had been trapped and climbed to its crest. Shielded by the dense jungle above the cliff, they descended to where they could overlook the scene of the attack.

Americans were walking upright, examining and searching the bodies of Japanese dead. Oba's stomach churned with hatred as he saw two Americans drag a body from the ravine by its feet, then call to others who gathered to gape at it. A bloodied shirt had been partially blown off, revealing a torso covered with artistic tattoos. Shaking with anger, Oba pulled his pistol and emptied it at the crowd around Horiuchi's body.

The Americans had not even begun to answer his futile attack with their own barrage of bullets when Oba slumped to the ground. He made no effort to resist the overwhelming sense of disaster and shame that drained him of all will to continue. It was over. He had lost. Japan had lost. Even the seemingly invincible Horiuchi had lost.

Awareness returned with Kitani's voice. "Sir, are you all right?"

He got to his feet. "Yes, I'm all right. Let's go."

Neither man spoke as Oba and Kitani followed the trail to Gakeyama and climbed the steep slope of the hill. They walked several meters apart, because neither wanted to start a path that would indicate the group's presence.

Aono was among the first to greet them in the natural fortress Oba had discovered near the hill's crest. He allowed her to dab a damp cloth on his cut hand but waved her off when she attempted to apply a disinfectant.

"Save that for those who will need it," he said, brushing her aside. "Go find Corporal Kuno and tell him to come here!"

"How many men did we lose?" he asked the corporal.

"Counting us and Nagato's people, who were not discovered, there are fifty-seven. Eighteen are missing."

"I counted eleven bodies from the top of the cliff. Captain Jimpuku was among them." Oba did not trust himself to talk about Horiuchi.

Three of those who returned had been wounded, two by bullets and one by hand grenade fragments. Oba walked to where Aono and Watanabe were treating them and asked about their condition.

"If we can prevent infection, they'll survive," Aono predicted. "But we need more medicine."

Oba nodded and walked dejectedly away. He still blamed himself for leading the force into the most disastrous attack they had suffered. And if it hadn't been for the nonsoldier, Horiuchi, none would have survived.

How long can we last? he wondered. Two months ago we were one hundred and fifty; now we are a little more than a third of that figure. The Americans know we're still here, and they won't quit until they've killed us all. Is it better to stay on the defense and die a little at a time, or should we stage a final attack that could avenge the deaths of our friends? Perhaps, he thought, they could carry out a well-planned attack in the name of the tattooed *yakuza* to whom they owed their lives, and take the rest of the American lives he would have needed to reach his goal of one hundred.

Distant explosions interrupted his thoughts, and he recognized them as mortars falling near the hill of the attack. At least they still think we're in the area, he realized with relief. Perhaps we'll have time to reorganize.

Six more men reached Gakeyama the following morning. Two were severely wounded, one in the mortar attack Oba had heard the previous afternoon.

The despondency and self-recrimination that had overtaken Oba immediately after the attack gave way to a new determination in the morning. We still have more than half a hundred fighting men, most of whom now have weapons, he reasoned. We met the enemy in a battle heavily tipped in their favor, yet probably caused as many casualties among them as we suffered. He admitted only to himself, however, that their most valuable fighter had died in the effort.

He busied himself reorganizing his sentry system, establishing defenses around the camp, sending details of men to Takoyama to retrieve food and supplies hidden before their departure, and scouting the enemy camps on the coastal plain to the west of Gakeyama.

The hill was topped by a ragged ridge of volcanic rock towering a hundred meters above its rounded dome. It was within a fissure of this ridge, a few meters above the jungle, that he established his camp. Large breadfruit trees in the thirty-meter-wide space between the rock walls concealed them from the air, and caves in the walls provided protection from the elements.

The steep ravines that cut into the eastern side of the hill made an attack from this direction unlikely and offered several emergency escape routes.

Enemy patrols had been increased immediately after the battle in which Captain Jimpuku and his platoon had been killed, but they were restricted to areas near Second Line,

Tapotchau, and Takoyama camps, all of which had been discovered by the Americans.

Three days after the battle, Warrant Officer Tsuchiya walked
into camp.

"What are you doing here?" Oba demanded.

"The civilians told me you were running short of food,"
he said as he slipped a bag containing rice and canned crab-
meat off his shoulder. "Then, yesterday, I heard from an
American that most of you had been killed. I've come to
help."

"The food we can use, but you can serve us better from
the compound. How did you get out?"

"They've replaced the American guards with Chamorros,"
the slightly built warrant officer replied with a smile. "They're
not too vigilant."

"But how did you find us?"

"The bodies of your men are still where they fell. When I
saw blood stains leading in this direction, I knew this was the
most likely place."

"You seem to know these hills pretty well," Oba observed.

"I should. We trained here for six months prior to the
invasion, keeping track of civilians and the Chamorros."

"What's happening with the war?" Oba unconsciously held
his breath while awaiting the reply.

"The Americans say they've captured Iwo Jima."

"I was afraid of that. Our planes have not attacked the
airfield here in over a month."

The knowledge that still another Japanese bastion had fallen
to the enemy was less shocking to Oba than he had expected.
He willfully closed his mind to the reason for his lack of
surprise.

"Stay here until nightfall, then return to the compound.
We'll remain here as long as possible, in case you have reason to contact us again."

Tsuchiya bowed, took a step backward, then walked to a
small lean-to where Aono was kneeling beside a man who
moaned deliriously. He ignored the stench that arose from
the man's swollen and green-colored lower leg and watched
as the nurse rinsed a cloth in a pan of water and laid it carefully over the infected limb.

"Can you save it?" he asked softly.

She shook her head. "In a hospital, maybe. But here . . ." She turned away. Tsuchiya laid a hand on her shoulder, then looked up as Oba approached.

"How is he?" Oba asked.

"He's dying. Just like Kojima-san and Onegawa-san died." She turned and cast a scathing look at Oba. "He's dying, not as a soldier, but as a . . . a . . ." and she fell silent. She fought to subdue a sob that had risen to her throat. When she had regained control, she said, "He was a good soldier. He would have been happy to die fighting the enemy. Instead, he dies like this because we don't have the medicine to save him."

Oba studied the defiant eyes of the girl a moment, then turned and strode toward the main camp. He hesitated at the infirmary area and briefly inspected the pitifully small collection of medicine that Aono and Watanabe kept in a canvas bag. Most of the bottles were empty.

Later, while most of the group slept to escape the afternoon sun, Oba asked Tanaka to send Kitani, Watanabe, and two others to his cave.

"Two men have died of gangrene in the past week, and Hayashi-san is about to die. We must have medicine to prevent more deaths like these," he told the four men when they had assembled. "Without it," he continued, "wounds that could be treated and healed within days, eventually will destroy us." He looked at each of them and, satisfied they understood the gravity of the situation, went on. "I want the four of you to go to the large hospital at the base of the mountain tonight and come back with the medicines we need."

"But how will we know what to get?" Kitani asked.

"Watanabe will know. Your greatest problem will be in locating the pharmacy and getting inside it."

"It is probably near the entrance," Watanabe volunteered. "Somewhere convenient to outpatients with prescriptions."

"Is there any drug that could save Hayashi-san?"

"There are medicines that could ease his pain," the medic replied, "but nothing that could save him."

Oba stared for a moment at the jungle outside the cave

entrance, then, nodding his head as the decision was made, said, "All right. You will go tonight. Carry empty backpacks and bring them back full!"

Watanabe sat outside the infirmary, writing in a small notebook, glancing inside occasionally to help recall the medicines they needed. At last he called Aono, asking her to check the list and to add any drugs he might have forgotten.

"Don't forget bandages and cotton," she said after checking the list. "The medicines won't help much unless we can dress the wounds and protect them from the flies." She returned to sit beside Hayashi.

Shortly before midnight, Oba spoke quietly to Kitani, Watanabe, and the two men who were to accompany them on the raid. Three carried Sampachi rifles, while Kitani, in addition to an extra canvas bag hanging from his left shoulder, had an American BAR slung on his right.

"You all know how important this mission is to our survival," Oba told them. "So be careful." He watched as they disappeared in the darkness. He arose and headed toward the path that led to his cave in the cliff, passing within a few yards of the infirmary.

Aono lay inside the structure, and her eyes followed the dark figure who made his way out of camp. The faint glow of a three-quarter moon filtered through the trees and allowed her to follow Oba's movements until he had walked from the clearing into his cave.

She waited a full minute before quietly getting to her feet, then started out in the direction Kitani and the others had taken. Once well away from the camp, she quickened her pace, trying to keep her balance as loose stones and rocks caused her to slip on the steep decline.

Ahead of her, walking more cautiously and slowly, Kitani and his small group followed a trail that would bring them to the edge of the jungle overlooking the U.S. Army 442d Field Hospital. The moon provided sufficient light to walk easily in open areas, but the three following Kitani had to rely on the sound of the man ahead to make their way through the more heavily jungled portions of the trail. Occasionally they stopped to listen for sounds of a possible enemy patrol.

The noise of a rolling stone somewhere behind them caused

all four to drop silently to the ground and turn their weapons to the rear. A few seconds later they heard more rolling stones followed by the sound of a body striking the ground and an exclamation: "Damn!"

"Who's there?" Kitani whispered loudly.

"It's me, Aono," she replied from the darkness.

The four listened as Aono made her way toward them. "What are you doing? Why are you here?" Kitani whispered when she had arrived in their midst.

"I'm going with you," she replied in a firm voice.

"Fool! You're not going anywhere. Return to camp!"

"No, I can help. I know which medicines we need. You may need me."

Before Kitani could reply, Aono placed her hand on his arm and, in a much softer tone, said, "Please, let me go with you. I won't be any trouble."

The hand on his arm sent a tremor through Kitani's body. Gruffly, he jerked his arm away and said, "All right, but stay directly behind me, and be quiet!" Then he turned and led the party toward the lights of the hospital.

Pfc. Walter Moldafsky was opposed to walking sentry duty but felt that if he had to do it, this was the best post to have. The nurses' quarters were just inside the perimeter fence, and he was high enough to see directly into the windows of either the first or second floors. At this moment, he was absorbed in watching a shapely nurse, who had returned to her quarters a few minutes earlier, prepare for a shower. His fingers were locked in the mesh of the three-meter fence, his rifle propped against it beside him.

The five Japanese also watched. But their eyes were on Moldafsky, not on the disrobed nurse. A silence of several minutes was eventually broken when the lights in the woman's room were snapped off and Moldafsky muttered, "Shit," picked up his rifle, and continued his patrol.

When he had rounded a corner and was well out of sight, Kitani handed Watanabe's rifle to Aono and in a low voice said, "Don't move from here, don't make a sound, and don't use this unless we need help!"

Silently, the four men made their way to the grassy area

that extended about five meters on their side of the fence. The others remained there while Kitani snaked forward on his stomach, then rolled on his side and removed a pair of wire clippers attached to his belt. Wrapping a cloth around the clippers and the lower strands of the fence, he quickly opened a panel through which they could enter. Security lights on the living quarters enabled the others to see his signal for them to join him.

Minutes later, all four crept in the shadows of the buildings toward the compound entrance. Twice they crawled behind shrubbery when they heard voices approaching, and waited until the Americans had passed.

"There it is," Watanabe whispered as they reached an intersection of walkways. A single bulb protected by a metal hood illuminated the word PHARMACY above the door of a building directly in front of them. "Stay with me," Kitani whispered and began crawling at a right angle to the building. Ten minutes later, they were at the unlighted rear entrance of the pharmacy. Using the crowbar that had gained him entrance to other locked American buildings, Kitani began to loosen the hasp that secured a large padlock to the door. The protesting nails squeaked loudly as they were pulled from the wood, causing the three men to cringe farther into the shadows. Then, with a slight splintering sound, the hasp broke free.

Once inside, with the door closed behind them, they found that nearby security lights illuminated the room enough for them to read the labels of the bottles and boxes that lined the shelves from wall to wall. Followed by the other three who held their canvas bags open, Watanabe moved along the shelves, selecting some boxes and ignoring others.

Aono was surprised that she felt no fear. It was the first time since escaping from the cave that held the bodies of her family that she had been this close to the enemy. She gripped the Sampachi and stared into the shadows of the hospital compound.

Then she was aware of movement to her left. Private Moldafsky, his rifle slung over his right shoulder, walked along the fence, his eyes turned toward the darkened windows of the nurses' quarters.

Aono could feel her heart beating within her chest. She thought again of the explosion that had killed her sister and her parents. A part of her warned her to remain hidden until Kitani returned, but a year and a half's worth of hate and the desire for revenge were stronger. Carefully, she laid the barrel of the long rifle over a rock, waited until Moldafsky was silhouetted against the security lights inside the compound, then slowly squeezed the trigger.

Watanabe dropped two bottles he was placing in a canvas bag as the rifle report stunned all four into rigidity. Kitani was the first to recover, rushing to the door and checking for activity. All four, carrying their partially filled bags, ran from the building and along the footpath toward the opening in the fence.

Shouts could be heard from several directions. Rounding a corner, Kitani ran headlong into a bathrobed man, knocking him to the ground. Another rifle explosion; definitely a Sampachi, Kitani noted almost subconsciously. It was answered instantly by the heavier reports of American M-1's and shouts in English.

Kitani squeezed through the opening they had cut in the fence, pulling a half-full backpack behind him. Once outside, he passed his pack to the man who followed him, unlimbered the BAR from his shoulder, and threw himself to the ground beside the fence. He saw the body of a sentry lying between him and the two soldiers who were directing their fire at the dark jungle above them.

Behind him, one of the men had become entangled in the loose strands of the fence and, pulling himself free, caused the entire link chain to rattle. The two sentries turned and opened fire. Watanabe, halfway across the outer grassy area, grunted, then twisted and fell, accompanied by a loud clanging of bottles.

Kitani released a burst of fire from the American rifle as the entangled man behind him broke clear and ran for the jungle. Unaware of Watanabe's body lying in his path, the man tripped over it and fell. Before he could rise, bullets from another BAR ripped into him and the pack of medicines he carried.

Kitani was aware of the higher-pitched crack of the Sampachi to his right. He could no longer see the sentries he had fired at, but he could hear the voices of others who were on their way to reinforce them. He jumped to his feet and, firing the BAR from a crouch, ran the five meters to safety. As he scrambled through the vines and undergrowth, he heard his name called by the one man who had reached the jungle.

"Get back to the camp!" he ordered. "I'll follow."

He directed his attention toward where he could hear the Sampachi firing amid the increasing volume of rifle and automatic fire. He was unable to see the sentries because of the jungle, but he could see an occasional spurt of fire from Aono's rifle. Fighting the undergrowth that pulled at his legs and rifle and ignoring the crashing sound he made, he pushed toward a point from where he could fire on the enemy.

Then he saw Aono. She had risen to one knee and was firing as rapidly as she could work the breach of her rifle.

"Get down!" he shouted. But his voice was drowned out by the roar of rifle fire. He saw Aono thrown backward.

"Aono!" he tried to shout, but the sound came out as a hoarse, unintelligible cry. Dropping his rifle and disregarding the American bullets, he ran to where Aono had fallen.

Half running, half crawling, he stumbled behind a rock next to where Aono had been thrown. He slid an arm under her shoulders and raised her until she lay in his arms.

"Why?" he said. Tenderly, he wiped a line of blood that ran from the side of her mouth to her neck.

She opened her eyes, and as she tried to focus them, they softened in a way Kitani had never seen. As they met his, her eyes brimmed with tears. With a half-smile and a slight nod of her head she raised her right hand until it touched his cheek. Then it fell, and her eyes closed; the smile remained frozen on her lips.

Sobbing and holding her close, Kitani was oblivious to the approaching sounds. Not until an American boot stepped on the Sampachi that lay at Aono's side and an M-1 barrel was thrust into his chest, did he raise his tear-filled eyes.

· 15 ·

THE WAR IS OVER

For a week the Americans had been strangely absent from the hills. No patrol had been reported by any of Oba's sentries.

"I don't like it," Oba confided to Tanaka after returning from a tour of sentry positions. "It's like the calm before a storm."

"Perhaps the navy is returning, and they know it. They may be concentrating on their defenses," Tanaka suggested.

The answer came the following morning when a single-engine monoplane flew over the hills just out of rifle range, trailing a cloud of leaflets that settled on treetops and wafted to the ground.

"The war is over!" they asserted in Japanese. "Surrender signed aboard U.S.S. *Missouri* by Japanese leaders." The document gave August 15 as the date of the surrender. It urged all Japanese soldiers to obey their Emperor by laying down their arms.

Oba was stunned by the news. "It can't be true," he said to Tanaka, who had brought a leaflet to Oba's cave. "It must be a trick. They've purposely kept their patrols out of the hills in an effort to make us believe this lie." He crumpled the single sheet of paper. "Have the men seen this?"

"They all have them," Tanaka replied. "They were dropped from an airplane early this morning."

"Tell them it's an enemy lie," Oba said, "and have them remain on the alert for an attack!"

Oba made the round of sentry posts each day for the following week. Neither they nor he saw any signs of enemy activity except a second deluge of leaflets three days after the first. By that time, he was tempted to believe their message.

If the war is over, he thought, we will be able to return to Japan. The prospect of living a full life, something he had long since put out of his mind as an impossibility, haunted his thoughts. Enemy security around their camps also was eased, he noticed, and food patrols now easily entered areas that had previously been well guarded.

Efforts to obtain information from the farmers were frustrating. They all had been told the war was over and that the Americans had won, but most refused to believe it.

The need to know what was happening brought him to a decision: someone would have to go to the civilian camp to find out. He announced his decision at a meeting of Tanaka, Suzuki, Iwata, and Tsuchiya, saying he would leave that night.

"But what if it's a trick and they capture you?" Tanaka asked. "As our commander, you shouldn't take the risk. Let me go, instead."

"No," Tsuchiya interrupted. "I should be the one to go. I've already made the trip twice, and I know all the compound leaders."

Oba thought about Tsuchiya's suggestion for a moment, then agreed. "All right. You will go tonight and return as soon as possible, preferably tonight!"

The tall military policeman arrived at the deserted farm area shortly after midnight and saw no evidence of the American guards who had formerly been posted there. Skirting the Quonset huts near the highway, he walked at the edge of Lake Susupe's marsh grass until he reached the breadfruit trees marking the compound's northeast corner. He went directly to where he had lived with a young widow before leaving the compound.

"Mitchan," he whispered as he entered the darkened room they had shared. A sleepy "Yes, who is it?" directed him to where she lay, and he reached for her hand and said, "I'm back."

His absence apparently had not been reported, he noted as he walked through the narrow alleys toward Motoyama's living quarters early the next morning. Most of those he greeted did not even seem to be aware that he had been gone.

Motoyama was brushing his teeth over a narrow ditch where water flowed from a bath area. "Welcome back" he said with a frothy smile. "Where are the others?"

"They're still in the hills. What's happening?"

"Haven't you heard? The war's over. The Emperor has ordered us to stop fighting. I heard it myself on the radio two weeks ago! Soon we'll be free to return to our homes."

Tsuchiya sagged visibly. He, too, had hoped deeply that peace had returned, but not in defeat.

"What will happen now?" he asked.

"Those in the hills will have to come down," Motoyama said gravely. "The Emperor has ordered it." He rinsed his mouth noisily, emptied the cup into the flowing water, and stepped toward the door of the hut he called home. "Please, come in. I'll tell you all I know."

Tsuchiya sipped tea and listened in silence as Motoyama related what he had heard about a new kind of bomb that had destroyed the cities of Hiroshima and Nagasaki, and how the Emperor had stopped the war to prevent further loss of civilian lives.

"How do you know all this is true?" the soldier asked finally.

"I don't. But I believe the Americans believe it. Those in the compound office have completely changed their attitude toward us. Suganuma-san, the camp interpreter, has been ordered to go with the Americans tomorrow to Pakanto-shima where they are to collect the weapons of Brigadier General Umahachi and his men."

"They have been fighting all this time?" Tsuchiya asked incredulously. He knew the small force on the tiny island seventy miles north of Saipan could not have withstood an American assault for more than a day.

"No, they were by-passed. They were never attacked."

"Where is Suganuma-san? I want to talk to him." A plan

had formed in Tsuchiya's mind. If a general who had not yet surrendered were to order Oba and the others to cease their resistance . . .

"I can't do it," Suganuma objected when Tsuchiya handed him a hastily written note addressed to General Umahachi. "The fact that I'm to accompany them is supposed to be secret."

"Motoyama-san," Tsuchiya turned to the civilian commander. "Explain to Suganuma-san that Captain Oba can only bring his men down by the order of a superior military officer. So far, we have only the word of the enemy that the war is over."

"It's as he says," Motoyama directed his words at the interpreter. "You will carry this note to General Umahachi and return with any orders he has for the soldiers still in the hills. The Americans are not to know of the note or of the general's reply."

Before dawn the next morning, Tsuchiya arrived back at Takoyama.

"It's true!" he said to Oba and those who gathered to hear the news. "The Emperor has ordered soldiers everywhere to lay down their arms." He related his conversation with Motoyama and Suganuma and explained that he had agreed to return to the compound in two days to receive the orders from General Umahachi.

"When you go back," Oba said, "tell Motoyama and Suganuma that I want to talk to them here in the hills. If the war is really over, they should be allowed to come freely. Tell them to meet me at the Second Line campsite the day after tomorrow shortly after sunrise."

He instructed Tsuchiya to go back to the compound that night, but to return immediately if he suspected an American trick.

Later that morning, he called all who were not on sentry duty and told them what Tsuchiya had reported. Inwardly, he was relieved that the years of killing were at an end. He was happy to think of seeing Mineko and little Kazohiro again. He knew, however, that most of the men were unable to accept the possibility that Japan had lost the war. He was careful not to reveal his inner feelings as he spoke to them.

"We have fought well, and we are undefeated. Yet, as soldiers of Japan, we only reflect the will of our Emperor. If, as we have been told, it is his divine will that we cease fighting, then we must obey. We will not stop fighting, however, until we receive official orders from a senior officer. I have therefore arranged for a message to be carried to Brigadier General Umahachi, who is still in command of Pakantoshima, north of here. I expect to receive a reply from him in two days."

A murmur of shock and surprise swept through the gathering as some realized for the first time that the rumor of losing the war was actually believed by Oba.

A navy chief named Hirose voiced the opposition. "It's a lousy lie," he shouted, and was followed by a rumble of support from many in the group. "The barbarians can't beat us, so they're trying to trick us into surrendering. You, Captain Oba, have been deceived, and now you're trying to pull us into the same trap into which you've fallen!"

"I've told you only what I have heard . . ."

"If you say once more that Japan has lost the war, I, by the strength of our divine Emperor, will kill you!"

Oba's face was impassive as he stared at the man who threatened him. He waited until Hirose's eyes wavered and broke contact with his own before ordering, "Dismissed!"

"He means it," Tanaka whispered as he fell into step with Oba. "He would probably kill you and then take his own life. I've had many long talks with him at Tapotchau, and I know him well."

"I believe you," Oba replied, "but I also believe what the Americans say may be true. If it is, he and all the rest must be convinced. I won't say any more until I'm certain, because I don't want to have a split in force at this point."

And, he thought, he certainly did not want to die if the war was really over . . . not after the hell he and the others had experienced for the past eighteen months.

"We're still Japanese soldiers," he said, "and if the war is truly over, it's our duty to return home and help build a new Japan. Our country will need us more than ever." He looked around him at the faces of Tanaka, Saito, Suzuki, and Iwata, all of whom had known the steps taken so far to learn the truth. They nodded and voiced their agreement. They would accept the truth, he knew, no matter what it was. The problem would lie with Hirose and those who shared his opinion.

"I will assume full responsibility for any order I issue," he said. "If you and the others go down because of my orders, and if I should be wrong, my first act will be to kill myself."

He no longer believed this was an American trick, but he knew that if it was, and if he were deceived into turning his men over to the enemy, he would have no alternative but to commit hara-kiri.

Oba spent the next night at the former Second Line camp, together with Tanaka, Suzuki, and Iwata. It was several hours after sunrise when they saw Tsuchiya and two others walk through the farm area toward the jungle. He recognized the portly figure of Motoyama.

The two civilians acted as if they were official spokesmen. "I have the duty to inform you," Motoyama said after a formal greeting, "that Brigadier General Umahachi, commanding officer of the Imperial forces on the island of Pakanto, has ordered that all Japanese military personnel, whether resisting in the jungle or pretending to be civilians"—and he glanced at Tsuchiya—"turn themselves and their weapons over to the American authorities as quickly as possible. This is in accordance with orders from His Imperial Majesty, the Emperor."

"I understand," Oba said softly. He had expected to hear those words but had not expected the shocking blow to his entire being that they dealt him. A wave of numbness swept through his body, and he feared for a moment that he would have to sit down. He forced himself to remain standing.

"Is Suganuma-san the man who carried Tsuchiya's message to General Umahachi?"

"That's right."

"Suganuma-san, did you speak with the general?"

"Yes, I spoke with him, and I passed Tsuchiya-san's note to him without the Americans knowing that I did it."

"Did he give you a written reply?"

"No, but he spoke the words that Motoyama-san repeated to you just now."

"How is it that you left the compound in daylight?"

"The Americans know we've come to talk with you. They allowed us to leave."

The meeting ended as formally as it had begun. The two groups bowed stiffly and each murmured their thanks and regrets for inconveniencing the other. Tsuchiya remained with the holdouts while the two civilians walked back down the hill.

Each of the five men was involved in his own thoughts as they walked from Second Line to Gakeyama. As they walked out of Second Line, Oba, as was his custom when moving through the hills, pulled his pistol, then returned it to its holster.

Halfway back, he stopped and turned to Tsuchiya. "You speak some English, don't you?"

"A little."

"Go down to the Americans. Tell them I want written orders from General Umahachi, and that we will not come down until I have them!"

Maj. Herman Lewis was writing a letter to his wife when the field telephone attached to the side of his desk interrupted his train of thought. He had just written that he would be on his way home in six weeks and, if he could wangle a flight on a returning bomber, might be there for Christmas. The ringing telephone returned his thoughts to Saipan, but he allowed it to ring several times before picking it up and identifying himself.

"Sir," a young voice said on the other end of the line, "a guard unit near Garapan has a Japanese who says he wants to talk to somebody about Captain Oba. . . . That's the guy in the hills, sir."

"I know who he is. Where is this guard unit?"

Lewis noted the location on a pad, broke the connection, and cranked the instrument.

"I want a jeep, immediately!"

He wished that Pollard was still around to savor this moment. The colonel had returned to the States two months earlier when the rest of the division had departed for occupation duty in Japan. He had gone without the general's star he had hoped for. And now, Lewis hoped, he was about to negotiate the surrender of the man who had been their nemesis for a year and half. He hesitated when he thought of the word *surrender*. No, he's not surrendering, he thought. How could he? He hasn't lost. He'll simply be negotiating his own peace . . . the end of his own well-fought war.

A cloud of dust enveloped Lewis and his driver as they braked to a stop at the headquarters of the guard company. It was located on a hill above Garapan, just below the jungle. Several soldiers stood around two others who pointed their rifles at an unusually tall Japanese who wore a hospital-type mask over his mouth and nose. Lewis noted immediately that the man did not scrape and bow, as had most prisoners he had seen, but stood straight and proud.

"I'm Major Lewis," he said to a first lieutenant who snapped a salute as Lewis approached. "Where did this man come from?"

"Don't rightly know, sir. He just kinda walked into camp. He speaks a little English and said something about a Captain Oba. Isn't that the guy in the hills?"

"Yes, it is."

"D'you suppose that's Oba?"

"I don't know, but let's get him in my jeep. I'll take him to headquarters."

The soldiers motioned the man toward the jeep. He walked to it and hesitated, as if unsure whether he should sit in the front or in the back. Lewis pointed to the backseat, and the man climbed in. Lewis threw an answering salute to the lieutenant, and as the jeep headed out of the parking area, he turned to look at his prisoner. Prisoner? he thought. The war had been over for more than two months. How could the man be a prisoner?

Neither of them made any attempt at conversation until they reached Lewis's office. There he called a clerk to record the interrogation in shorthand and sent another to bring Commander Ito to his office. The soldier, who had removed his face mask, watched impassively as Lewis explained to the clerk what he wanted. His face registered surprise a few minutes later, however, when a uniformed Japanese navy commander, still carrying his sword, walked into the room.

"Commander Ito," Lewis said after returning the man's salute, "this man was just picked up after walking out of the hills. Will you first identify yourself to him, then assist me in questioning him? I would like the entire conversation taken down in shorthand, so please be sure anything you say is repeated in English."

"Yes, sir," the Japanese officer replied. Then, to Tsuchiya, he said in Japanese, "I am Commander Ito of the Okinawa Naval Base Force. I have come here by order of Major General Sasaki to remove any doubts about the war's end." He repeated the statement in English.

"The Emperor has ordered us to cease fighting," he continued. "I am here to see that order carried out."

Any lingering doubts in Tsuchiya's mind were removed during the next hour as the three men discussed the events leading to the war's end. He explained to them that Captain Oba needed proof to persuade his men, and that he would not come down until they all were convinced.

At Lewis's suggestion, the commander agreed to accompany Tsuchiya into the hills to meet Oba. Both Ito and Lewis had pointedly refrained from asking the location of Oba's camp, for which the warrant officer was grateful.

Later, the three men lunched at the officers' club. The commander was kept busy answering Tsuchiya's questions as Lewis, with his limited Japanese, tried to follow the conversation. Tsuchiya relayed Oba's demand that the order from General Umahachi be in writing, with his *han* mark, before he would consider coming out of the hills, or could convince his men to lay down their arms. He continued to think of questions throughout the afternoon and into the night, until Ito turned out the lantern in the tent they shared and good-naturedly ordered him to sleep.

Early the next morning Lewis escorted the two Japanese to the edge of the jungle, then watched as they disappeared along a trail south of Tapotchau. It was the second time he had watched two men enter the jungle to meet with Oba, but he was certain these two would succeed in bringing the elusive captain down.

• • •

Sentries reported the arrival of Tsuchiya and the Japanese commander long before they reached Takoyama. When Oba learned that the officer was wearing a sword, he wondered if it could be General Umahachi or one of his command. He changed into the uniform he had been saving for the day of the navy's return and ordered his men to clean the camp and themselves. He sent runners to all sentry posts, ordering all to return to Takoyama immediately.

"There's no doubt now," he told Tanaka. "If a Japanese officer is coming to us from the Americans, it's truly over."

When the two men walked into camp thirty minutes later, Oba, in his white uniform, stood before the two platoons of his force and saluted the commander. After they had exchanged greetings and identified themselves, Ito said in a voice loud enough to be heard by all present: "I have been directed by the high command to inform you that His Imperial Majesty, the Emperor, has ordered all Japanese armed forces to cease the war against the Americans and to turn over all weapons to them.

"I have been flown here from Okinawa by the Americans to give you this message, and have spoken with the Americans here, as has Warrant Officer Tsuchiya. We will be available to answer any questions you have."

He waited, but there were no questions. The men were stunned by hearing the report confirmed by a source they could not question. Oba broke the silence by saluting once more and inviting Ito to have a cup of tea from the stock supplied by the farmers. Tsuchiya joined them and handed Oba an envelope bearing a letter from Maj. Herman Lewis. Accompanying the note in English was a translation in Japanese.

"To Captain Oba from Maj. Herman Lewis, USMC," it read. "This will introduce Commander Shinji Ito, of the Okinawa Naval Base Force, who has been flown here to inform you that hostilities between our countries have been terminated, and that all Japanese soldiers have been ordered to stop fighting. As your representative, Warrant Officer Tsuchiya, will tell you, we treated him as a commissioned officer—even though he is an enlisted man—and hope that you will accord Commander Ito, my representative, the same courtesies.''

I hope you will be able to report that we offered you all the amenities of our camp,'' Oba said to Ito as they shared a papaya and sipped tea. ''But as you see, they are limited.''

The naval officer smiled. ''I'm impressed that you have survived under these conditions so long. Major Lewis had high praise for the manner in which you have fought.'' He hesitated, then added, ''Will you and your men return with me tomorrow?''

Oba looked at the jungle below their hidden stronghold and slowly shook his head. ''No, not yet. If it is true that General Umahachi has not yet surrendered on Pakanto Island, he is the ranking officer of the Marianas and, as such, my commanding officer. Please tell Lewis that I will come down only if I receive written orders from him. Until I come down and until he surrenders, we still are soldiers of Japan and must act accordingly.''

''I understand your feelings,'' Ito said solemnly. ''These are difficult days for all of us.'' He raised his head and looked directly at Oba. ''I have allowed my own feelings to become numb. I neither feel nor think deeply. If I did, it might be impossible for me to carry out this mission.''

''We all do our duty,'' Oba said, and accepted a cigarette the other proffered.

''Major Lewis learned of your demand for written orders from Tsuchiya-san and told me last evening that he had requested the navy to obtain them as quickly as possible. He said they should have them in two days.''

''In that case, I will send someone down then to bring them to me.''

''The major also said they would like to have a meeting with you tomorrow afternoon. He says he will come unarmed and asks that you do the same. He suggested the camp where Tsuchiya first came down, but would meet anywhere you say. He will come with no more than four persons.''

Oba did not answer immediately. His instinctive distrust of an enemy warned him of the danger of a trap. Wouldn't walking unarmed into an enemy camp be the same as surrender? What if the man sitting in front of him were really an American Nisei, and the whole story was a lie? But Suganuma had been to Pakanto and had spoken to General Umahachi . . .

"All right," he said finally, "but not at an American camp. I will meet him just inside the jungle, above the civilian farm. I'm sure he knows of the camp we once had there."

Ito agreed to relay the information to Lewis and said he hoped to be among those in the American party. He spent the rest of the evening answering many of the same questions Tsuchiya had asked about the course of events during the past year and a half.

The next morning Tsuchiya accompanied the commander to the same camp at which he had been held at gunpoint a few days earlier and waited until Ito had explained to the lieutenant that he wanted to telephone Major Lewis. The officer moved to stop Tsuchiya as he turned to leave, but Ito explained that negotiations were still under way and that Tsuchiya's return to the hills was an important part of them. The lieutenant, anxious to play a role in the capture of Captain Oba, ordered two of his men to accompany Tsuchiya to the jungle's edge.

"Just to make sure none of my trigger-happy people take a potshot at you."

That night, small fires blazed throughout the narrow canyon in which Oba and his men camped. For the first time in a year and a half they relaxed their vigilance and sat around the fires discussing a future none had ever expected to see. They had talked their way through their initial shock during the long afternoon and now began to believe that they would return to their families. Long-submerged thoughts of loved ones began to surface and seek release in conversation.

Oba did not order sentries to their posts the following morning, although some of them went out of habit. The day passed slowly. The normal tension of eighteen months was gone, and the hours dragged until noon, when two of the men who had voluntarily manned sentry posts returned, one of them with a bullet wound in his shoulder. The tension returned.

As the men gathered around the wounded soldier, many became convinced that it proved the Americans had been lying. Oba, too, had his doubts until he questioned the

wounded man's companion and learned they had been returning from a post overlooking Garapan and had met two American soldiers on the trail. One of them had fired before both
turned and ran in the opposite direction. He instructed the
man to tell the others exactly what had happened, hoping that
most of them, at least, would realize it was an accidental
encounter.

An hour before the appointed time, Oba, Tanaka, Suzuki,
and Tsuchiya walked the two kilometers to Second Line, then
watched from the jungle as two jeeps stopped at the low side
of the farm and three men began walking across the tilled
land.

Oba scanned them closely with his binoculars to be sure
none carried weapons. He recognized Commander Ito, uniformed but without his sword. A second Japanese, in an
American uniform, apparently an American Nisei, walked on
the other side of a tall American whose height was accentuated by the shorter stature of the two Japanese.

With his glasses, Oba swept the terrain on either side of
the farm, looking for hidden troops. Seeing none, he motioned to the others and they strode back to Second Line.
They removed their weapons, placing them where they could
be recovered after the meeting. Oba stood in the center of
the clearing with the other three behind him, as the two
Americans and Ito entered the campsite. They stopped two
paces in front of him.

Oba bowed, but purposely refrained from saluting because
the tall American was technically still an enemy. He was a
little surprised when the American joined the other two in
returning the bow, albeit awkwardly. The Nisei spoke first.

"Major Lewis has asked me to thank you for this meeting.
He is pleased to meet you under these conditions and hopes
the understanding reached here today will result in an end to
the fighting on Saipan."

Both Oba and Lewis frankly appraised each other as the
Nisei spoke. Lewis was surprised at how healthy and fit his
very special enemy appeared after eighteen months of resisting every type of warfare that could be thrown at him. He
knew American patrols had stripped papaya trees of their
fruit, shot holes in every container they could find, and taken

every other possible step to deprive the Japanese of food and water.

"If the war is truly over, I am willing to discuss the terms under which I will bring my men out of the hills," Oba said.

"Will you come down on the first of December?" Lewis asked, adding, "That is five days from today."

"Only if I have written orders from General Umahachi on Pakanto-shima. I will obey his orders. But if I do not receive his written orders, I will not come down." He waited until the Nisei had repeated his statement in English, then continued. "If we do come down, I want a tour of the island to satisfy myself that other Japanese are not still fighting, and I want my men to remain together as a unit."

"I have already requested our navy to ask the general for written orders," Lewis replied, "and we should have them within two days. As for your other two requests, I promise you will be given a tour and that your men will remain together. I understand you have forty-seven men with you, is that correct?"

"That is correct," Oba responded. "But one of them was wounded yesterday by one of your soldiers. I want him removed to a hospital immediately, and I want your assurance that no other American soldier will enter the hills for the next five days."

"I apologize for the shooting." Lewis was visibly surprised to hear that his orders of three days earlier, that no American forces were to enter the hills, had been violated.

"I will take every possible step to see it does not occur again. If you will tell me where I should send a jeep, I will see to it that the wounded man is taken to a hospital."

"There is one more matter," Tanaka spoke from behind Oba. "If there is to be peace between us, it should be written in a treaty to which we both agree, which should be signed by both sides."

Oba was surprised by Tanaka's demand. It was something they had not discussed.

Lewis asked something of the Nisei to clarify Tanaka's request, then said in badly accented Japanese, "That I cannot do. A peace treaty has already been signed by representatives of our two governments aboard the battleship U.S.S. *Missouri*. We cannot sign another treaty here. I'm sorry.''

Tanaka started to speak again, but Oba turned and glared at the lieutenant, who bowed almost imperceptibly and kept silent.

After selecting a point at which a jeep could pick up the wounded man, the two delegations bowed, and the three from the American side turned back to their jeep. Oba and his group watched them depart, then retrieved their weapons and began following the trail to Takoyama. Oba withdrew his pistol and resumed his normal cautious manner of traversing the hills. Despite the major's assurance, he did not want to be caught unaware by a last-minute souvenir hunter. .

A stretcher was fashioned by Tanaka's soldiers for the wounded man. The Americans promised a hospital jeep would be dispatched to the agreed-upon location within an hour of their return.

"If you have no objection," Tanaka said to Oba just before they departed, "I would like to accompany Nagano-san to the hospital, then return immediately."

"Good idea," Oba told him. "Let me know what you see." He then spoke briefly to the wounded man, assuring him that he was not surrendering, but was going to receive treatment for his bullet wound, which was already showing signs of infection.

Suzuki and Iwata, meanwhile, were surrounded by soldiers to whom they were giving a word-by-word account of their meeting with the two Americans and Ito.

A hospital jeep rigged with racks for two stretchers was waiting on the narrow dirt track just below Takoyama when Tanaka and those bearing the wounded Nagano arrived. Two men stood beside the vehicle, and one of them started forward as the Japanese approached. He said something in English that Tanaka did not understand, but his manner and the stethoscope that hung from his neck made it apparent that he was a physician.

After a brief examination of the wound, he inserted a hypodermic needle in Nagano's arm, then indicated that he needed help transferring him to one of the jeep's stretchers.

As the two prepared to leave, Tanaka stepped forward. "I want to go with him," he said.

When the physician failed to understand, Tanaka repeated his request and made it understandable by pointing to himself, Nagano, and the jeep as he spoke.

The American responded by gesturing for Tanaka to take a seat on the narrow bench parallel to the two stretchers. But as Tanaka started to board, the physician barred his way, pointed at the pistol on the lieutenant's belt, and shook his head.

Tanaka withdrew the weapon, handed it to one of the men who had accompanied him, and with an ironic smile, climbed into the jeep.

As they passed through what had once been the city of Garapan, Tanaka could hardly believe what he saw. Rounded metal buildings, aligned along roads and streets that had not existed before, had completely replaced the quaint Japanese-style city he had known.

They drove south parallel to the beach. Beyond the shore, rusting American tanks and other vehicles canted crazily in the water where they had been blasted into immobility by Japanese artillery eighteen months earlier.

A few minutes later they turned into a crushed coral driveway surrounded by a cluster of the rounded structures. Uniformed Japanese nurses and some Americans removed Nagano from the jeep and carried him into one of the buildings.

The wounded man was placed on an examining table where the physician who had met them took his blood pressure while another washed and examined the bullet hole just below the shoulder.

Tanaka turned to an attractive nurse who stood nearby. "What kind of a hospital is this?" he asked.

"It's the Japanese hospital," she replied as if he should have known. "It's run by the American navy, but the patients and most of the staff are Japanese."

The American doctor who had been examining Nagano turned to look at Tanaka, then spoke in English to another nurse. She answered, but Tanaka did not understand.

"The doctor wants to know if you are also wounded," she explained in Japanese.

"No, I'm his friend. I will go back now."

His statement caused a mild flurry of excitement in the small room as the Americans' attention was directed to him, and their conversation was obviously about him. Tanaka grew nervous and wished he had not left his pistol behind. It had not occurred to him that the Americans might try to take him prisoner. He wondered if the Japanese nurses would help him escape if he was forced to fight his way out.

The examining physician turned toward him. Tanaka stood unmoving, his muscles tense. He was ready to break for the door. The man said something to the nurse who spoke English. She nodded, then turned to Tanaka.

"Doctor Malone says he understands that you are to return, but asks if you would wait until after lunch. He also asks your name."

"I am First Lieutenant Tanaka, of the One Thirty-sixth Infantry Regiment." His military tone faltered as he realized he was being invited to lunch by the American he had been prepared to kill a moment earlier. He had to force himself to accept the fact that the man was trying to be friendly.

"Please stay," the girl said with a smile. "You will be taken back to the hills after lunch."

"All right. Thank you." Tanaka could think of nothing else to say.

It was the first time he had eaten fresh meat in many months. The food was strange, but edible. It took him a moment to recognize that the white mound placed in front of him for dessert was a bowl of ice cream.

The nurse who doubled as an interpreter, Kikuchi Takako, sat at the table he shared with the two physicians. He was kept so busy answering questions about his experience in the hills that he had little time to ask his own questions. Initially he was surprised at the friendly and informal way in which Takako conversed with the two American officers. Then it occurred to him that during the year and a half he had considered them his enemy, this girl and the others who worked for the Americans had come to consider them friends.

Is this how it would be in the future? he wondered. Would

all Japanese be able to befriend the enemy so easily? Will we completely give up? Will our spirit be forever destroyed? These thoughts jumbled with unexpected impressions from the hospital visit, stayed in his mind as Tanaka rode in a jeep to the point just below Takoyama.

He reported to Oba that Nagano was scheduled for surgery that afternoon and that the physicians had told him he would recover. He was unable, however, to reveal his thoughts and fears about the future.

Two days later, on November 29, Tanaka went back to the world of the Americans, this time with instructions from Captain Oba to return when he had received the written orders from General Umahachi. He went directly to the guard camp visited earlier by Tsuchiya. Though he wore his pistol, the soldiers made no move to disarm him as they led him to the lieutenant who commanded them.

"I will hold your weapon until you return," the officer said through an interpreter before he raised the telephone to call Major Lewis. Tanaka complied and handed over the weapon after unloading and clearing its chamber. The lieutenant placed it in a drawer of his desk.

After Lewis arrived, Tanaka told the interpreter he had come to receive the written orders from General Umahachi that had been promised by this date. The lieutenant relayed the information to Lewis.

"General Umahachi and his men will return to Saipan within a week," Lewis told Tanaka in stilted Japanese as he handed over an envelope with Oba's name, both in English and in Japanese. "He said he expects to meet Captain Oba and his men at that time and hopes that you all will have come out of the hills by then."

Tanaka promised to relay the information, together with the written orders, to Oba.

"Please tell the captain that I suggest we meet in the clearing just north of this camp at nine o'clock on the morning of December 1, the day after tomorrow. If he agrees, ask him to have someone notify Lieutenant Norris"—and he indicated the guard company commander—"by tomorrow afternoon."

Tanaka agreed, then watched as the lieutenant retrieved his

pistol and handed it to him, butt first. He returned it to his holster without reloading it and left to return to the hills.

Oba looked at the two versions of his name on the envelope Tanaka had just handed him. He knew that his life and the lives of his men would be changed by its contents. Carefully, he tore off one end.

He glanced first at the signature. It was that of Brig. Gen. Ano Umahachi. Beside it was affixed the personal stamp of the general's *han*. He read the Japanese script.

"In accordance with the order of the Emperor," the paper read, "the Imperial Government of Japan surrendered to the supreme commander of American forces, Gen. Douglas Mac-Arthur, on September 2 in the twentieth year of Showa. I order you, all military and civilian personnel under your command, as well as any others who are still resisting on the island of Saipan, to cease fighting immediately, and to turn yourself and your weapons over to Vice Adm. Francis M. Whiting, the commanding American officer of Saipan, of the Mariana Islands, or to any person representing him."

The English translation, on a separate sheet of paper, was typewritten. It did not bear the general's signature, but that was not necessary. The war was over. Japan had lost.

He fought to maintain his composure and to hide the turmoil within him as he walked to his belongings and removed a knife. Aono, of them all, would have refused to obey, he thought as he used her blade to post the paper on a tree.

He knew he should assemble the men and read the order aloud. But he knew that he could not. A captain of the Imperial Army must not break under his emotions.

Oba turned to Tanaka. "Have the men read this." A tightening in his throat prevented him from saying more. Slowly, with lowered head, he walked to his cave. He sunk to a sitting position, and his shoulders heaved with mute sobs.

By the next morning, the unbelievable had to be believed. If it was the Emperor's will, it had to be accepted without question. Several of the men had bowed deeply at the posted order, both before and after reading it.

Once the order had been digested, an amazing transformation took place. There was an air of lighthearted joviality among the men, which had never existed before. Oba ordered them to wash their clothing and themselves, preparatory to meeting the Americans the following day. Then he used the needle and thread, given to him by Okuno, to repair tears in his uniform. Throughout the morning, the men sat around joking and discussing plans for the future as they cleaned the rifles they would turn over to the Americans the next day.

A single large fire was lighted at dusk, and the last of their food was prepared by the best cooks among them. After the meal, which consisted of stolen American canned goods, several bottles of freshly made *yashizake* were passed from hand to hand as the men talked about the ordeal that was about to end and the unknown future that lay before them.

Songs, both military and from their civilian days, echoed from their mountain stronghold throughout most of the night. Captain Oba, who had had his share of the fermented *yashi* juice, contributed little to the singing of civilian songs but took the lead in military numbers, particularly his favorite, *"Hohei no honryo"* ("The Heart of the Infantry").

Although the party lasted until a couple hours before dawn, the entire group was up and shaving with the first light.

"Lieutenant Tanaka!" Oba called to his muttering junior officer, who was trying to scrape his face clean of accumulated beard with a dull and rusty razor, "Have the men ready to stand inspection at oh eight hundred hours."

Oba returned to his cave and unwrapped the maps, drawings, and notes on American defense positions that he had accumulated over the past months. The navy had no need for them now. He crumbled each piece of paper after reading it briefly, then struck a match and watched them burn. My reason for being here is gone, he thought as the flames turned the white paper to gray ash. Then he picked up the small packet wrapped in white cloth that he had kept since the day of Banno's death months earlier. He knew the Americans would never understand his reasons for keeping his friend's thumb, nor would they allow him to return it to the lieutenant's family. Reverently, he placed it on a niche in the rear wall of his cave and bowed his head for a moment in silent prayer.

Then he heard Tanaka ordering the men into ranks outside. He donned his sword and pistol belt and inspected his uniform. He placed his spare pistol with Banno's thumb, then turned and walked into the sunlight.

He stopped abruptly just outside the cave's entrance. In front of the assembled men, waving gently in the breeze, was a sight as beautiful as it was unexpected: a Japanese flag.

Tsuchiya, who had walked from the compound the previous night in order to take part in the ceremony in his true role of an army warrant officer, had brought the flag as a gift from Motoyama.

The rippling red and white silk was nearly two meters long. It hung from a staff slightly longer than that, which was held by Hirose, the navy officer who had once threatened to kill Oba for saying that Japan had lost the war. Automatically, but with an emotional choke in his throat, Oba snapped to attention and gave the emblem of Japan a long salute.

His men looked more like soldiers than he had ever seen them before. They stood at attention in the tattered remnants of their uniforms, each with a rifle at his side.

"Prepare for inspection!" Corporal Suzuki shouted at a nod from Lieutenant Tanaka.

Oba stopped in front of each man as he walked up and down the ranks, trying to burn the memory of each face onto his mind. He was sad that his association with these men was about to come to an end. It wasn't until one of them returned his bow that he realized he had been unconsciously bending slightly from the waist before moving to the next man in line. After completing the inspection, he stepped to a position from which he could address them. He returned a salute from Tanaka and told them to stand at ease.

For a long moment he allowed his eyes to focus on the faces of the men with whom he had shared such an important part of his life. When he began to speak, it was as if he were speaking to each individually.

"I am proud to have served with you. You have fought well, and in keeping with the spirit of Bushido. Today, by order of our Emperor, we will end our war. But we will end it as undefeated soldiers of Japan."

Then he raised both hands and shouted, *"Tennoheika, banzai!"* and was joined by nearly fifty voices in a rousing salute to the Emperor. There were tears in his eyes and in the eyes of some of his men. Twice more the salute echoed through the valley.

"Now, in memory of our comrades who gave their lives . . ." He nodded to Tanaka, who in turn bowed slightly toward Naito. All lowered their heads as the former Buddhist priest chanted the *ireisai* prayer for souls of the dead, and thought of the friends who had played such brief but important roles in their lives.

Oba stared at the ground, thinking of the smiling, good-natured Banno, of the barrel-chested Kitani, who might or might not be dead, of Aono, whose lust for revenge had, in the end, taken her own life, and of Horiuchi, whom society had branded an outlaw, but who had lived by his own code of ethics and had saved all of their lives.

Again, Oba nodded to Tanaka.

"Attention!" Tanaka shouted. As one, the men complied with the order. "Port arms! Load!"

Oba watched the men work the bolts of their rifles and insert live cartridges. On Tanaka's order, they would fire their weapons for the last time, not at the enemy, but in a salute to their fallen comrades.

Tanaka turned and saluted when the noise of the moving bolts had subsided. "Ready, fire!" Tanaka repeated the order two more times, and the explosions of nearly fifty weapons reverberated through the hills, echoing all the way down to the American camps, nearly two kilometers distant.

At another sharply barked order, the men removed and pocketed the cartridge clips and pulled their triggers once more to verify that their rifles were empty.

At fifteen minutes before the appointed hour, the procession began winding its way down Gakeyama with Hirose at its head, carrying the huge flag of the rising sun. Tanaka followed, leading the first platoon, followed by his mixed platoon of soldiers and sailors. Oba, the last man in the column, walked directly behind Tsuchiya. As they passed the last of the banyan trees, he began to sing *"Hohei no honryo,"* almost to himself. Tsuchiya, then others, hesitantly joined in, and soon all were singing lustily in the spirit that made the Japanese army the exceptional organization that it was.

As they emerged from the jungle near the guard camp, a dozen American soldiers stood with rifles aimed at the marching Japanese. Hirose's steps faltered as his eyes swept back and forth over the threatening soldiers. He suddenly became convinced that the entire negotiation had been an American charade leading them to a slaughter that was to begin now. They were trapped without a bullet among them! Tanaka's voice, directly behind him, kept him in line. "Fool! Keep marching!"

Then Tanaka increased the volume of his singing and turned to be sure the men behind him followed his example.

The Americans, who had been startled by the earlier rifle salute and by the sound of singing from the jungle above them, stood and gaped at these soldiers who ignored their readied weapons and, without unslinging their arms, marched disdainfully through their midst.

"I'll be a sonofabitch!" one of them exclaimed as he lowered his rifle.

Oba was unaware of the reason for the increased volume of singing until he stepped into the clearing and could see the stupefied soldiers. He understood immediately and smiled at the courage of his men.

Tanaka ordered the men to form two ranks as Oba reached the clearing where the Americans waited. He recognized Lewis and Ito, but the men who clustered in the background were strangers.

He walked to a point slightly ahead of Tanaka and Hirose—who still held his flag defiantly—and the two ranks. The men stood at attention, holding their unloaded rifles beside them. He turned to Tanaka. "Order the men to lay down their weapons."

Tanaka barked the order, and the two ranks, as one man, laid their rifles on the ground, took one step backward, and resumed standing at attention.

A young American in civilian clothing stepped in front of Tanaka, raised a camera, and photographed the highly emotional lieutenant.

"*Bakayero!*" Tanaka growled and took a threatening step toward the photographer. The man scurried back to the safety of the small knot of onlookers.

Lewis walked to a point one pace in front of Oba. For a long moment they looked at each other, each with his own thoughts.

Oba's left hand moved to secure his scabbard, and his right gripped the hilt of the sword he had carried proudly for eight years. Lewis's eyes followed the motion, and the fingers of his right hand touched the holster that held his government-issue .45 caliber pistol. Lewis flinched as Oba withdrew the gleaming blade and it passed within inches of his face. With its tip pointing toward the sky, Oba brought the sword's hilt to his forehead in salute.

Lewis was choked with emotion as he raised his hand to return the salute. The two of them, he and this man who had outfought, outwitted, and outmaneuvered him for a year and a half, were about to end the battle for Saipan. He lowered his right hand, then extended both to accept the sword that Capt. Sakae Oba, one of Japan's heroes, offered at arm's length.

WAR BOOKS
FROM JOVE

0-515-08674-6	**BLOODY WINTER** John M. Waters	$3.95
0-515-09030-1	**A DISTANT CHALLENGE** Edited by Infantry Magazine	$3.50
0-515-08054-3	**INFANTRY IN VIETNAM** Albert N. Garland, U.S.A. (ret.)	$3.95
0-515-08365-8	**HITLER MUST DIE!** Herbert Molloy Mason, Jr.	$3.95
0-515-08810-2	**LITTLE SHIP, BIG WAR: THE SAGA OF DE343** Commander Edward P. Stafford, U.S.N. (ret.)	$3.95
0-515-08682-7	**THE END OF THE IMPERIAL JAPANESE NAVY** Masanori Ito	$3.50
0-515-07733-X	**THE INCREDIBLE 305th** Wilbur Morrison	$2.95
0-515-08066-7	**THE KAMIKAZES** Edwin P. Hoyt	$3.95
0-515-07618-X	**KASSERINE PASS** Martin Blumenson	$3.50
0-515-08732-7	**PORK CHOP HILL** S.L.A. Marshall	$3.95
0-515-08940-0	**THE LOS BANOS RAID** Lt. Gen. E. M. Flanagan, Jr.	$3.50
0-515-08913-3	**FOUR STARS OF HELL** Laurence Critchell	$3.95
0-515-09066-2	**DROP ZONE SICILY** William B. Breuer	$3.50
0-515-08896-X	**BLUE SKIES AND BLOOD** Edwin P. Hoyt	$3.50
0-515-09005-0	**PAK SIX** G. I. Basel	$3.50
0-515-09230-4	**THE BATTLE OF LEYTE GULF** Edwin P. Hoyt	$3.95
0-515-09159-6	**ACE: A MARINE NIGHT FIGHTER PILOT IN WWII** Colonel R. Bruce Porter with Eric Hammel	$3.95
0-515-09074-3	**RINGED IN STEEL** Michael D. Mahler	$3.95
0-515-09367-X	**DEVIL BOATS: THE PT WAR AGAINST JAPAN** William Breuer	$3.50
0-515-09511-7	**WE LED THE WAY: DARBY'S RANGERS** William O. Darby and William H. Baumer	$3.50
0-515-09485-4	**76 HOURS: THE INVASION OF TARAWA** Eric Hammel and John E. Lane	$3.95
0-515-09543-5	**AMBUSH** S.L.A. Marshall	$3.95
0-515-08887-0	**PATTON'S BEST** Nat Frankel and Larry Smith	$3.50
0-515-09643-1	**BATTLES HITLER LOST: FIRST PERSON ACCOUNTS OF WORLD WAR II BY RUSSIAN GENERALS ON THE EASTERN FRONT** Marshalls Zhukov, Konev, Malinovsky, Rokossovsky, Rotmistrov, Chuikov and other commanders	$3.95

Please send the titles I've checked above. Mail orders to:

BERKLEY PUBLISHING GROUP
390 Murray Hill Pkwy., Dept. B
East Rutherford, NJ 07073

NAME _____

ADDRESS _____

CITY _____

STATE _____ ZIP _____

Please allow 6 weeks for delivery.
Prices are subject to change without notice.

POSTAGE & HANDLING:
$1.00 for one book, $.25 for each
additional. Do not exceed $3.50.

BOOK TOTAL	$_____
SHIPPING & HANDLING	$_____
APPLICABLE SALES TAX (CA, NJ, NY, PA)	$_____
TOTAL AMOUNT DUE	$_____

PAYABLE IN US FUNDS.
(No cash orders accepted.)